Angel's Revenge

Happy Annivesary

Don Helin

The Big 50

Don Helin

Publisher Page
an imprint of Headline Books, Inc.
Terra Alta, WV

Angel's Revenge

by Don Helin

To order additional copies of this book or for book publishing information, or to contact the author:

Headline Books, Inc.
P.O. Box 52
Terra Alta, WV 26764

www.HeadlineBooks.com
800-570-5951

Publisher Page is an imprint of Headline Books

ISBN 13: 978-1-882658-60-2

Library of Congress Control Number: 2016939184

PRINTED IN THE UNITED STATES OF AMERICA

Dedication

To Elaine for her love and support – love always

Remembering Bill, a thoughtful friend taken from us
way too soon.

Acknowledgments

Thanks to my critique group – Carmen, Cathy, and
Laurie, and to Dennis and all the members of the
Pennwriters Fourth Wednesday Writers Group.

To Cathy, Ashley, and all the staff at Headline Books
You are the best.

1

Cape May, New Jersey, Sunday Evening

Lieutenant Colonel Brian Toomey stirred, first opening his eyes, then focusing to clear his mind. His head ached. He tried to lift his arm. *Why couldn't he move?* Leather straps bound his hands and legs to the table. His pulse quickened.

Except for a flickering candle, darkness surrounded him. Some sort of classical music sounded in the background. *Where was he?*

The pounding in his head beat on him. His throat was dry—he licked his lips. Closing his eyes, he tried to remember. Couldn't. *Drugs maybe?* He tried to fight it. Push himself up. Couldn't.

The sweet smell of incense invaded his senses. A breeze played across his body. Shit, he was naked. *Come on,* he thought, *push yourself up.* When he couldn't, his mind raced and his stomach clenched. Panic set in and he started to sweat.

Sounds. *Footsteps?* Toomey turned his head toward it. Shadows surrounded him in the semi-darkness. A hooded figure materialized out of the darkness and glided toward him. A female voice said, "Ah, Colonel Toomey, I see you're awake."

Was this someone's idea of a joke? A fraternity prank? "Who the hell are you?"

The female replied, "Someone who wants to talk with you."

"Let me up, or I'll have your ass."

The hooded figure moved closer. "I don't think so. I think you've gotten all the ass you'll ever get."

Toomey felt embarrassment, helpless anger, naked in front of this hooded female. He concentrated to slow his heartbeat. "What's that supposed to mean? Where are my clothes? Why am I tied down?"

"First, I'd like to take you back three years to an event, an event in which you caused pain to my friend standing next to me."

Toomey's heart beat faster, his head still pounded. What was going on? "I don't understand what you're saying. Who else is there with you?"

"Oh, I think you do." The hooded face got closer, almost breathing in his face. "Do you remember Sergeant Margo Collins?"

He smelled perfume. His mind whirled, searching. Finally a hit. Collins, that prick teaser. "Yes, I went out with Margo a couple of times."

Her arm moved and a blade scraped up and down his arm, then moved to his chest. Oh, no, the bitch has a knife.

"How about your date on that April 23rd?" the woman asked. "Remember that?"

His eyes widened, understanding seeping into his consciousness. What to say. "Ah, I don't remember anything special about it." He did, though. She'd refused to put out and he'd gotten sick of it. Maybe pushed her a little. Only a little.

"You took advantage of her, didn't you?" the hooded female replied. "Raped her and left her along the side of the road. Told her if she tried to report it, you'd see that she'd get busted for lying about what happened. Big deal colonel and a lowly sergeant. You had her. Nothing she could do."

The blade scraped up to his chest, then down to his stomach. *Oh, Jesus. What had he gotten into?* "That's not true." His voice broke. "I wouldn't hurt her."

Another shadow moved into his line of vision. A shorter hooded figure.

"Maybe if you saw her again," the woman said, "it would help you remember."

The shorter woman took off her hood and stood before him.

"Now do you remember? You raped this woman. Stole her pride. Destroyed her self-esteem. Made her feel unfit for any other man. You did it, then made sure she'd never be able to blame you. You were her boss and you covered it up. Got a couple of your officer buddies to testify she was easy. She tried to file a complaint but who would believe her? Just a sergeant."

The sharp edge slid down his stomach, across his scrotum, trailed down his right leg, then back up his left leg.

"What do you have to say for yourself? What can you say to Sergeant Collins?"

He stuttered. Couldn't talk.

The blade moved up to his lower stomach. "Say something to her, you bastard."

Toomey nodded, the movement sending pain radiating through his skull. "I'm sorry. I'm so terribly sorry. What can I do to make it right?"

The hooded figure leaned over him again. "You're going to make it right by her and you're going to do it now."

He leaned forward at little, straining at the bands holding him so he could see the woman. Sergeant Collins. Yes, Margo Collins.

The hooded woman standing next to Collins lifted his penis, held it, the knife moving toward it. "You're about to see your last woman. And, you're not going to enjoy it."

"No, no! I said I was sorry. Please, please, I'm so sorry."

The hooded figure placed the knife at the base of his penis. "Not good enough, asshole. You're one of so many and we're going to make it right. Then we're going after your officer buddies who lied to help you. None of you will ever do that again."

Searing pain shot up his body. He screamed. "No, no, please no."

The pain, oh no, the pain . . .

2

Arlington, VA, Monday, 5:45 a.m.

Colonel Zack Kelly shut off the alarm, yawned and pushed up out of bed. He glanced out the window into his backyard and marveled at the colors. Late June. Not too hot yet in D.C. Trees and plants all in bloom. A great time of the year. It's going to be a busy week, but then a long weekend with the July 4th holiday coming up. Do something with Laura. Maybe suggest a short road trip. Some camping in the Shenandoah Mountains along the Skyline Drive.

He enjoyed home ownership. Having his daughter move in with him even better. At least most of the time. Bachelor Officers Quarters living at Fort Myer really sucked.

He pulled on a robe and wandered down the hallway to the door of his daughter's bedroom. She was supposed to be up, but no noise sounded from inside. Knocking on the door, he called out, "Hey, you're going to be late if you don't get moving."

A moan, then her voice, "Yeah, I'm up."

"Better be, because next time I'll be back with a bucket of water."

The door opened a crack and Laura peeked out. "You wouldn't dare."

He laughed. "But you're not sure, are you? Come on, get it in gear and I'll make you an omelet. Something to help you start your week in style."

The door closed again and he heard, "That's a deal."

Laura had come to live with him when Zack's ex-wife ended up in jail for selling drugs back in Minneapolis. He loved the idea of her living with him and going to GW. Her friends were fun. Brought life into the house.

Zack figured he'd better hit the jogging trail to keep his weight at 195 pounds, so he slipped into his shorts and T-shirt, then hurried downstairs.

In the kitchen, he got out the frying pan and eggs, then whipped up a three-egg ham and cheese omelet, his specialty. By the time Laura bounded down the stairs, Zack had pulled an English muffin from the toaster and set it on her plate.

"Thanks, Pop." She flopped down as only teenagers can and started to shovel.

"Hey, take it easy. Those eggs aren't going anywhere."

She pushed hair from her face and smiled up at him. "Oh, but I am. I've got soccer practice this morning. We've got a game to-night."

Laura played in the summer northern Virginia soccer league and would be starting her practice with the George Washington University team in August.

Her blue eyes sparkled. "You're coming to my game, right, coach? Five o'clock on field four."

"I'll be there." He watched her, marveling at how beautiful she was. Tall, slender, long brown hair, and that cute smile. He loved to help coach her team.

She glanced up. Caught him. "All right, what are you staring at? I bet you're going to say something about what a beauty I am or some dumb thing like that."

"Nope. I was only wondering how you can polish off an omelet that fast."

"No choice. Mary Ellen will be picking me up in" – she looked at the clock – "no, ten minutes." She jumped up, gave him a kiss. "Gotta go brush my teeth in case some handsome hunk wants to kiss me. Maybe some extra mouthwash."

Zack jerked. "Huh?"

She headed for the stairs, laughing. "Got ya. Busy day?"

"Yeah, I'm headed out for a jog, then going to meet Colonel Garcia for breakfast. She's got something going on and wants me to help."

"Tell her hi for me."

While Zack cleaned up the dishes, the front door slammed.

He finished and headed toward the door, wondering what Garcia wanted.

———————

Zack turned his truck into the parking lot for Mom's Restaurant, cut the engine and hopped out. Located just two miles west of the Pentagon along Columbia Pike, Zack enjoyed having a chance to BS with friends over a cold beer after work.

Garcia waved from the back as he entered. He walked over to the booth and slipped in across from her. "Hey, Zack, thanks for coming on such short notice."

A slender, petite woman, Rene Garcia had grown up in Texas and now wore the rank of a lieutenant colonel. They'd worked together for about eighteen months. A great partner. "No problem. But, let me get some coffee first so I can think."

After they'd ordered, Zack took a couple of sips of coffee. "I saw your Harley out back." Only five four, she had told a number of big guys she'd blacken the eye of anyone who told her she stood too short for the bike. Zack believed her. "Okay, my mind's ready to process information."

Garcia smiled. "Never catch a guy without his coffee."

Her smile so darn infectious, Zack found himself smiling back at her. "Good advice."

"I'm not quite sure where to start," Garcia said. "So how about at the beginning. I got a call from my brother last night."

"Your . . . ?"

She cut him off. "I know, I know, I never told you about my brother. His name's David. The twit my parents spoiled rotten because he happened to be a boy. Since I left home for the University of Texas, I haven't seen him more than two or three times in the past ten years."

Zack waited as she looked away and when she didn't continue he asked, "Do I gather you and your brother aren't particularly close?"

"Understatement of the year. He's thirty-three years old, loves computers, and must have set the record for being a jerk growing up. When he called me last night, he asked if we could meet."

"Did he say why?"

"Apparently there's some problem at work and he needs my help because it deals with a contract his company has with the Pentagon."

Zack took a sip of coffee. "Where does he work?"

"Some computer outfit here in Fairfax." She put her head in her hands and sighed. "Oh man, I hate to admit I don't know much of anything about David."

Zack reached over and put his hand on her arm. "Don't feel as if you owe me an explanation. You're my friend. You wanted me here and here I am."

They stopped talking when the waitress arrived with their breakfast. As Garcia sliced into her omelet, she glanced up and mumbled, "Here he comes."

Zack slipped out of the booth and stood in time to see David Garcia arrive. His black hair trailed halfway down his back and he wore dark framed glasses with narrow lenses. A pair of gray cords, long-sleeved T-shirt, and running shoes filled out his wardrobe. Zack did see a resemblance between brother and sister, although Garcia wore her black hair much shorter.

Zack held out his hand. "Zack Kelly."

The man took the outstretched hand. "David Garcia." Glancing at his sister, he said, "Hi, Rene. Thanks for coming."

"Hello, David." She stood and gave him a half-hearted hug, then motioned with her hand toward a seat. "Sit down."

After they were seated, she said, "Zack's my partner on the national security advisor's special task force. When you said you had a problem with your job and the Pentagon, I thought Zack might be able to help out, too. How about some breakfast?"

"No, thanks. I already ate and have to leave shortly to get to work." He looked at Zack's cup. "Maybe some coffee."

Zack turned to catch the waitress's eye. "Could we get another cup, please?"

When the waitress left, David said, "I work at a software company, Sterling Software."

Zack made a mental note of the name, but didn't say anything.

"We've developed a new security system that should be a great leap forward for the industry."

"Why is that?" Zack asked.

"The design will allow companies to block hackers from breaking into their system."

Garcia dropped her fork with a clatter. "Look, David, can you move this along. Zack and I have a lot of things we need to do today and learning the details of your system isn't on the top of my list."

David held up his hand, palm toward her. "Wait a minute. Let me explain. I'm sure you're both aware of the problems the services are having in meeting the need for intelligence, surveillance, and reconnaissance or ISR capability."

Zack took a sip of coffee. "Right, ISR was a big problem in Afghanistan. Still is."

"In June, 2005, the Air Force established Creech Air Force Base in Nevada as the home base for its remotely piloted aircraft systems program with a mission to fly the ISR drones across the globe."

"Okay," Garcia said, "I'm with you so far."

"They started with the Predator Drone and eventually moved toward the much larger and more capable drone, the Reaper."

Zack had to hand it to him. The guy knew what he was talking about. "Where do you fit in on this?"

"The drone program has been very successful and a number of corporations have expressed interest in establishing drones for commercial use. As a matter of fact, the Federal Aviation Administration recently announced that six states will develop test sites for drones, a critical next step for integrating unmanned aircraft into U.S. skies. Alaska, Nevada, New York, North Dakota, Texas and Virginia will host the research sites."

Interested, Zack set down his fork. "I've heard something about this."

"Drones have been mainly used by the military, but state and local governments, businesses, farmers, and others are looking at ways to use them for peacetime missions." He started to cough and took a sip of water. "Many universities are starting or expanding drone programs. These test sites will give us valuable information about how best to ensure the safe introduction of this advanced technology into our nation's skies."Garcia glanced at her watch. "Sounds as if things are moving along."

"The FAA doesn't allow commercial use of drones domestically yet. But it's working to develop operational guidelines. The FAA projects some 7,500 commercial drones could be aloft within five years of getting approval access to American airspace."

Zack whistled. "Wow, big deal."

"There's a lot of pressure to get this moving," David said. "An industry-commissioned study has predicted more than 70,000 jobs would develop in the first three years after Congress loosens drone restrictions in U.S. skies."

"I bet the civil liberty folks are gonna be upset," Zack said.

"Absolutely," David replied. "They feel that giving drones greater access to U.S. skies moves the nation closer to a surveillance society in which our every move is monitored, recorded, and scrutinized by the authorities and who knows what else."

"Oh, boy," Garcia said, "gonna be a big fight."

"It turns out that at the end of 2013, a multi-agency program was launched at Camp Shelby's Joint Forces Training Center. This is one of the first efforts to bring together unmanned vehicles technology with open source software."

Garcia took another bite of her eggs, then leaned back. "I'm glad you're in the middle of something really good. Why do you need us?"

"Sterling Software won the contract to do the cyber-security for this new research project. My company has the capability to hack into the most sensitive portions of this project and steal computer secrets from not only the DOD agency but also the member companies who are doing the work."

"If you control their security fence, isn't it your job to stop that?" Garcia asked.

"Exactly right. But, I've overhead our company managers say they plan to steal those government and company secrets and sell them to the highest bidder. And who knows what else they might try and do with those drones?"

Zack stared at David for a moment. He couldn't believe what he was hearing. "You're saying that your company plans to steal government secrets?"

"That's exactly what I'm saying and I need your help to stop it."

3

The White House, Washington, D.C., Monday, 2:30 pm

The staff car carrying Zack and Garcia passed through the northwest gate of the White House and pulled up in front of the West Wing entrance. A secret service agent met them at the side door and escorted them to the national security advisor's outer office.

When they entered, Admiral Steele's senior administrative assistant, Evelyn Brody, glanced up from her desk. "Hi, Zack, sorry we had to push back the meeting. The boss will be with you in a minute. Please take a seat. How about some coffee?"

"Oh man," Zack replied, "that'd be great. Let me get it."

He walked over to the pot and poured a cup for himself and one for Garcia, then sat next to her on the couch. Zack took a few minutes to organize his thoughts.

While they waited, their partners on the special task force, T.J. Wilson, Blake Lannigan, and Barclay Morrison hurried into the office and took seats opposite them on the other couch. Wilson mopped his brow. "Damn traffic almost did us in."

Admiral Steele stepped out from his office and motioned for the five to enter and sit at his conference table. "I don't have much time. Another appointment at three o'clock." He pointed at Garcia. "Okay, what have you got?"

Garcia summarized the conversation with her brother from that morning.

When she finished, Admiral Steele sat for a moment. "I was in a meeting with the president a few weeks ago when the head of the FAA briefed him on the initiative. He supports it and sees this program as the wave of the future. We have too many separate agencies in the middle of our drone program, and we've got to get it together before the program runs away from us. How valid is what your brother says?"

"Like I told Zack, Admiral, I don't think he would make this up. He believes what he told us and thinks there is real danger the clowns at Sterling Software will hack into that database and steal national secrets. And who knows what they may be able to do with them."

Steele sat back for a moment stroking his chin. "What do you recommend?"

"I'm not sure," Garcia replied. "I don't have any contacts in this new program I trust with this sort of information. David is way out on a limb. If he's wrong, they'll undoubtedly fire him, but if he's right then someone is going to try to stop him. There must be a lot of money on the table."

Steele sipped his coffee. "Probably the best course of action is to ask General Harding to join us for a discussion. She's the Pentagon's point person on the initiative."

Barclay Morrison leaned forward. "I have a contact in the DOD who's working with General Harding. I trust he'll tell me what he knows and keep it a secret."

"Okay, that's good," Steele replied. "See if you can get with him today. Once we hear what he has to say, we can evaluate whether or not to bring in Harding. In the meantime, I met an FBI agent a couple of weeks ago who recently took charge of cyber extortion for the FBI. I'll ask Evelyn to contact him and set up an appointment for Garcia. We'll meet tomorrow morning and see where we are. Not something we can sit on."

Garcia arrived at FBI headquarters and parked her Harley in a lot across the street. By the time she reached the front door, it was almost time for her appointment. A classic summer day in Washington, warm and sunny with low humidity, at least not yet. Today would be a great day for a long run; not another meeting.

She cleared the security checkpoint and the metal detector, then took an elevator to the seventh floor. When she arrived at room 702, a young blonde looked up from her desk. "Are you Colonel Garcia?"

Garcia wanted to point to her name tag but decided to play nice and simply nodded. "I have an appointment with a Senior Agent Frank Harper."

The woman buzzed her intercom and soon a tall, well-built man in a dark suit, white shirt and tie came out from one of the offices. "Colonel Garcia, I'm Frank Harper. Please come in. Coffee?"

"That would be nice."

When they were seated, she took a sip. "Hum, not bad for government issue."

Leaning back, Harper put his feet up on a footstool, then brushed a piece of lint off his suit pants. "How may I help you, Colonel?"

"My brother, David, told me his computer company may be planning to steal classified material from this new initiative on drones the FAA has put together. I wanted to tell you about it to see what you recommend. If you agree, it may be prudent to put a wire on him and see if we can record his meetings."

Harper watched her for a moment, tapping his fingers on the desk. "You're a military police officer. You know we can't tape conversations without probable cause a crime has been or will be committed. We don't want to stumble into another NSA mess and have the press all over us. Americans value their privacy."

Garcia shifted in her chair. "I'll be honest with you, Agent Harper. My brother and I haven't been all that close over the years, but I believe him."

16

"What exactly does his company do?" Harper asked.

She shared with him what David had told her.

"All right. Admiral Steele speaks very highly of you and asked me to help out in any way I could. First of all, let me tell you a little about what I do. I'm Director of the Computer Crimes Division. I took over four weeks ago, so I'm still learning my way around the system. Minneapolis is a long way from Washington."

"Minneapolis is that," Garcia replied. "I grew up in Austin. Even farther away."

"Let me call in my deputy, Special Agent Fairchild. She's been here longer than I have and keeps me on the right track." He picked up the phone and talked to someone.

In a few minutes, a woman who looked to be in her mid-thirties, square shoulders like a weight-lifter's, and dressed in a tailored navy-blue suit, stood in the doorway. Her blond hair was spiked on top, then the rest swept back on the side of her head. Looked tough as hell.

Harper motioned to a chair. "Colonel Garcia, let me introduce Special Agent Tara Fairchild." The two women shook hands. "Colonel Garcia is here because of what appears to be a problem in the Pentagon. Admiral Steele has asked if we could help. Colonel Garcia, why don't you summarize what you told me?"

Garcia wondered why Harper hadn't gotten Fairchild in here earlier, but she kept a smile on her face and repeated her story.

When Garcia finished, Fairchild seemed to stare right through her, then she said, "All right. Have your brother come in. If he passes our screen and his statement seems valid, we should be able to argue our case before a judge and obtain a warrant to wire him. Then we can plant him at this Sterling Software."

Garcia thought about that. "Could be pretty dangerous."

"That's true," Fairchild replied, "but so is stealing government secrets."

Garcia nodded. "Okay, I'll see if he'll do it."

4

Washington Lee High School, Field Four, Monday, 5:30 pm

Zack pulled up in front of the ball field in time to hear the crowd roaring. Blue sky, sun shining, but thankfully not too hot. He hustled to the bench and greeted the coach.

"You made it," Coach called. "Why don't you focus on defense? I'll take the lead on offense."

"Will do," Zack replied. He paced the sidelines, watching each player move the ball, searching for weaknesses in the other team they could exploit. He loved to watch Laura, smooth, fluid in all her movements.

The two teams were evenly matched and the game rolled on, neither side getting the upper hand. At the break, Zack shared a flaw he'd spotted in the other teams' defense, one of their players slower on the left wing. The coach agreed, so they set up for Laura to take the ball down that side of the field, shadowed by the center.

Shortly after the start of the second half, Laura broke to the right, the center following slightly to her left. The two did a masterful job of moving the ball. Laura came at the goalie from a right angle, slamming the ball into the net to a round of applause from the crowd.

Laura ran back toward the center line, giving her dad a thumbs-up as she ran. Zack smiled and gave her a thumbs-up. God, he loved that girl.

His cell rang. *Ignore it*, he thought, but something told him he'd better take it. He pulled it out of his pocket. "Kelly."

"Zack, this is Linda Christensen."

Zack had to pause for a moment before he could process the name. Then it came to him. Linda Christensen, a navy lieutenant commander, and Brian Toomey's wife. Toomey had worked for Zack during his second tour in Afghanistan. "Hello, Linda. I'm kinda busy. Can I call you back in a while?"

"Zack, I need your help."

He could hear the stress in her voice. "What's the matter?"

"You know Brian and I had our differences."

Hell yes, they'd had differences. She'd left him, fed up with all of his running around. Then when the sexual abuse scandal hit, she'd finally divorced him. Toomey was a strong officer, but turned out to be bad news with females. "Look, I'm in the middle of my daughter's soccer game."

"It's Brian. He's dead."

Zack sucked in his breath. "What? Brian's dead?"

A muffled cry. "Yes." Another sob.

"What happened? An accident?"

"It looks like someone killed him Sunday night, then left his body along the beach in Sea Isle City, New Jersey."

"What the hell . . .? Why there?"

"I don't know. Brian really hurt me. Then we split. But to have someone kill him. Oh, it's horrible . . ." She sobbed again.

Zack walked away from the bench. "What can I do to help?"

"Would you come with me tomorrow to Sea Isle City? I need to identify the body."

Zack thought about it. Things were busy and he had Laura to consider. But, Linda needed help. "All right, I'll drive you there."

"Thanks so much, Zack. It's awful. Someone killed him, then they . . . they, they cut off his penis and stuffed it in his right hand."

Barclay Morrison walked into the diner and spotted Zamir Nabhas sitting in the back, looking at a menu. Barclay checked to see if he recognized anyone else before he slid into Zamir's booth.

Zamir looked tired and kept glancing around the restaurant. "I don't think this is a good idea. If anyone finds out about us, my old man will have a fit. He's been searching for a young woman from India for me to marry. Talk about a guy caught in the past. But damn, I hate to break the news to him about us."

"No kidding," Barclay said. "Look, Admiral Steele insisted I meet with you tonight. This is too big an issue and he doesn't wait worth a damn."

Zamir put his hand on Barclay's arm and gave it a squeeze. "I understand. Let's just have a quick cup of coffee and a roll, then slip out of here before anyone spots us together."

Barclay raised his hand. He usually did the ordering for the two of them.

When the waitress arrived, he said, "Two coffees and two of your best chocolate chip muffins. And could you hustle that order, please? We need to get a move on."

When she walked off, Barclay whispered, "Let me tell you about the meeting I attended with Admiral Steele this afternoon. You're familiar with Sterling Software and their role with the FAA initiative and the new agency at Fort Shelby."

"Hell, yes. They provide security for our computers. Why?"

"Lieutenant Colonel Garcia briefed our task force this afternoon. Apparently her brother works for Sterling."

"Sure, David Garcia. Not much of a dresser, but he seems like a nice enough guy and all signs are that he's competent."

"What do you know about the contractor, this Sterling Software?"

"We've been pretty happy with Sterling's performance to date."

"How long have they been providing computer security for the program?"

"We brought them on board about eighteen months ago. There have been problems with hackers in the past. We needed an iron-clad program to protect the system. Why?"

Zamir motioned for Barclay to be quiet while the waitress set down their coffees and muffins.

After she left, Barclay said, "Tell me a little about them."

Zamir lowered his voice. "I did much of the research on the original contract. Jason Sterling founded the company in 1994. According to their prospectus, they specialize in engineering and logistical solutions for corporations as well as the federal and state government. They've developed a suite of products including sensors and other electrical materials. I can get you more."

Barclay smiled. "Damn, what a memory you have. Sounds to me like a typical government beltway bandit."

Zamir took a bite of his muffin. "Sterling did about fifty-four million dollars of business last year, specializing in developing security programs for various companies. They have this new anti-virus system that does it all. Our idea is to use their program for as many of our systems as possible."

"I don't get it," Barclay said. "They're not a big company. Did they win the contract on a competitive bid?"

Zamir finished chewing. "That's the interesting part. The vice president herself came down from the mountain top to one of our meetings and suggested we select them."

"No shit. Millicent Townsend sponsored this contractor?"

Zamir nodded. "Now, I'm not saying they're incompetent or anything like that. They're good, but we didn't do a thorough search. I wanted to check out a number of other contractors, but General Harding rolled over for the VP."

"I can understand that. She can be pretty persuasive from what I understand. Do you know what she did before she became the veep?"

"I believe she ran some big deal energy corporation, then was elected to the U.S. Senate from Texas before joining the ticket."

Barclay looked around. "Here's the deal. Sterling may have the capability to hack into the most sensitive portions of this new research program and steal computer secrets not only from the agency, but also member companies who are doing the work."

"Wait a minute, It's their job to prevent hacking."

"But according to Colonel Garcia, her brother overheard the leadership of the company say they plan to steal those government and company secrets and sell them to the highest bidder."

"Holy shit." Zamir's eyes widened. "They might be able to steal a drone."

"I don't know what the truth is, but that's what David told his sister. Zack Kelly sat in on their meeting to witness the discussion."

Zamir played with his muffin for a moment. "We've known each other for a long time. I've got to trust you."

Barclay reached under the table and put his hand on Zamir's thigh. "You know you can."

Zamir put his cup down and lowered his voice even more. "I think it's possible. Hell, anything's possible."

"All right. What do we do about it? And what about David Garcia?"

Zamir grimaced. "I have no idea, but I gotta get out of here."

Barclay watched him leave. Took a sip of coffee.

5

Sea Isle City, NJ, Tuesday, 8:00 am

It had taken Zack a little over four hours, in his truck, to negotiate the interstates with Linda Christensen from D.C. to Sea Isle City. An early start had gotten the two of them through D.C. and past Baltimore before the rush hour hit. But the traffic slowed between Baltimore and Wilmington on Interstate 95. Once they reached New Jersey, traffic lightened and they made good time.

His GPS led them across the bridge to JFK Boulevard, the main drag into the small town, then directed Zack to turn right on Central and drive to the police station.

The two stepped out of Zack's truck and walked across the parking lot to a temporary building, tucked in behind an old school. Much of the Jersey Shore still worked on recovery from Hurricane Sandy.

Linda took his arm as they walked. "Thanks so much for coming with me. I'm not sure I could have done this on my own."

Zack still couldn't believe it. "Remember, Brian and I worked together. He was my friend, too."

When they stepped inside, Zack asked the uniformed officer at the desk for Lieutenant Powell. Expecting the normal hard-boiled detective, it surprised him when an attractive young woman, short, with her brown hair pulled into a bun on top of her head walked up the hallway. "Good morning, I'm Maxine Powell. May I see some identification, please?"

Zack and Linda pulled out their military IDs and showed them to the lieutenant.

Powell took the IDs and led them down the narrow hallway and into a small conference room. "You'll note our headquarters leaves a lot to be desired. Hurricane Sandy did a job on the permanent building, so we're here until they fix our new digs."

A blockish-looking man, his black hair streaked with gray and combed directly back on his head, sat at the rectangular table. His bored expression probably indicated he'd seen it all.

Powell pointed toward the man. "This is Albert Sprite, the representative from the Cape May County prosecutor's office. His office will be leading the investigation into Colonel Toomey's murder."

Sprite managed a half stand, weak handshake, and a mumble.

After introductions, Lieutenant Powell summarized what they knew thus far. "A jogger discovered Colonel Toomey's body on the beach near 54th Street Monday morning a little before six o'clock."

"Not till six o'clock?" Zack asked. "I'm surprised someone didn't see him earlier."

"The number of folks on the beach is picking up as we head into the season," Powell continued. "At first, the jogger assumed the man had fallen asleep because he was sitting in a beach chair, head slumped to his chest. When he saw the man was dead, he called us."

"How did he determine that Brian had died?" Zack asked.

"Toomey didn't respond to the jogger calling out to him, then when he got closer" – she seemed to shudder – "he noticed the man was naked, saw dried blood on his crotch, and his penis stuffed into his right hand. The words 'Dark Angel' were tattooed across his chest."

"No," Linda cried. "Oh, no."

Powell handed Linda a box of tissues. "I'm sorry, I've been a terrible host. Would you like some coffee, maybe tea or a glass of water?"

"Coffee and water would be great," Zack replied.

"I can arrange to have a social worker here for you to talk with if you'd like"

Linda shook her head and blew her nose. "No, that's all right. Brian and I divorced a little over a year ago. He could be difficult, but my lord, no one deserves that."

"Of course," Powell replied. "What do you mean he could be difficult?"

"We were married for almost five years. The first four seemed great. We had an enjoyable two-year tour in the Pentagon, then a joint assignment to Iraq."

Powell made a note. "Where were you assigned in Iraq?"

"At the joint military headquarters in the Green Zone. Brian deployed on a number of operational assignments in the field during our tour . . . he was a ranger like Zack. But all in all, the months flew by. I was assigned to the naval liaison section."

"What happened then?" Powell asked, her pen poised.

Linda took a sip of coffee, hesitating, seeming to debate what to say.

"You need to tell her everything," Zack said.

"All right." Linda squared her shoulders, obviously preparing herself for the next part of the questioning. "The rumors began shortly before we left Iraq."

"Rumors?" Powell looked up from her paper.

"I didn't pay much attention to them because Brian was always so sweet with me."

Sprite seemed to come alive. "This is an investigation. You need to provide us details."

Powell's gaze searched Linda. "I can't imagine how difficult this must be for you, Commander Christensen, but we need to know everything that could be helpful in finding out who did this terrible thing."

Linda blew her nose again. "Thank you." She glanced at Powell and managed a faint smile. "About two months before we rotated back to the States, the rumors surfaced that Brian had been" – she swallowed – "you know, abusive to women."

"What exactly do you mean, Commander?" Sprite demanded. "Please be specific."

Zack wanted to slug the guy. "Give her a chance, Sprite."

Sprite glared at Zack. "I'll clear the room if you interrupt again."

Powell held up her hand. "That won't be necessary. Colonel Kelly is only trying to help Commander Christensen through a very difficult time."

Linda took another sip of water and cleared her throat.

"Three women came forward just before we left. Two of the complaints were his using, you know, sexual innuendos. But the third woman was a sergeant who claimed that Brian had raped her."

Powell nodded. "What did the investigation show? Was your husband exonerated?"

"Ex-husband," Linda said.

Sprite leaned forward, tapping his pen on the table. "We'll need a copy of that investigation. I'll forward a request to DOD."

Linda stayed quiet for a moment. She glanced at Zack.

"The army never conducted a formal inquiry," Zack replied. "The sergeant worked for Brian. He said she was upset about not being selected for promotion. By the time the incident came to the attention of higher command, Brian and Linda were departing the command."

Powell made a note. "Are you saying the army never investigated her complaint?"

"There was an informal inquiry," Zack replied, "but it was the sergeant's word against Brian's and the matter eventually got dropped."

"Do you remember the name of the sergeant?" Powell asked.

"I'll never forget it," Linda replied. "Sergeant Collins, Sergeant Margo Collins."

Everyone in the room sat silent, each of them looking down, probably searching for what to say.

Finally, Zack asked, "You mentioned the Dark Angel. What does that mean?"

"I'm not sure," Powell replied. "Maybe that's who is taking credit for the murder."

Rene Garcia sat next to her brother at the conference table, Agents Harper and Fairchild across from them.

Fairchild opened her small, spiral notebook. "Your sister has explained to us your concerns, David. These, of course, are serious allegations. We need to obtain proof of what you've told us. Would you be willing to help us by wearing a wire so we could hear these discussions?"

David rose from his chair, staring at her. "I'm not lying to you, Agent Fairchild. Look, I came forward voluntarily. The easiest thing for me would have been to drop it, then move on to another job."

Fairchild glared at David. "Sit down. I've got to verify what you say to take any action against these people. I realize what we're asking you to do here. Somewhere down the line you'll need to testify against your former employers. I know that won't be easy."

Garcia put her hand on David's arm. He sat back down. "I'm not an idiot. I understand the ramifications of what I'm doing."

Fairchild watched him. "No one is calling you an idiot."

Harper leaned forward in his chair. "I know it wasn't easy to come to us, but it was the right decision."

"I'm not so sure," David said, looking at his hands.

Fairchild closed her notebook. "We need to set up a system so you'll be able to contact us without being detected by the people at Sterling."

David nodded.

Fairchild pulled a form out of her briefcase. "This document authorizes us to place a recording device on your body." She handed it to David. "You'll need to read it at your convenience, then sign it."

David nodded, then looked up at her.

She handed David another sheet. "Here's a second document for you to read and sign. It's a cooperation agreement. It says that we won't prosecute you for any information you provide us. In return for that agreement, you must always be truthful. If you lie to us or are not completely honest, you could be prosecuted for perjury or even obstruction of justice. Do you understand?"

"I know you have to do this," Garcia said, "but you're making it sound as if David is the bad guy here."

"These forms are a standard requirement. Both Agent Harper and I appreciate what David is doing and we will do everything we can to assist him. It's just that sometimes, people get in over their heads and start lying to us. I don't want that to happen and I'm sure David doesn't either."

"All right," David said. "What's next?"

"Let me show you what we plan on using." She handed him a small metal item, thin, about the size of a cigarette case. "Our device doesn't use tapes, it is digital. This will allow the conversations to be uploaded later and played on a computer. Do you have any questions?"

"No," David replied, his voice sharp. "Can we get started? I don't want this to drag on."

Garcia leaned forward and put her hand on her brother's arm again. "Take time to read all the documents and make sure this is what you want to do."

He pulled away from her. "Don't you think this is all I've thought about for the past five days? I want to start."

Fairchild glanced over at Harper who nodded.

"You're sure?" Harper asked.

"I'm sure."

Fairchild picked up the phone. "I'm calling the agent who will help you put this on and test it for you. While we're waiting, I suggest you finish reading, then sign the forms. I should be able to obtain formal authorization this afternoon."

David looked at his sister, then sat down and began to read again.

6

The White House, Tuesday, 4:00 pm

Zack dropped off Linda Christensen at her house about three o'clock, then raced to the White House to brief Admiral Steele.

When he arrived, T.J. Wilson, Blake Lannigan, Garcia, and Barclay Morrison waited at the conference table in the admiral's office.

A blond with a few streaks of gray in her hair, stood in the corner of the room talking to Steele. When she turned, Zack saw the two stars on her U.S. Air force uniform and the name tag, Harding. Oh, yeah, General Harding, the military coordinator for the military's stateside drone initiative.

After Zack pulled up a chair, Steele said, "Okay, let's hear it."

Zack went over the details of what had happened with Toomey, gathering grimaces from each of the attendees. "Powell, the detective from Sea Isle City, seems like she'd be pretty good to work with. But this Sprite, he's from the prosecutor's office in Cape May, looks to be a real pain in the ass. Very harsh on Linda, I think far more than he needed to be. Unfortunately, his office will be in charge of the murder investigation."

Steele stood and started pacing. He always seemed to think better on his feet. "I invited General Harding to sit in on the discussion about the possibility of a cyber security issue. Garcia, could you give us an update?

"Sure." Garcia briefly summarized what her brother had told her and the FBI.

When she finished, Harding said, "That's impossible. I personally screened Sterling and accepted them based upon their qualifications and also the word of the vice president.

Garcia's eyes widened. "Vice President Townsend?"

"Right. Apparently Sterling had done work for her when she was with some energy corporation in Texas. According to the vice president, they were professional, highly qualified, and very helpful." Harding turned to Garcia. "How do you know your brother didn't make all of this up?"

"Well, we'll be able to verify David's story once we hear the tape."

"Okay, enough of that," Steele said. "Let's return to a discussion of the murder. What about motive?"

"I knew Brian fairly well," Zack said. "He was in my battalion during my second tour. A good officer, but from what I understand, on his tour in Iraq, he went off the deep end on sexual abuse."

"How do you mean?" Blake asked.

"You know, sexual innuendos with females in his battalion. I don't believe he stomped down hard enough on other guys in the battalion when they did the same thing."

Steele stopped pacing. "We have too much of that, but it doesn't appear to be enough of a motive for someone to kill him."

"Probably not," Blake replied. "But it makes for an awful atmosphere for females to try and do their job. I wouldn't stand for it."

"Blake's right," Zack replied. "If I understand it correctly, during his last tour, a sergeant in his battalion accused him of raping her. It appears he may have covered it up."

"No investigation ever held?" Blake asked.

"Brian and Linda were close to their rotation time back to the States so nothing ever came of it. No investigation."

"What happened to the sergeant?" Blake asked.

"I don't know." Zack replied. "A Sergeant Margo Collins. I'll see if I can find out."

Blake grimaced. "Damn army, they're getting an awful reputation concerning sexual abuse. Really pisses me off. You think the big boys would listen to what's going on around them."

"One hell of a problem," General Harding said. "A number of officers charge it off to 'boys will be boys' or that the 'girl asked for it'."

"Disgusting," Blake said. "Do they have any leads as to who might have done it?"

Zack shook his head. "He had the name Dark Angel carved on his chest. The preliminary forensics exam indicates it may have been carved before he died."

Steele grimaced. "All right, let's stay with this. I'll brief the president on what we know so far. Be sure and keep me advised of any new developments."

––––––––––––

Zack walked in the front door to see Laura sitting at the dining room table, iPad on one side, books scattered around her on the other. "Hey, sweetheart, how ya doing?"

"Summer school is a pain in the butt. I guess I'm not cut out to be a math major."

"I wish I could help you, but math never was my strong suit."

"Well this is a warm up for college algebra in the fall. Guess I'll be glad then I'm doing this now." Laura leaned back and took a swig of her soda. "How was the trip today? Where did you go?"

"I drove Linda Christensen up to Sea Isle City, a little north of Cape May, New Jersey."

"Sure, I remember her. We met someplace."

"Probably one time when we were at the Fort Myer Officers Club. It turns out her ex-husband was murdered. The police think it happened on Sunday night."

"Oh no, that's awful."

"It was very bad. Apparently whoever did it tortured Brian before they killed him."

"What do you mean tortured?"

Zack shuddered when he thought about it. *Should he share the truth? Well, maybe part of it.* "The murderer carved initials in his chest. The medical examiner thinks it was done before he died."

Her hands flew up to her face and she moaned. "Why?"

"Brian may have been involved with mistreatment of some of his female soldiers."

"You mean sexual abuse?"

Zack nodded. "He may have even raped a female sergeant who worked for him and was successful in covering it up. The police are trying to find the sergeant and see if she knows anything about the murder."

Laura fell silent for a minute. "Last year, we had a group of guys at school who were abusive to one of my friends. The poor girl, she's kinda heavy, they'd say awful things about her, bump into her so she'd drop her books, sometimes even grope her. Pretty bad."

"Did she report them?" Zack asked.

"Oh sure, and the principal called these guys into his office, but they're the big jocks in the school and they only had their hands slapped. Then the harassment only got worse. The girl said she felt like committing suicide."

"She needs help. How about her parents?"

"They're not very involved."

Zack hated to hear about parents like that. "I wish I had known. Would have been glad to talk to the principal. That's no way for anyone to be treated."

Laura's face lit up. "I wish I'd told you. I felt so sorry for her."

"The principal has a problem and doesn't realize how serious it is. The harassment is just going to get worse if he doesn't do something about it and the earlier the better." Zack stopped for a moment. "Does anyone do stuff like that to you?"

"Nah, they leave me alone. The dumb shits know I'd kick 'em in the balls if they tried anything."

Zack had to laugh. "Well, that's one way to solve the problem."

"You bet and it's very effective. Oh, Dad, Rodney's coming over in a little while and we're headed off to a movie."

Every time Zack thought about Rodney, he remembered what an ass he'd been. Zack had prejudged Rodney because he looked like a human pincushion with all the rings hanging from his nose, ears, and who knew where else? It turned out the kid was a good guy and really cared for Laura. Big lesson learned.

"Tell him hi for me." Zack turned and walked up the stairs to change, thinking about sexual abuse and how he might be capable of killing someone who did that to Laura. He shuddered.

———————

The phone rang in his apartment. The man lifted his head from the woman's breast. "Why does the damn phone always ring when I'm in the middle of something good?"

"Let it ring, honey. We've got more important things to do. Kiss me again like you did before. That felt really good."

Shit, might be the boss. He untangled himself from the current sweetie on his bed and struggled into the living room to answer the phone. "Yeah."

"I've got a job for you," a female voice said.

"Better be plenty of money involved."

"Have you ever known me to not take care of you? Now, listen up. You need to eliminate someone who could cause trouble. This guy must meet with an accident. It needs to happen right away. In the next twenty four hours."

7

Falls Church, VA, Wednesday, 5:50 a.m.

David Garcia pedaled hard, hunched over his handlebars, bat-tling the morning winds. The breeze buffeted him as rush-hour traffic whizzed past. He relished the burn in his legs, the sweat trickling down his back. Focus. Forget your frustrations. Pedal.

As he biked, memories flashed across his brain – his wife, a new baby, hell, a chance for a new beginning. Make things right. At least, try.

He glanced at his watch. Ten minutes to six. Just enough time to get back to the house, take a shower, and get ready for work. Check-ing his mirror, he stuck out his left arm to signal a turn. A maroon pickup truck trailed him. "Move over, buddy," he murmured, "you're crowding me."

His muscles tightened. He slowed the pumping of his legs and waited for the truck to pass. Checked the mirror again. Damn pickup wasn't passing. The truck's grill, chrome reflecting the morning light, loomed directly behind him.

"Turn," he cried. "Oh, god. No. No . . .!"

The truck's bumper smashed into his bike. Tightness gripped his chest. Pain exploded in his head. Tumbling. Falling . . ..

The sound of screeching metal enveloped him. Then darkness.

The ringing telephone shook Zack out of a sound sleep. He checked his clock. Five fifty-five. Time to get up. Damn, he'd almost overslept.

He grabbed the phone. "Kelly."

"Colonel Kelly, it's Lieutenant Powell in Sea Isle City. We found another dead male, looks like the same MO. Body stashed on one of our beaches in a lawn chair. One of his private parts removed. Appears to be a sharp knife."

Zack couldn't believe it. Another one. "Do you think it's this Dark Angel again?"

"Yep, the name's carved on the poor bastard's chest. We've managed to identify him. Name is Frank Butler. He's – that is, he was – a Marine Corp major."

"I'll be there as soon as I can. And thanks for the heads up. We've got a killer who doesn't like military officers."

"Perhaps the understatement of the year. Let me know when you'll arrive and I'll meet you."

"Will do." Zack hung up and called Steele. When he answered, Zack said, "Sir, Zack Kelly. Lieutenant Powell in Sea Isle City called a minute ago to tell me they've found another body. This time it's a Marine Corp major by the name of Butler. The name 'Dark Angel' is carved on his chest and they cut off his penis."

"You'd better fly up there and see what's up. Garcia is busy with her brother. Why don't you call Blake. See if she can go along."

"Will do, sir. He hung up and dialed Blake Lannigan. As the phone rang, he wondered what would happen next.

"Lannigan."

"Hi, Blake, Zack Kelly. Lieutenant Powell in Sea Isle City called. Another dead officer. Admiral Steele wants me to fly up there and thought you'd be willing to come along."

"Oh, no, not another one. Ah, okay, I've got to cancel a couple of meetings. This is more important. I'll meet you at the Pentagon as soon as I can get there. Give me an hour."

"Let me call T.J. Maybe he can fly us up there."

He stood and stretched. *I'd better shake out Laura and get her moving, too.*

———————

Lieutenant Colonel Rene Garcia shut the door of her condo and hurried through her backyard toward the one-car garage, eager to make it into the Pentagon. *Beat the rush.*

She opened the wooden garage door and stepped inside. Her Harley stood ready, a 2012 Super Glide Custom. She'd bought it six months before and rode it every chance she could. *A little cool out there today, but she wore her leathers.*

The bike had tank-mounted gauges, solid stainless steel pull-back handlebars, mid-mounted controls that made it easy for her short legs to reach the pedals and best of all, gave her 53 miles to a gallon.

She rolled the Harley onto the cracked cement driveway, closed the garage door, and glanced at her watch. Twenty minutes after six. *My damn curmudgeon neighbors won't like the noise, but that's tough. Duty calls.* Hopping onto her bike, she cranked it up, shuddering when it fired. She gunned it to get out of there as fast as possible.

Her condo in Old Town Alexandria made it a fast run up the George Washington Parkway to the Pentagon. Unless she got caught in a traffic jam she'd be there in twenty minutes, thirty at the outside. A chance to check with David and see how he's doing before he gets to the office. Garcia had to admire him for his willingness to wear that wire. *Maybe she'd misjudged him. No, he was that little prick growing up, but,* she smiled, *maybe he'd matured. Who knew.*

As she turned onto the Parkway, the ear bud in her helmet rang. She pushed the button on her left wrist and spoke into the microphone. "Garcia."

"Colonel, this is the social worker at Fairfax Hospital."

Hospital? How did this guy get her number? "Yes?"

"Do you know a David Garcia?" He asked.

Uh, oh, did something happen with the taping? "Sure, my brother's name is David."

"There's been an accident," he said. "We found your business card in his wallet."

Garcia sucked in a quick breath. "An accident? What sort of accident?"

"He was . . .."

"Wait. Let me pull over." She found a place to stop. "What sort of accident? Tell me."

"He was riding his bicycle on Columbia Pike when a truck hit him."

"A truck? Is he all right?"

"It would be best if you talked to his doctor."

"Look buddy, you called me. Don't jerk me around. Tell me what the hell happened and do it right now."

"All I know is a truck hit him a short time ago. He's on his way into surgery as we speak. The doctor will have to tell you more."

"You're at Fairfax Hospital?"

"That's right, Colonel. Do you know where we are?"

A mental road map of Fairfax County flashed through her brain. "Yeah, I know. I'm on my way."

Garcia disconnected and made a quick left turn onto Route Seven heading west, ignoring the horn of some clown behind her. She'd never forgive herself if this was tied to the taping.

8

Fairfax Hospital, Wednesday, 8:00 a.m.

Rene Garcia sat in the surgical intensive care waiting room, stewing. When she first arrived, she'd checked in with the charge nurse, then called the office to let the Sergeant Major know what had happened and she'd be in as soon as she could.

Tired of waiting, she figured she could check again. At the nurse's station, Garcia asked, "I'm wondering when I'll get information on my brother?"

The nurse put her pencil down, a tired smile stuck on her face. "His name again?"

"David Garcia."

She consulted a sheet of paper. "He's in surgery. I don't know when the doctor will be done, but he will talk to you as soon as he can."

Garcia hated hospitals. She'd been here a number of times interviewing soldiers or visiting friends. "I'm sorry to bother you, but I'm concerned. All I know is a truck hit him this morning a little before six o'clock. I'm worried and nervous. Don't mean to be frustrated with you."

"That's okay, Colonel. I'm sure the doctor will be out soon."

Garcia walked back to her chair and plunked down. She was supposed to be at the White House for a meeting with Admiral Steele and here she sat, twiddling her thumbs.

Lieutenant Pamela Scott, a homicide detective with Fairfax County, stood in the doorway. Garcia had worked on a couple of cases with Scott. She waved her over. "Hey, Scott, what brings you to the hospital this early on a Wednesday morning?"

Scott opened her tan trench coat and pulled loose the purple scarf draped around her neck. "I'm here on a case. What about you?"

"Some jerk in a truck hit my brother, David, while he rode his bike this morning."

"When I saw you, I figured you might be related to David Garcia. I'm sorry about your brother. How's he doing?"

"Still in surgery. Man, it's hard to wait."

Scott took out a notebook. "Can we talk for a few minutes?"

This startled Garcia. "Why?"

Four of the people in the waiting room looked away as if they were intruding on a secret meeting. The fifth, a gray-haired woman sitting on the orange couch in the corner, squinted at Garcia over her *Vanity Fair* magazine.

Scott pulled wire-rimmed reading glasses out of the pocket of her trench coat, perched them on the end of her nose, and made a note in her notebook. She motioned toward the corner. "Let's go over there for a few minutes. I'd like to ask you a few questions."

"Okay." *Wait a minute, wait a damn minute*, she thought. *There's more here than Scott is saying.* She knew Scott. *But with homicide . . .?*

A voice over the loudspeaker called for Doctor Spencer.

When they were seated again, Scott asked, "I understand your brother works at a place called Sterling Software."

What to say about David? What could she tell Scott? "Ah, that's right."

Scott pushed her glasses back again. "Can you tell me a little about him?"

Garcia hated to have this out in the open, but it would probably happen soon anyway. "Not a lot. He's thirty-three years old, loves computers, and must have set the record for being a spoiled brat growing up."

"Are you aware the truck that hit your brother this morning didn't stop?"

Garcia shook her head. A headache started to thump in her forehead. She debated telling Scott about the taping, but decided to hold back. She remembered the army motto during an Inspector General inspection. Just answer the asked question and never volunteer a thing.

"We have a description of the truck, but no license number, at least not yet." Scott smoothed the tailored brown slacks and shifted her shoulders to adjust her tan jacket. "Does your brother have any enemies?"

"Why?"

Scott watched Garcia over the rim of her glasses. "We haven't confirmed this yet, but a witness walking her dog along the frontage road swears the pickup truck appeared to swerve toward your brother."

"Scott, what exactly are you telling me?"

"This witness believes the truck purposely hit your brother."

———

Zack glanced at his watch. Eight thirty-five. He stared down at the small ocean-side town as the helicopter dropped down to land in an open area two blocks from the police station. His brain swam with questions. Who the hell was this Dark Angel? Why military guys?

Blake leaned over his shoulder to look out the window. "I used to spend a lot of time during the summers in Strathmere, a little burg north of here when I was growing up. My folks owned a place there. Mom and I would stay for much of the summer, then my dad commuted back and forth to work in D.C. A long time ago."

Zack had learned to not say anything about Blake's dad. A real jerk, he'd shot and killed Darcy Quinn, the president's national security advisor last spring, then kidnapped Zack's daughter in revenge for Zack's testimony against him. The bastard was serving a well-deserved life sentence in jail. Hopefully no chance for parole. "Lucky you. Bet it was fun. I used to go fishing in one of our many lakes in Minnesota when I was growing up, but never spent much time at the ocean."

T.J.'s voice came over the intercom. "We'll be landing in about five minutes."

"Could you fly down the beach once?" Zack asked. "Maybe we can spot the place where someone murdered the second officer."

"Piece of cake," T.J. replied over the microphone.

The chopper angled to the right and they saw it right away. Police cars. Yellow crime scene tape. People milling around.

"Looks to be close to where they found Brian Toomey on Monday," Zack said.

"Okay, my friends, hang on," Wilson responded. "We're dropping down and will be on the ground in a minute."

Zack glanced at Blake and saw her watching T.J. The two had a thing going and it seemed to be working for both of them. Made Zack happy for her. Blake deserved whatever breaks she could get. Darcy Quinn had been Blake's aunt and Zack knew Blake missed her dearly.

When they landed, two police cars waited. After T.J. cut the engines, Zack jumped out and spotted Lieutenant Powell. She wore a navy-blue shirt over a light blue sweater and a beige skirt. Her long brown hair spilled down over her shoulders today, framing her face and accenting her brown eyes. Damn, she did look good.

Zack introduced Blake and T.J. Wilson.

Wilson shook her hand. "My copilot will stay with our chopper so we can get going."

Powell brushed a strand of hair out of her eyes. "Colonel Kelly, I'm sorry to call you so early, but I couldn't believe it when I received the call. Nothing like this ever happens in Sea Isle City and here we have two murders in only two days."

Zack stretched his legs. "Can we drive to the site where they found the body?"

Powell nodded. On the way, she briefed them on what she knew. "On his way to work about five o'clock this morning, one of our beach maintenance guys found Major Frank Butler. Like before, his first thought was the man had fallen asleep on the beach. But once he got close to Butler, he realized what had happened and called 911. Everyone knows about Colonel Toomey, so when another one happened, well, people are scared. I suspect the news will go national soon."

"It already has," Zack said. "By the way, where's Sprite?"

"He had to brief the governor." She smiled. "He sends his regards."

"Be sure and tell him how much I missed him."

Powell turned and moved toward the cars. "Yeah, right."

In five minutes, they arrived at the beach. Police cars with red lights flashing blocked the street, yellow crime scene tape circled the area, and this time a crowd of people stood around, talking.

"Almost the same place?" Zack asked.

"We found Colonel Toomey on 54th street. We're on 49th, only a few blocks north."

The medical examiner had already left with the body. Zack wanted to take a quick look around the area. As if reading his mind, Lieutenant Powell said, "We checked carefully. Nothing."

"Any witnesses?" Zack asked.

"Not that we know of so far," she replied, "but we're running a door-to-door screen of the houses facing the beach. It's quiet in the early morning, but picks up pretty quickly cause we're into the beach season. Merchants are afraid people will get scared and leave."

Once they arrived at the police station, Lieutenant Powell led them into a conference room. A pot of coffee sat on a warmer.

After they had 'coffeed up', Zack asked, "What do you make of this?"

Powell took out her notebook. "I had my folks do a check of Butler's military file and found he also had been accused of raping a military woman. Apparently she was a navy enlisted person. Seems that because of a lack of evidence, no formal charges were ever brought. It appears the military moved Butler to another post."

"A case of another guy getting away with raping a woman," Blake said.

"Looks that way," Powell replied. "Course if the rape had something to do with his death, then you can't say he got away with it."

"Do we know the name of the woman he's alleged to have raped?" Zack asked.

"I checked that out," Powell replied. "The woman is a Chief Petty Officer Rosemary Edelman."

"Where . . . ?"

Powell waived away Zack's question. "She's left the military and lives somewhere in Northern Virginia. We're trying to locate her now."

"We need to make it a high priority action." Zack said. "Like right away."

"I'll can get a copy of her records," Blake said. "Maybe her file will give us a lead."

9

The White House, Wednesday, 3:00 pm

Zack, Wilson, and Blake arrived back at the White House at three o'clock, in time to brief Admiral Steele on their findings. When Zack spotted Garcia he asked, "How's your brother?"

She shook her head. "No change."

Zack opened with a quick update for Steele on what they'd found at Sea Isle City and in the meeting with Powell. "It's possible we may have a serial killer on our hands. Someone's going after military officers who've been accused of sexual abuse."

"Let me add to that," Blake said. "It appears we have a second case of an officer who has ducked being held responsible for committing sexual abuse"

"Blake," Garcia said, "you sound really angry."

"You should be too, Garcia. These guys rape unsuspecting woman, then are able to run off and hide behind their rank." She looked at the rest of the attendees. "I know I sound pretty cold, but it does piss me off."

"I understand what you're saying," Steele said, "but nothing justifies killing someone, then cutting him up."

"Of course not, sir" Blake replied, "but guys keep getting by with it."

The office door opened and Vice President Millicent Townsend strolled into the room. A tall, thin, blond woman, with silver streaks in her hair and her oval face was threaded with fine wrinkles. An attractive woman, probably in her early sixties.

Everyone jumped to their feet including Admiral Steele. "Madam Vice President, welcome. We were just talking about the cases in New Jersey where two military officers have been murdered."

"I'm sorry to burst in on you like this, Admiral Steele. I heard you were being briefed on the awful business in Sea Isle City and I wanted to sit in."

Steele motioned her toward a chair at the conference table. "We would have been happy to come over to your office and update you on what we know. I believe you know most of my special task group."

She looked around the office. "Let's see, I've met Colonel Kelly, Colonel Garcia, Ms. Lannigan, and Mr. Morrison, but I don't believe I know this gentleman."

"Major Wilson, Madam Vice President," T.J. said. "Not sure I can agree on the gentleman bit, but it is a pleasure to meet you."

"I have a healthy respect for your team, Admiral. I was delighted when Darcy formed this group, and I'm glad you've kept them. It's nice to have a small group of dedicated professionals to cut through the bureaucratic tangles and get to the bottom of things."

Zack pulled out a chair for Townsend. He had met her a couple of times before and remembered those pale green eyes could look right through you. Today she wore one of her trademark dark suit jackets with a tweed skirt.

"Thank you, Zack."

Once they had settled, Steele motioned toward Zack. "Why don't you summarize things for the vice president?"

Zack began with his arrival in Sea Isle City and discussed everything he knew about Toomey and Butler. "I didn't know Major Butler personally, but I knew Toomey. When he worked for me as a major, he did a good job. His wife, a navy lieutenant commander, told me Brian changed, became more abusive toward women. It seems he may have raped a female sergeant, then covered it up."

Townsend's glasses hung on a thin gold chain around her neck. She reached down and slipped them on. "I want you to keep me up to date on these awful incidents. Things like this can take on a life of their own. You know there's a move in Congress to take the authority away from commanders to investigate sexual abuse allegations and turn it over to independent lawyers."

"Do you think that will work?" Zack asked. "I'm not so sure."

Townsend wheeled around. Her glasses had slipped down her nose and she watched him over the glasses. "Well, it's got to be better than the current system. There were an estimated 26,000 cases of sexual abuse this past year and only 3,000 formally reported." Townsend's gaze over those glasses made Zack uncomfortable.

"That's right," Blake replied. "And only about 300 were ever prosecuted. Dammit, we need to stop it."

"I'm not disputing that point," Zack replied, "but I'm not sure an independent lawyer will be any better. He's farther from the incident."

Blake bit her lip. "Which means more of these young women will report this crap. Sorry, Zack, but I feel pretty strongly about this."

"All right," Townsend said, "this isn't getting us anywhere." She turned to Garcia. "Now, tell me about your brother. I understand from General Harding there may be a case of cyber terrorism here."

Garcia briefed her on the meeting with her brother, then the FBI sting operation.

"It'll be interesting to see what's on the tape," Townsend said. "Do you know when we'll have copies of the first report?"

"I'm afraid we may never get to hear the tape. A truck hit my brother this morning. He's in a coma in Fairfax Hospital."

"Oh, no, I'm so sorry. Do you think someone found out and struck him on purpose?"

"I talked to a homicide detective from Fairfax County this morning. She told me a witness believes the truck purposely hit my brother."

"Oh, my, that's awful. Let me know how he's doing." Townsend looked at her watch, then stood. "Please keep me advised on both of these incidents. The president has asked me to lead the administration's response in dealing with these cases of sexual abuse in the military."

After she left, Steele said, "Keep working these issues. My gut tells me one or both of them is going to blow up."

"Sir," Zack said, "people in Cape May are scared and on the verge of a full-fledged panic. I'm going to touch base with your press guy. I suspect we'll end up having to meet with the press."

Steele nodded. "Good point. I'm afraid I agree."

On the way out the door, Zack had the uneasy feeling these two events could be somehow related. Coincidence they both started at the same time. But if they were, how? And why?

———

Sergeant Margo Collins paced back and forth in her motel room. She'd arrived in Fairfax, sad and lonely after leaving her friends in New Jersey, frustrated at being kept separated in this place, not able to talk with anyone in case she might slip, tipping them off as to what she was about to do.

She watched the stars out of her window, wondering when she'd leave. The time for her mission had come. She felt ready. Tired of the depression that engulfed her and sick of everyone looking at her with sorrow about the rape.

Men. Her best friend didn't want to touch her. As far as he was concerned, she'd been branded soiled goods. All because of Toomey and his buddies. Colonel fucking Toomey. The Dark Angel had paid him back, now it was up to her to get the others. She would make the Dark Angel proud.

Collins turned away from the window and got down on her knees to pray for strength. Strength to forget the weakness of the body. After her prayers, she rose. She had no friends now except for the Dark Angel and her sisters.

Collins needed to stay alert. Her watch read quarter to eight. Soon she would begin her journey. A journey to meet her destiny.

After Toomey's death, she had dedicated her life to the Dark Angel. Her sisters were waiting, looking for her to lead. She would be the first. They were all ready to sacrifice everything for the Dark Angel, the only person who really cared for them. Cared what had happened to each of them. This provided her with a sense of calm.

A knock sounded on the hallway door. She turned away from the window, picked up her bag, and, not wanting to take any chances, glanced through the peep hole in the door. A slender woman with bushy dark hair and a narrow face stood, waiting. Collins opened the door.

The woman looked up and down the hallway. "Come with me, it's time."

Collins sighed, then straightened. "I'm ready."

They walked down the darkened hallway and stopped at a side exit. The woman opened the door, stepped outside, and looked both ways. She motioned with her right hand. "This way. Hurry."

The night air felt cool to Collins and the stars shone brightly above her. She shivered as she walked, wishing someone special could be there to share the beauty of those stars with her. But forget the thought. All that is over.

She followed the woman down the sidewalk and past the trees swaying in the evening breeze. The woman stopped and glanced around. "Wait here, I'll be back in a moment. We have a long drive ahead of us." She hurried toward the parking lot and brought the car around.

As Collins slid into the front seat, the woman pushed in a number on her cell phone. After a moment, she handed it over. "It's her."

Collins picked up the phone and with shaking hands put it to her ear.

"Are you ready, Margo?" the Dark Angel asked. "Ready to strike back for all those who can't? Ready to right the wrong done to you by those two men? The way they lied about you."

Margo straightened in the seat. "Yes, I'm ready. I won't fail you or my sisters."

"This briefcase is the first step on our path to regain our rightful place. With that, people will know. They will no longer forget what has happened. Those bastards will not be able to do their evil deeds any longer and get away with it."

Tears filled Margo's eyes. Overcome with emotion she couldn't talk.

"Our prayers go with you. You must drive through the night."

Collins whispered, "I will not fail."

10

Fairfax Hospital, Wednesday 8:10 pm

Rene Garcia sat by her brother's bedside, holding his hand and talking to him. She wasn't sure what to say, but the doc said to keep on talking so that's what she did.

She sensed rather than heard movement at the door, then turned to see her parents standing in the hallway. Emilia Garcia entered first. A slender woman, her mother's jet black hair had become lined with streaks of gray. Her brown eyes red and puffy, she held a tissue to her nose.

Garcia walked over and hugged her mother. "I'm glad you're here."

Her father stood behind her mother, half in the room and half in the hallway. His black horned-rimmed glasses and tweed sport coat with patches on the elbow gave him the look of the college professor he'd been for his entire career.

Garcia reached over to hug him. "Hello, Father."

He pulled back from her and shook his head. "How could this happen to David? How?"

Uh, oh, this is not going to be good. "I don't know, Father. Come and sit. You must be tired."

Her parents stood next to the bed, looking down at David and both now sniffling into tissues. Bending over, her mother kissed his cheek. Garcia walked around the bed and helped them to draw up chairs.

"I received the call at a little after six this morning as I was driving to work." No need to tell them she had a motorcycle. That would only spark her father's anger. "I came right away and finally got to see the doctor. David is in a coma and they're not sure when he'll come out of it."

"But he will . . ." her father said.

"The doctors don't know. They had to release pressure in his head so it wouldn't build up from the injury. Now it's up to David. He might wake up in a couple of minutes, or it could be days."

Jose Garcia's eyes got wide. "Days?"

Garcia nodded. "No one knows."

"Tell me, Rene," her mother asked, "how did this happen?"

"David rode his bike this morning like always before he went to work. A truck hit him." She paused for a moment, debating whether or not to tell them about the microphone, then decided against it. This next statement would be enough of a shock. "The police think the driver of the truck may have purposely swerved to hit David."

She let that fact settle for a moment. Her parents did not deal with shocks well, particularly her father. "To be honest, that's all I can tell you now."

Her mother blew her nose. "Oh, Rene, this is terrible. Poor David."

Her father jerked up and walked to the window. He looked out, his body shaking and hands trembling, probably getting ready to unload something. Probably aimed at her.

"When is the last time you saw him?" he asked.

Garcia tried to measure her response. "We had breakfast together yesterday morning. He told me about some concerns at his work." She let it drop.

"Concerns?" Emilia Garcia asked.

Before she could answer, Garcia's father turned and pointed a finger at her. "Why didn't you help him? You're his older sister. You're supposed to care for him. He's lying in that bed . . .."

The heat built inside her, threatening to explode like a volcano. Enough. She cut him off. "He contacted me two days ago. Asked me to have breakfast with him. I did. He has a problem at work and I tried to help him. Up until then, I didn't even know he lived here. I thought he still lived in Austin."

"I know, dear . . .," her mother started again. "I know, and I'm sorry."

Her father's hands formed into fists and his face turned red. "What did you do to help him? Couldn't you have done more for him in your position?"

Her mother rose quickly and stood between the two of them. "Now, that's not fair, dear. We didn't tell Rene about David's move to Washington and we should have."

Garcia couldn't take this crap. "No, mother, David should have told me. He's thirty-three years old. He could have picked up the phone and called me. Quit treating him like a baby and me like a babysitter. I'm tired of it."

She glared at her father, turned on her heel before she said anything else, and stalked toward the door. She stopped with her hand on the knob. "You don't care how I feel. All you care about is the body in that bed."

She hurried down the hallway, bumped into a nurse, slammed the stairway door as she stormed down the stairs, eyes full of tears.

Head down, gaze fixed on the floor. a slender man pushed his mop and bucket down the fourth floor corridor of Fairfax Hospital and through the double doors of the ICU. The right wheel on the bucket squeaked each time it turned. He wanted to rip the damn thing off.

He'd put on a blue denim work shirt and navy pants, standard uniform for the cleaning staff. If anyone asked, he was standing in for the day, you know, flu season and a bunch of the regular folks out sick.

He had missed the target once. This time there would be no mistakes, no slip ups. He only needed a minute or two. Lights out for one David Garcia. Then he could get back to the sexy broad simmering back in his room. So damn inventive. Kept him on his toes.

He slouched down as he passed the nurse's station. He'd timed it well. Both nurses stayed on the move handing out their drugs. What if one of them worked in the man's room? No sweat, he'd deal with it when he got there.

Three lights blinked on the switchboard. A phone kept up an insistent ringing, the sound grating on his nerves.

He reached the third door on the left and looked in. No one else was in the room. With the ventilator and all the tubes, it looked as if David Garcia had only recently returned from surgery. This was his chance.

He pushed the bucket into the room, cursing the damn squeak, patted the mustache to make sure it held in place in case the nurse came in. His fake gray ponytail swung whenever he turned his head. He hated wearing glasses, but the dark frames gave him a whole different look.

Okay, the little prick's good as dead. Watch out for the damn nurse. Don't want to tangle with her.

He stepped to the door and checked the hallway once more, then slipped back to the bed. The ventilator's soft hissing caught his attention. Connected to the throat. Could he cut off the air? It'd be quick and easy. He pulled on latex gloves and reached over to close the line.

Looking back out into the hallway once more to double check for the nurse, he pinched the line shut with his fingers. An alarm sounded and he jumped back. A red light flashed on the monitor.

He dropped the line as if it were a snake. Rushed over to where he'd left his mop leaning against the wall. Footsteps echoed in the hallway. He grabbed the mop, bent over to start scrubbing.

A nurse hurried into the room. She looked at the monitors, then traced the lines to the sockets in the wall. Checking the patient's pulse, she called, "What happened?"

He shrugged. Tried to look calm. Wiping sweat from his fore-head, he turned away and pushed the mop into the corner. His heart pounded so loudly he figured the nurse must be able to hear it.

She ran her fingers over the cords on the ventilator, then she dialed the phone. "I need you to come up and check one of our oxygen lines. The alarm went off." She hung up and studied the rest of the dials.

The nurse turned. Her eyes widened when she saw him. "Are you new?"

Keeping his head down, he mumbled, "I'm a temp. The regular is out sick today." Thank heavens he'd lifted an identification badge from the janitor's locker room when he stole the clothes. "It scared me to death when the alarm went off. I almost ran out to find you, then here you are." He risked a smile. "You're fast."

"Everything seems okay now," the nurse replied. "Respiratory therapy is on the way up to check all the controls. Better hurry. I've got a number of other patients to see before the shift change."

After she left the room, he walked over to the bed. Reaching behind him, he pulled the curtain partially shut so he could still see the door, then picked up a towel.

He looked down at the man, still and peaceful. He hated to kill a person up close. Much easier when he did it from a distance and couldn't see his victim's face. Well, better get it over with before another fucking alarm rang.

He placed the towel over David Garcia's face and pushed down on the veins in his neck. The body convulsed. Hold on, buddy, this won't take long. He pushed harder.

Footsteps sounded. He turned to watch the door. An older, dark-haired woman entered the room and stood in the open door-way. He started dusting the bedside table with the towel, trying to block her view of the bed.

"What is going on with my son?" she asked. "I heard the alarm all the way down the hall when I was talking to the doctor. I'm so worried about my boy."

He dusted the legs of the table. "Some problem with the ventilator. The nurse came in and checked it out. She says everything is working okay now." He pushed his bucket out into the hall, the squeak following him like an unwanted ghost.

"My goodness, wait a minute," the woman called.

He stopped, heart beating fast, throat dry. He began to sweat again. Should he run? He felt for the pistol tucked in his belt. "Yeah."

She followed him into the hall, holding a sponge at arms length. She placed it on his bucket. "You almost forgot this."

"Ah, yeah. Thanks." He pushed his mop and bucket down the hall and out through the double doors of the ICU. "You were lucky this time, buddy," he whispered. "Next time, you won't be."

———————

The special cell phone vibrated on her left hip. She got up from the desk, walked to her office door and pushed it shut with her foot. She didn't need any prying ears for this call and couldn't take any chances, even at this time of night. "Yes."

The voice sounded strained. "I'll have to try again. I had a foolproof plan, but I went in too early. Should have waited a couple more hours. Almost had him, but I got interrupted. Won't happen again."

"I've assured the boss this task would be completed by now. You've failed twice. The boss doesn't tolerate failure. I don't either."

"Don't sweat it. This Garcia guy has nine lives, but I'm about to stomp on the last one."

"You'd better." She disconnected the cell phone and slipped it in the gray bag in the back of her desk drawer. She pulled out another cell phone and attached it to her belt.

She should call the boss, but she'd wait until her operations man had succeeded.

Wiping sweat from her forehead, she took several deep breaths. She wanted this over.

11

Army War College, Carlisle, PA, Thursday, 8:15 a.m.

Sergeant Collins leaned forward in her seat as the driver turned left off the main road and pulled up to the front gate of Carlisle Barracks. It had taken about four hours to drive to central Pennsylvania from Fairfax, Virginia. The guard in his blue uniform held up his hand. The driver stopped and flashed her military ID card.

The gate guard asked Sergeant Collins for her identification.

Collins reached into her purse and pulled out her ID, her hand shaking slightly. "Oh sure, here it is."

Relax, she thought, *he has no reason to think anything might be wrong.* Both women had active duty army identification cards and it was too soon for the car they were in to be reported stolen from Fort Myer.

Collins been a member of the army team, a valued member. Little did the guard know that she no longer felt part of the team. The team had destroyed her and she was about to strike back.

After inspecting their cards, the guard stepped back and waved them through.

The driver stayed well below the fifteen-mile-per-hour speed limit on the base. The driver turned left before the theater and stopped across the street from Root Hall.

Collins saw a number of military officers moving toward the building for classes. She looked for the two men who had lied to help Toomy, but didn't see them. Well, she knew they were here. Knew they would be in this class. Well, no more, no more would this go on without reprisals.

The driver reached over and put her hand on Collin's arm. "Good luck, my friend. You'll be entering those doors and showing your ID to the guard. He should suspect nothing. Classes are just beginning. You know which classroom the two men are in. The discussion will be starting. Stand in the back. Quietly. Then you know what to do."

Collins nodded. She reached around and picked up the briefcase from the back seat. Carefully she got out of the car, walked across the street, up the five stairs and along the walk to the front door. A couple of joggers ran along the street behind her. Two women passed her, both women walking their dogs and chatting. She missed the normalcy of this daily routine. Well, things would change in a few minutes.

When she opened the door, the guard looked up. Her heart lurched. Would she be able to do this? Yes, she remembered her story. In transit from her last assignment in Afghanistan, she soon would be leaving for an assignment in the Pentagon. She wanted to buy a book which had been recommended by her friend and hoped the bookstore had it on their shelves.

She handed him her identification and he studied it. Then he glanced up at her face. She smiled back. Two officers hurried by, talking to one another. What had these two done? Anything? Well, it was time for them to realize they would be safe no longer.

"Can you open your briefcase for me?"

Collins smiled again. "Sure. It's a little messy."

The guard checked quickly but didn't notice the false bottom. "Thank you."

She started to tear up.

"Are you all right?" the guard asked.

"Yes, I'm fine. It's just my mother is sick, cancer you know. It's hard to see her waste away to almost nothing."

The guard nodded. "I understand. Same thing happed to my dad. Cancer is awful."

He seemed nice. Margo looked at his hand. No ring. Maybe if she'd met someone like him, someone kind and gentle, things would have been different. He waited for her to say something. "Yes, it is. Thank you for your thoughts."

Two more officers rushed by, late for class. One of them glanced at her. He didn't look at her face. Only her legs. And probably her butt. Men. Dumb shit men.

This gave her strength. A quick look at her watch. Eight thirty-five. Realizing she couldn't put it off any longer, she picked up her briefcase and walked down the hall toward the classroom. She eased open the door and stepped inside. An officer in the back looked up.

"I'm looking for my husband," she whispered. "Our child is sick."

The officer nodded.

She saw the two men who had lied about her, helped Toomey and destroyed her life. Here they sat in the school for army leaders. What bullshit. "May I have your attention, please."

Everyone turned to look at her.

"My name is Sergeant Margo Collins. I've been in the army for twelve years. This was to be my life until an officer raped me. It was a brutal rape and until now he never paid any price for it." She looked at the two men who had lied. "You two have never paid any price for your lies."

One of the two officers, a lieutenant colonel, stood and hurried toward her. "Wait a minute, sergeant. We can talk this over."

"It's too late for talking," she said through her tears. "Time for action."

She bent down and opened the briefcase, said a short prayer and pressed on the red button.

With a flash of light and a loud explosion, the entire briefcase exploded, sending shrapnel flying in all directions.

Lieutenant Scott waited at the Sterling Software information desk. She looked at her watch, eight forty-five. Tiled floors and beige walls surrounded her in the one-story building. Place looked pretty new and in good repair.

Men in sports shirts and slacks, women in blouses and pants hurried up and down the hallway, papers in hand. Four Impressionist paintings hung in the lobby. *Not bad,* she thought. *Business must be booming.*

A man lumbered down the hall toward her. His tie stopped short over his extended belly. He reminded her of Buddha. A fringe of gray hair surrounded his bald head, fuzzing out in all directions.

He held out his right hand. "Welcome to Sterling Software, Lieutenant Scott. My name is Samuel Foster."

She shook his hand, and showed him her badge. "Thanks for seeing me on such short notice, Mr. Foster. I'm sure you're a busy man."

"Of course." Foster turned and pointed. "This way to my office."

She followed him down the hallway, looking into each office she passed. Staff typed on computers and papers lay scattered on most of the desks. A number of people talked on phones, some using headsets. "Busy place, Mr. Foster."

"Our business continues to grow." Foster held his office door open for her. "Have a seat, Lieutenant. Would you like some coffee?"

Scott stepped into the carpeted office, sat on one end of the three-cushion couch, and scoped out the office. "That would be nice."

Foster had decorated his office with antique furniture. The desk held a half-empty glass coffee cup, a pipe rack, and on one corner stood a picture of a smiling wife with two small children. A laptop with keyboard sat on a square table to the left of his desk.

The sounds of traffic moving along Arlington Boulevard floated through the partially-open window. "This won't take long, Mr. Foster."

He poured a cup of coffee, handed it to her, then sat in a rocker next to the couch. Certificates attesting to his community participation lined the wall behind him. "Now, what may I do for you?"

Scott crossed her legs and straightened the seam of her pants. "You're aware a truck struck David Garcia yesterday morning during a bike ride?"

"Yes, yes, a terrible thing."

Sipping her coffee she said, "A witness at the scene believes the driver swerved intentionally to hit Mr. Garcia."

Foster leaned back, his eyes wide. "Are you sure? David could be forceful at times, but from what I could see, he didn't have any enemies."

Well, Scott thought, *he must have had at least one.* She pulled a pen from her pocket and decided to keep pushing him. "How long have you been at Sterling, Mr. Foster?"

"Seven years. And please call me Sam."

"Where did you work before Sterling?"

"I spent fifteen years with Coastal Energy Corporation."

She made a note to check that out. "And what did you do there?"

"I ran their WAN. My responsibilities kept me pretty busy since Coastal is an international corporation." He blew on his coffee and took a sip. "It's a Wide Area Network. Are you familiar with a local area network?"

Does he think I'm some sort of dumb shit? "Sure, we use a LAN at the station."

"Exactly. The computers in one building can be tied together with a local area network, whereas the computers at various sites around the country, or internationally, would be linked by a Wide Area Network."

The guy seems kind of condescending. Okay, keep him talking. "Why did you leave Coastal?"

Foster tapped his fingers on the arm of the chair. "The owner here offered me the position of vice-president."

He seemed nervous. Why? "Isn't it unusual for someone to step into the vice president's position from outside the company?"

Foster sipped his coffee, watching her. "I married the boss's daughter. Maria didn't even tell me until we had been dating for three months that her father owned Sterling Software."

Yeah, I'll bet. Scott smiled. "Mr. Foster, I noticed you're the president. Did Mr. Sterling recently retire?"

"No, sadly he died about two years ago in a traffic accident."

Lieutenant Scott raised an eyebrow and made a mental note to check it out. "What are David Garcia's duties?"

Foster kept tapping his fingers on the chair. "David was a computer analyst. He ran our troubleshooting group until about eighteen months ago when he took over the new security system. He was a bright young man."

"What kind of a manager is he?" And she wondered, *what kind of a boss are you?*

"David had an innovative approach and developed answers where others had failed. But he could be very demanding. You know, intolerant of those who weren't as quick as he was. I had complaints from three employees over the past year. We always worked it out without any major problems."

"I'll need the names and contact information of those who complained. Now, Mr. Foster, tell me about this new security system."

"It should be a great leap forward for the industry."

"Why is that?"

"The design will allow companies to block hackers from breaking into their programs."

Scott debated how to proceed. "How does it work exactly?"

"I'm afraid I can't tell you much more. Proprietary, you know. You can check our website, or we have a DVD which explains the basics of the program. The important thing is we give our customers a huge competitive edge and this should be quite a boon to my company."

Could this be a motive? "I'd like a copy of that DVD."

Foster hesitated. "All right. I'll have it messengered over to your office."

"You say Mr. Garcia took charge about eighteen months ago. When do you expect the system to be on the market?"

"We've been beta testing it with a new research agency," Foster replied. "The results are very promising and there are a number of companies who want to experiment with it."

"Won't David Garcia's loss slow down your timing?"

Foster folded his hands over his stomach. "No, we'll keep moving ahead. This has to be above any one person."

"I imagine you'll be in charge?"

"I'm moving up another member of the staff, Ms. Megan Alcott, to take over as project manager. She's worked with David for the past year."

Interesting. Alcott has a motive to push Garcia out of the way. "I'll need to speak with her."

Foster leaned back in his chair again and stroked his goatee. "Why?"

Scott watched him. "It's only routine." Scott rose from the couch. "Could you see if Ms. Alcott is in now?"

"Ah, she's been traveling a great deal as our client is based in Mississippi as well as the Pentagon, but I'll check for you." Foster pushed a number on his phone, let it ring. He hung up. "I'm sorry, Lieutenant, it looks as if Megan's not at her desk. She may have already left for the Pentagon."

"In that case, let her know I'd like to speak with her." Scott stood and turned toward the door. "Thank you for your time."

"No problem, Lieutenant, I want to help in any way I can."

Scott opened the office door and strode down the hall. Something funny about Foster. She'd need to meet with Alcott, then give this place a lot more thought.

12

The White House, Washington, D.C., Thursday, 10:40 a.m.

When Zack and Garcia arrived at Admiral Steele's office, his administrative assistant told them he had been called to a short meeting with the president. She motioned toward the door to his office. "The others are already here. You can go in. I'm sure he'll be right back."

"Okay." Zack poured himself a cup of coffee. "Would you like some, Garcia?"

"Thanks for the offer, but I'm okay."

Admiral Steele hurried into the office. "Sorry I'm late, but when the president calls, you have to go. He wants to be kept up to speed on the two murders in Sea Isle City and the bombing this morning at the Army War College."

Zack handed the admiral a copy of the initial police report from the bombing as well as the police report from Sea Isle City. He waited while the boss scanned the papers.

"Sir, we've got more questions than answers," Zack said. "But let's start and see where we go."

Steele nodded.

Zack spent about ten minutes summarizing what he knew about the two incidents. "Sir, at this point, I believe the incidents are related. Collins is the common denominator between the two. We know she alleged Toomey raped her. A witness in the hall claimed she yelled that two of the officers in the class had lied about her."

"All right," Steele replied, "seems reasonable, so let's take this in pieces. First of all, what do we know about Collins?"

Zack looked down at his laptop. "I've got her efficiency reports on my computer. From everything in her folder, she appears to be an outstanding soldier. Promoted to Staff Sergeant early. Served in the Pentagon as well as the joint military headquarters in Iraq."

"That's where she met Toomey?"

"Yes, sir. She worked closely with him for almost a year before the alleged rape incident."

"So what does this tell us?" the admiral asked.

"They had a close daily working relationship," Zack replied. "That can lead to trouble."

"Doesn't excuse what he did," Blake said.

"No, of course not," Zack replied. "The interesting thing is that Brian's wife lived with him during much of the tour. Linda says she didn't pick up on anything unusual from him, but after the accusations by Collins, Brian seemed to change."

Admiral Steele sat, fingers pointing to his lips. Zack knew better than to interrupt his thought process. The group would know soon enough. "Okay," he said, "what about the press?"

Travis Plank, the admiral's press secretary, leaned forward. "A reporter at *The Washington Post* called me. He's put together the probable synergy between the two incidents and is itching to release a story highlighting the Dark Angel and what appears to be her cause. That's gonna capture the attention of the whole country."

"Can we hold him a little longer if we promise him an exclusive?" Steele asked.

Plank frowned and shook his head. "Maybe a few hours, but this thing is so big it's going to blow."

"All right, here's what I want to do," Steele said. "Schedule a press conference for six o'clock. Work up a release. Keep it as minimal as you can."

"Yes, sir," Plank replied. "Who's gonna lead the conference?"

"Let me talk to the Chief. He may want the Secretary of Defense to do it, if not I'll probably conduct the conference."

"Yes, sir. I'll get a statement ready for you."

Steele turned to Zack. "Give me your best thoughts"

"Sir, it seems to me we have three courses of action. First, work with the police in Sea Isle City to figure out exactly what happened and what we can learn about this Dark Angel. I can do that. Second, follow the investigation of the bombing and see if we can find out what Sergeant Collins had been doing in the past few months. Third, check out her apartment and see what we can find."

"I can work with the FBI on those last two actions, Admiral," Garcia said.

Steele nodded.

Zack knew from experience the nod meant agreement and for him to outline proposed action items. "Sir, we've got to get our satellites focused on Sea Isle City. See if we can spot something in advance. Let the intelligence guys earn their pay." Zack stopped there. Give the boss time to think.

Steele turned back to Zack. "All right, I agree. See if you can find out why this Dark Angel chose Sea Isle City. There must be a reason for that location." He glanced at Barclay Morrison. "What did you find out about the potential for a hacking attempt at the Fort Shelby Research Activity?"

Morrison cleared his throat. "I talked to my contact. Now, this is interesting. Sterling is a small company. They got the contract because of who pushed for it. And that someone is the vice president."

Steele's eyes widened. "She interceded for them?"

Morrison nodded. "That's right. Now, they've done a great job, but there really wasn't a competitive bidding process according to my contact."

"I want you and Garcia to go over and brief General Harding about this. Tell her we want to keep it quiet but with what happened to David Garcia she needs to know."

"Will do, Admiral," Morrison said.

Steele stood and everyone jumped to their feet. "I don't need to tell you the priority on this action. If we don't stop this in its tracks, it'll grow into an even bigger nightmare." He pointed at Zack. "Be careful. It's going to get messy."

As everyone turned to leave, Steele asked, "Garcia, how's your brother?"

"Still in a coma. The docs are doing everything they can."

"I understand someone may have hit him on purpose?"

"That's what a witness says. The Fairfax police are leading the investigation, but because the FBI set him up with a wire, they're involved."

"Take whatever time you need to be with your brother, but keep me advised on how that investigation is going."

"Thank you. I'll let you know what I find at Collin's condo. We need to figure out why the sergeant chose the Army War College. If the rumor she shouted about two of the officers in the room lying against her is true, that could be a motive. I need to check on that."

"All right," Steele said. "Keep me posted."

Turning off Columbia Pike, Lieutenant Scott pulled up in front of David Garcia's house. The rancher looked like one of those modular homes so popular during the 1990s. One large pine tree dominated the front right of the yard and a cracked cement driveway edged up the left side.

No junk littered the street or the various yards. Didn't look like the kind of neighborhood where people got murdered, but you never knew.

Scott walked up the sidewalk to the front door and pushed on the doorbell. No answer. Pushed it again, then tried the door knob. Locked.

She peeked through a rectangular window next to the door. Typical living room furniture. Actually everything looked to be run-of-the-mill suburban.

Walking around to the back, Scott stopped when she reached the wooden deck. A breeze fanned her sport coat so she pulled it tighter around her waist. Thought she heard a noise from inside the house. She walked around to the front and rang the bell again.

This time a woman opened the door, but not the screen. Young and dark-skinned with long black hair, her eyes gave her an Asian look. "Yes, I help you?"

Scott flashed her badge. "I'm Lieutenant Scott with the Fairfax Police Department. I would like... ."

The door slammed shut.

"What the hell . . .?" Scott opened the screen and pushed on the door, but the woman had locked it. Scott raced around to the back of the house to see the young woman running through the woods. "Wait," she yelled, "I only want to talk to you."

She pulled the portable radio out of her coat pocket as she ran and called over the radio, "Officer needs assistance." Shouted the address. "Woman running south behind the house in the woods. Send a car to block her."

After a hundred feet or so of running through brush, Scott stopped. Breathing hard. Damn, she needed to give up cigars. She turned back toward the house, knowing the squads would be the best bet to catch the woman. *Who was she? Why had she run?*

Scott reached the back porch and pushed open the door. Pulling the pistol out of her holster, she slipped inside, looking from side to side. She worked her way through the kitchen, into the living room. Sparsely decorated but clean and neat. The dining room held a round table and four chairs. Smelled of Chinese food, maybe noodles and something. Actually smelled good. Reminded her she needed to get something to eat.

The house felt empty. *What did the Asian woman have to do with David Garcia? Girl friend? Significant other? Wife?*

Off the living room, she spotted a short hallway. Keeping the pistol pointed ahead, she crept through the doorway. The bedroom on the left looked like a master bedroom, bed made and everything neat. Hell, neater than her own.

The smaller bedroom on the right contained a crib and baby furniture. When she stared down into the crib, a baby smiled up at her.

A baby? What the hell?

13

On the way to Sea Isle City, Thursday, 1:15 p.m.

Rain pelted Zack's truck as he sped northeast along Interstate 95, about halfway between Baltimore and Wilmington. His wipers swished back and forth across the windshield, that noise was accompanied by the sound of water thrown backward from his tires against the undersides of his truck. Lightning danced across the sky with the roar of thunder not far behind. The storm had hit fast. It hadn't even been raining in D.C. *Must be one of those coastal storms.*

Zack checked his watch. Another two hours plus before he'd reach Sea Isle City. He'd made an appointment with Lieutenant Powell for four o'clock. Should make that unless the traffic at the damn toll booth stopped him cold. Interstate 95 was known to do that. But thank heavens for E-Z Pass.

Something drew the Dark Angel to Sea Isle City and Zack needed to figure out the lure. He had to admit he liked working with Maxine Powell. A good-looking smile matched with a great intellect.

The rain finally let up as he turned southeast onto Route 40 toward Cape May. A few remaining lines of lightning lit the sky, but the streaks were waning and the roll of the thunder was dropping off.

A large semi rumbled past on his left, splashing water onto his windshield. *Why the hell do they do that? Pass when it's been raining. Jerk.*

Zack had to smile as a state police cruiser pulled out and took after the truck, red and blue warning lights flashing silently. *Take that, you clown. Finally some justice.*

It took a little over an hour before he drove across the bridge into Sea Isle City. He turned right onto Central, splashing his way out to 46th Street through the standing water. *Must be high tide.*

He parked and walked up to the door. The officer on duty called for Lieutenant Powell.

In a moment, she hurried down the hallway, a bright smile on her face. "Hi, Colonel Kelly, glad you're here. What a mess with this rain. Come on back and let's talk."

Zack followed her, pulling off his jacket and shaking out a few drops. "I guess you heard about the bombing at the Army War College, the bomber none other than Sergeant Margo Collins."

She nodded. "I saw it on CNN a little while ago. How about some coffee?"

"That would be great."

"Now, what do you make of all this, Colonel Kelly?"

"First of all, it's Zack. If we're going to be working together, I think Colonel Kelly will get old, fast."

"Okay, Zack, and I'm Maxine, although my friends call me Max. Now that we've settled names, I picked up a couple of muffins at WaWa. Can I offer you one?"

"Wow, great. Didn't eat much for lunch." As Max lifted the muffins and napkins from a white paper bag, Zack pulled his notebook from his breast pocket. "We're in the middle of some sort of plot against military officers. Now I'm not defending what these guys did, or that the army shouldn't do more to stop it, but innocent people died at the Army War College this morning. And worst yet, I'm concerned more will die if we don't get this Dark Angel stopped."

She handed him a muffin, partially wrapped in a napkin. "I agree."

Zack took a bite. "Chocolate chip. My favorite. Thanks."

"I'll have to remember that."

"Any leads on Petty Officer Edelman?"

"We've been trying to locate her without success. The Virginia state police stopped at her apartment, but it turned out to be empty. Her next door neighbor said she'd been depressed ever since the rape incident with Commander Butler. She left about two days ago with a suitcase and told her friend she'd be gone for a while."

Zack took a sip of coffee. "Not much to go on."

"What worries me is she gave her cat to a friend about a week ago. Her friend assumed she had received military orders and would be deploying overseas. But we checked and she's left the military so not on any orders." Max bit at her lip. "Why would she give her cat away? I wouldn't. Why did she?"

"Good question. My partner, Rene Garcia is going to check out her place. Maybe she'll come up with something the state guys missed."

"I hope so," Max said, "but I'm not optimistic."

Zack sipped his coffee. "My concern is why the Dark Angel picked Sea Isle City?"

"Good point. I've got a couple of guys screening the rental offices to see if any groups of women have rented a place nearby."

"How about if she owns it?"

"We're going through the property tax records, but it's a little like looking for that proverbial needle in a haystack." She took a bite of muffin, chewed, swallowed. "Ah, that's good. It's harder now because we're at the height of the season and almost all of the houses are full. Rentals are up. Property owners are here. In the winter, the population is only about twenty percent of the summer."

Zack grimaced. "Swell."

By the time Scott and her team finished searching through the house and lining up Social Services for the baby, it was 4:30 and she still hadn't had a damn thing to eat. She tried to tie together what she knew so far. The woman had fled on foot. Three police cars searched the area but hadn't located her yet.

Scott checked the desk in the living room and discovered the woman's name was Yun Hee Soon. Paperwork in the desk showed she had come to the US from South Korea about five years ago. Scott figured she might be an illegal, but why here at David Garcia's house?

A search of drawers revealed the two shared the master bedroom. *The baby's mother? A lover.* Hell, who knew, but Scott had to find out. *And the baby. Who'd leave a baby?*

Her cell phone rang. "Scott."

"Lieutenant, this is FBI Special Agent Frank Harper."

Scott sighed. "Oh, great, the Feds. That's all I need."

Harper laughed. "It's not that bad."

"Says you."

"I'd like to talk to you about David Garcia. Do you have some time this evening?"

Gotta eat. Maybe a quick burger at Reilly's. "I'll be back in the office in about an hour."

"Would it be all right if I stopped by?"

"And if I said no?"

"I'd probably stop by anyway."

"That's what I figured. Let's make it two hours."

She clicked off her cell and took one last look around the house, then motioned to one of the police officers standing by the front door. "Stake out the place overnight. This Yun Hee Soon has no coat or anything else and it'll turn cool after dark. She's gotta come back. She'll want her baby. When she does, bring her down to the station. I want to talk with her."

Scott had found a key and gave to one of the officers. "Get copies made and let me have one. I want you to go over the house once more. Search everything. We need to find out what her part is in this. As soon as you're done here, let me know."

After she finished with the officers, Scott checked out the backyard once more, then returned to the front to get in her truck. *Fast food time. Get a grease hit.* But first, she had to call Colonel Garcia and see what she knew about the woman and the baby. Scott had the feeling Garcia didn't know a thing about any of this. *What if she had a niece she didn't know existed? Big time shock.*

Out front, a woman pushed a stroller down the street. The woman seemed startled when Scott came out of the house. Scott called to her and flashed her badge. "I'm Lieutenant Scott with the Fairfax Police Department. I didn't mean to surprise you."

The woman, hunched over the handle of her daughter's stroller, visibly relaxed after she saw the badge. "Hi, I'm Betsy Roberts. I live on the other side of the hill. I saw all the police cars and wondered what happened."

"I'm investigating the David Garcia incident. "

"I heard about it from one of our neighbors who saw it. How is he?"

"In a coma at Fairfax Hospital. Too early to tell how he'll do." Scott bent down. "And who is this lovely young lady?"

Roberts pushed her baseball cap back on her head. "This is my daughter, Elizabeth. She's having trouble napping. I'm hoping she'll fall asleep in her stroller."

Scott ruffled Elizabeth's hair, then looked up at the mother. "Tell me about David Garcia. Has he lived here long? Is he a good neighbor?"

Roberts smiled. "Oh, yes, they're both wonderful people."
"Both?"

"David and Soon. I know Soon better than David. He works long hours. Soon is the sort who will do anything for anyone. Elizabeth has some health issues and Soon has volunteered to babysit for her a number of times. Soon's a princess."

"What can you tell me about them?"

"David moved in about two years ago. He works for some software outfit here in Fairfax. Soon joined him about ten months ago and Lee Ann was born about six months later."

"Are they married?" Scott asked.

"Well, to be honest I don't know. Didn't want to pry, you know. They don't talk about it and I figured it's none of my business."

Scott made a note on her pad. "What can you tell me about their relationship?"

"Oh, they're in love. David always has his arm around her and they hold hands. I'm sure the baby belongs to both of them."

"How about David?"

"He's nice, but much quieter than Soon."

Roberts looked away for a moment, then back at Scott. "Did I hear right? The rumor in the neighborhood is whoever hit David might have done it on purpose?"

"Why do you ask?"

"Well, a funny thing happened two nights ago."

Scott's antenna shot up. "What do you mean?"

"I was out walking Elizabeth late and spotted a blue car cruise by their house. The driver drove to the end of the block, then turned around and came back. When he saw me, he drove off."

"Can you describe him?"

"Not really. It was dark and I didn't want to stare."

"What kind of a car was it?"

"I think it was a late model Toyota, dark blue. My husband and I have been looking at used cars and we're checking Toyotas. We've got to get rid of our gas guzzler." She paused. "You don't suppose . . .."

14

Fairfax, VA, Thursday, 5:00 p.m.

Garcia and FBI Agent Tara Fairchild arrived at Petty Officer Second Class Rosemary Edelman's condo a little after five o'clock. Harper had suggested Garcia take Fairchild along and Garcia agreed. Would give her a chance to get to know Fairchild.

Garcia banged on the landlord's door. A thick, balding man opened the door. He smelled of some sweet cologne. Not good.

The man looked at Garcia. "Yeah?"

"I'm a military police officer and this is FBI Agent Fairchild." She showed him the warrant. "We have a warrant to search Petty Officer Edelman's apartment."

He glanced at it, then pulled a key off the wall. "Second floor. Room 212. Bring the key back when you're done."

"Is she in?" Garcia asked.

The guy started to push the door shut. "Don't think so."

Garcia stuck her foot in the doorway to block it. "When is the last time you saw her?"

"Probably this past weekend, maybe Saturday."

"Is there anything you can think of that might help us find her?"

He shook his head. "State cops were here a while ago. Told them the same thing. Not my job to keep an eye on tenants."

"Okay, thanks for your time." Garcia looked back as she headed for the stairs. The man watched Fairchild, giving her a look up and down.

Fairchild must have felt it. She turned and glared at him. "Something wrong?

He straightened. "Ah, no."

"Then don't be a prick and stare at my butt. If I catch you doing it again, I'll knee you in the balls. I guarantee you won't like it at all."

As they walked up the stairs, Garcia murmured, "Bastard."

Fairchild nodded. "Yeah."

Garcia spotted chipped paint on the walls and a number of places with missing portions of staircase railing. "Looks like the place could use a little maintenance."

Fairchild nodded. "Lots of maintenance."

Garcia unlocked the door. It opened into a living room about ten by twenty feet. To the right, a door led to a tiny balcony. Two chairs were placed under the one window with a tattered couch along the wall. No carpet. A card table stood in the center of the dining room with two folding chairs arranged around it. No decorations on the walls, no anything to show who lived here.

Two bedrooms were off the hallway from the dining room, one totally empty, the other housing a single bed with a cover thrown over it. Garcia stripped back the cover to discover only a stained mattress pad over the mattress. She checked the closet and found four sets of navy uniforms. Again, nothing on the walls.

Pulling open the dresser drawers, Garcia noted T-shirts, underwear, and maybe a dozen pairs of socks. Checking drawers, looking behind cupboards, she came up empty. "This is not a home to anyone," she murmured. "Nothing personal on the walls, very little in the kitchen and the pantry. Hard to believe anyone lived here."

"Listen, Garcia, Edelman was brutally raped. I understand a couple of other officers handed pictures around of her naked. Posted them on the Internet. She got no help from her unit and I bet she ended up depressed. Somehow she found a group of like-minded souls. If that had happened to me, I wouldn't give a shit about living in a Better Homes and Gardens scene. Fucking men really screwed her over. I can't blame her for wanting revenge. I would."

"But you can't blame all military officers for the actions of a few."

"Bullshit. Men can be a real pain in the ass. All they want is a little ass, then they go on to sup nectar from the next flower."

"No question there's some pricks around, but don't go overboard."

Fairchild stood looking at Garcia, hands on hips. "I wish I could believe that, but I've met too many assholes. Makes me cry for Edelman. Hell, I have to get out of here. Harper wants me at another meeting in an hour or so."

"Yeah," Garcia said. "I've got a meeting at the Pentagon in a little while to talk about computer security."

"Good luck," Fairchild replied. "Let me know what you find out."

Zack took another sip of his coffee, damn stuff getting cold, and the police station getting on his nerves. "What do you say we get out of here and go look around."

"I'm ready for that," Max said. "How about if I drive?"

"Works for me."

Max drove Zack to the two sites where the bodies were discovered. They got out of her unmarked police car and walked the beach.

Zack spotted nothing out of the ordinary. "You know, we keep using the pronoun she for the Dark Angel. Any chance it could be a man?"

"Guess it could be. I always think of angels as women. A woman would have the motive for killing these guys."

"That's true." Zack laughed. "But don't forget about the Arch-angel Michael."

"Ah ha, someone with a little religious background."

"The operative word is a little. What brought these two officers to the beach? If I remember right, Brian was assigned in Washington. Why would he be here?"

"We contacted the D.C. police," Powell said, "and they dispatched detectives to interview his neighbors, friends, people he worked with. As far as anyone knew, he's never been to Sea Isle City before and they had no idea why he would have driven here." Powell pointed toward the town center. "Let's head that way. Maybe we'll see something else."

"He may have been kidnapped and brought here," Zack said. "When was the last time anyone saw him?"

"Friday at the Pentagon. He didn't seem particularly concerned about anything. Just another work day."

Zack snapped his fingers. "I wonder if he went to a bar Friday night. Maybe someone spiked his drink? From what it sounds like, he could be lured by the ladies."

"That's an interesting thought. So, the guy goes out on the town and is followed by a couple of good-looking babes. They hit on him and wham it's all over."

"Wham?"

Max laughed. "Yes, wham. You know, come on, buddy, come with us. We'll show you a fun evening."

"If that happened, Brian would be putty in their hands. What about Butler?"

"He's assigned to the Pentagon also. Whoever we're looking for may live in D.C. They pinpoint their targets, find out where they hang out . . ."

"And then, *Wham*," Zack finished her thought.

She laughed. "Yeah, *Wham*. But for these two guys, not such a fun thing."

"I'll contact Blake. See if she can put something out to alert military officers in the D.C. area. Check with the legal guys for a list of those accused of taking advantage of their rank with women. That's who the Dark Angel seems to be going after."

Zack checked his watch. "I almost forgot, Admiral Steele has scheduled a press conference for six. Where's the closest television set?"

"Are you hungry?" Max asked. "We could drive up to the Strathmere Inn, watch the press conference on television, then get something to eat."

"Sounds like a plan."

"But just dinner." She poked him in the ribs. "No *Wham*."

Agents Harper and Fairchild arrived at the Fairfax Police Station a little after six. Scott had put on a pot of coffee before hurrying down the hallway to meet them. She wondered what the agents were up to.

As she escorted them back to her office, Scott asked, "Are you the Frank Harper who played football for the Washington Redskins a few years ago?"

Harper nodded. "Guilty as charged."

"I've been a big 'Skins' fan for years. Sorry about the knee."

"Not half as sorry as I was. But that's football."

She led them into a small conference room. After they were seated at the six-person conference table, Harper said, "We have an interest in David Garcia. I understand you investigated his accident this morning. Could you summarize for us what happened?"

Scott squinted at him, thinking how much to tell them. "Guess I could do that. I've got a pot of coffee brewing. Should be ready in about ten minutes. I stopped by the hospital this morning and talked to his sister, an army lieutenant colonel named Rene Garcia."

"We met Colonel Garcia," Fairchild said.

Now what's that all about? Scott wondered. "He's in a coma and the doc doesn't know if he'll live or die. It appears the next twenty-four hours will be critical. But first, let me ask why you want to know about him? What exactly is your interest?"

"He's what we call a 'Person of Interest,'" Harper replied. "I can't say any more than that, at least for the present."

Scott sat up straight, her feet hitting the conference room floor with a loud thud. "Fucking feds, I might have known." She leaned forward and pointed at him. "You know, this is what gives you guys a bad rap with the locals. You expect us to share with you, but you don't want to help us do our job. Well, the hell with you."

Harper raised his hand. "Wait a minute, I'll share. I just want to know what you have so far."

Scott grimaced. "All right, I'll do it for old time's sake and the Skins.' But if you jerk me around, I'll clam up faster than you can say 'Skins.'" She grabbed a sheet of paper off the table and shared the basics of the accident. "Maybe somehow his job figures into what happened."

Fairchild made a note then asked, "Why do you think that?"

"According to the people I talked to today, he's a strong-willed guy, doesn't tolerate inefficiency worth a damn. Sorta like me. But the lady who lives across the street from his house seemed shocked something like this could happen, particularly if it were intentional." She decided to not mention anything about the baby or the car for now.

"What you say jibes with my information," Fairchild said.

"How did you get your information?" Scott asked.

"I'm afraid we . . . .."

"I know," Scott snapped, "you fuckers can't share with us commoners."

Fairchild lurched back. "Now wait a minute . ..."

"No, you wait a minute, both of you. I'll be damned if I'll give you a shit load of information to help you do your job if you sit there and plead the fifth. You can hit the road and don't let the door slam you in the ass on your way out."

Harper put his hands on the table. "Look, I have a confidential informant and I'm in the middle of a possible sting operation. I can't reveal the identity, at least not yet. Please believe me, I would like to partner with you in your investigation."

Scott watched Harper. "Have you interviewed any of the staff at Sterling?"

"The FBI doesn't have grounds to do any interviews yet," Harper replied.

"I met with the company president earlier today." Scott reached in her pocket and pulled out a package of cigarillos. She held up the package. "Want one?"

Both agents shook their heads.

"Not supposed to do this in an office building, but it helps relieve tension and the Feds always ramp up my tension level." She lit up a cigarillo and took a puff, leaning back to blow a smoke ring in the air. "I don't think I can go any further than what I have said at this time."

"All right," Harper replied, "I get your point. Let me tell you what I know We received a tip David Garcia had some concerns his office may be trying to hack into the Pentagon computers."

Scott's eyes widened. "What? His boss gave me a big deal about the security this new system could provide to DOD."

"That appears to be the point," Harper said. "Kinda like the fox guarding the hen house."

Scott leaned back in her chair and took a puff. "Well, I'll be damned, a Fed with brains. His concerns could provide a motive for whoever hit him with the truck."

Harper stood and turned toward the door, Fairchild following suit. "We'd better get going, but I'd like to stay in touch with you on this one."

"Samuel Foster, the president at Sterling, gave me a DVD they use to market their new system. He called it Red Dog. Let me get it and we'll take a look. And the coffee should be about done."

Fairchild sat back down. "On second thought, got any popcorn to go along with your movie?"

15

Strathmere, NJ, Thursday, 6:00 p.m.

Zack Kelly and Maxine Powell parked in the tiny parking lot adjacent to the Strathmere Inn. They hurried inside in time to see the beginning of the press conference on the restaurant's large screen television set in the bar. There had to be sixty or seventy reporters sitting or standing in the White House press room, with a number of news cameras spread across the back wall. Zack spotted ABC, NBC, CBS. Fox News and CNN. They smelled blood and wanted in on all the gory details.

At six o'clock sharp, Admiral Steele stepped up to the microphones. The lights reflected off the rows of decorations on his dress blue uniform. "Good Afternoon, I'm Admiral Steele, the president's national security advisor. I'd like to read a statement, then I'll take your questions." He covered the basics of the murders of Toomey and Butler, plus the attack at the Army War College. "Our hearts go out to all those who have been injured or lost their lives today as well as members of their families. We will do everything possible to catch the people who planned and carried out this terrorist act."

As soon as Steele finished his statement, the questions started. Questions about the dead officers in Sea Isle City. Then John Mercy from the *New York Times* asked, "I keep hearing about this Dark Angel. Who is that?"

Steel paused for a moment. "To be honest we're not sure. The name Dark Angel was tattooed on the chest of both men who were murdered. We're assuming that's the person, as yet unknown, who is taking credit for the murders."

"Do you have any leads?" Mercy asked.

Steele shook his head. "I'm not at liberty to comment on an ongoing investigation."

Then a reporter from the *Washington Post* asked the question Zack had expected. "Is the same person, maybe this Dark Angel, behind both the murders and the bombing?"

"We're not ruling anything out at this point," Steele replied.

Around the room, reporters tapped on smart phones and tablets. Travis Plank stepped forward and replaced Steele at the microphone. "Thank you, Admiral. A press statement is on the back table along with my business cards. We will keep you up to date as we learn more."

Steele made his way out of the press room, a number of shouted questions following him. As the press conference concluded, Zack turned to Maxine and asked, "What do you think?"

"The admiral did well. I've learned brevity is the best approach in a situation like this. When you say too much, you're stuck. You can't ever go back with the press."

"It's especially important with the Washington Press Corps," Zack replied. "They have the ability to get a guy going, throw him or her on the ropes, then completely ruin your day."

Max smiled that winning smile of hers. "Believe me, I'm extremely careful what I say when there are reporters around."

Once they were seated in the dining room, Zack ordered a beer and Max a glass of red wine. It took a few minutes for the waitress to bring their drinks. Zack proposed a toast. "To a lady who I enjoy working with even if this is ghastly stuff."

Max's face reddened. "Why thank you, Zack, I do enjoy your company. Why don't you tell me a little about yourself?"

"Not much to tell, really." He decided to not say anything about Laura yet. "I played a little football in high school, started college and found it wasn't right for me, then joined the army. Been hustling army rangers ever since. How about you?"

She smiled. "Well, I guess I might as well get it out. My mom was born in Romania, then moved to Vermont as a youngster."

"Wow," Zack said, "Romanian. You don't have any accent."

"I'm not really Romanian," Max replied, "but Roma."

"Roma?"

"Yes, Roma. You know, we're the gypsies you've probably hear so much about and don't know any real live ones."

Zack was a little taken back and didn't know quite what to say. Then he blurted out the truth. "I've never met a gypsy before."

"Be careful or I'll put a spell on you." She laughed then her face straightened. "Actually there are about twelve million gypsies world-wide. We're the largest ethnic minority in Europe."

"I've heard gypsies move around a lot."

She took a sip of wine and dabbed her mouth with a napkin. "Really out of necessity. In many places we're not allowed to own land or work in professions, so most of my family became seasonal laborers. My mom was a free spirit from the '60s so didn't bother with a marriage or a husband or anything silly like that. She and her best friend were groupies to a number of rock bands, so I never knew who my dad was. Probably someone from one of the bands. That's where the name Powell came from. I won't tell you my real name."

Zack didn't know what to say, so this time he kept his mouth shut.

"I appreciate your silence. A lot of guys don't know what to say, but at least you didn't say anything stupid like I'm sorry. I had a great childhood. My mom worked hard and got me through college, although I always had lots of uncles hanging around who liked to spend the night with her."

She took a sip of her wine. "Poverty is a big challenge for gypsies because of all the discrimination and persecution in Europe. My mom could never figure out why, but I always wanted to be a cop. I took criminal law in college, then worked on a small town police force before moving to Sea Isle."

Zack started to stutter. "I'm not sure how to ask this."

She laughed, a fun engaging laugh. "Don't worry, I've heard it all. Yes, it's hard to be accepted onto the force as a new guy on the block, particularly a female."

"Actually, an attractive female."

"I get hit on a lot and yes, I get tired of it. All I want to do is my job, but all these big tough guys want to take me under their wing and who knows what else."

"I can also sense what else."

He finished his beer and motioned to the waitress. "Would you like another one?"

"Ah, ha, you're trying to take advantage of me."

"Never crossed my mind. Besides, who'd be crazy enough to try and take advantage of a hard-boiled cop who could put a spell on you? I'm not ready to disappear into thin air yet."

Zack ordered the seafood platter and Maxine the salmon. A southpaw, she ate hunched over like she was protecting her food, her left arm out at an angle. Looked sweet.

As they ate, they talked over what they had discovered. "You know," Zack said, "when it comes right down to it, we haven't got a damn thing. Nothing from the APB on Petty Officer Edelman?"

"With all she's been through, I'm surprised we haven't found her yet." She paused. "Now I have a question for you."

"Shoot. Oops, forgot who I was talking to. Should have said, go ahead."

That got another smile. "Why do you drive that big gas guzzler truck? Why not something a little easier on our environment?"

"I've always loved a truck. Plus, I sometimes do work around the house and need to haul stuff. How do you like your Prius?"

"Love it and I get almost sixty miles to a gallon."

"Sure can't say that for my truck."

"Aren't you sorry for contributing to global warming?"

Zack didn't have an answer for that.

Garcia had to cut short her time at Petty Officer Edelman's apartment so she could hustle back to the Pentagon to meet with General Harding. She needed to find out what she could about the new research program into the use of drones in the United States and the contract with Sterling Software. Barclay Morrison had a conflict and couldn't join her at the meeting.

When she arrived, the sergeant major looked up. "Colonel Garcia?"

"Yes. I have an appointment with General Harding."

He let her to a doorway and motioned for her to enter. "The general is waiting for you. "

Harding looked up from her desk as Garcia entered and saluted her. Garcia had done her research and found the general to be one sharp officer. A jet pilot, she'd received her PhD in electrical engineering from MIT as well as having graduated from all of the air force's top schools.

"Please take a seat, Colonel Garcia. I don't have much time, but Admiral Steele told me you needed to see me." She pointed at the slender, brown-haired man in the corner chair. "This is my staff judge advocate, Zamir Nabhas."

A dark skinned, slender man with a goatee and dark rimmed glasses, stood. Garcia shook his hand, assuming him to be Morrison's contact.

Garcia sat. "I'm following up on our earlier meeting at the White House." She reviewed David's concerns and the plan for him to wear a wire while meeting with others at Sterling. "I'm becoming more and more concerned about Sterling Software."

"Wait a minute," Harding cut in, "isn't he in the hospital?"

"Yes. Unfortunately, a truck hit David yesterday morning. He's in Fairfax Hospital in a coma." It surprised Garcia how hard the comment hit her.

"He seemed like a very nice and competent young man." Harding placed her fingers to her chin. "Is it possible the truck hit him to shut him up?"

"Yes. A witness claims the truck swerved into David."

"If there's a possibility of compromise in our security, it would be a very serious problem," Harding said. "Our research project is a gigantic undertaking and it would be a real black eye for not only the project but the Federal Aviation Administration if this were to leak out. Are you familiar with the program?"

"Somewhat."

"I think with all that's going on, it's important you are." Harding took a sip of coffee. "Let me explain. The FAA approved six sites around the country to test commercial drones and explore what technological, legal and logistical challenges their commercial use in the United States would represent. We expect the first test drones to be in the air by late 2015 or early 2016. My task is to keep a close eye on developments at the test site at Fort Shelby, Mississippi. I'm not sure why Sterling might be interested in sabotaging our efforts? Do you?"

Garcia shook her head. "I assumed their motivation would be money. As a cop, I've always believed you should follow the money. Maybe their plan is to sell national secrets to other governments or other corporations. This project is the wave of the future."

"Absolutely. Drones will require some sort of artificial intelligence in the event their controllers lose contact with the vehicle for any substantial period of time. They'll be sharing the skies with other drones and of course, manned aircraft. If this program is compromised, it could set commercial aviation back years."

"Have there been problems?" Garcia asked.

"Oh, yes. More than 400 large military drones have crashed in major accidents around the world since 2001. The problems seem to be either mechanical, human error, or sometimes bad weather. Our military drones have slammed into homes, farms, highways, and in one case, an Air Force C-130 Hercules transport plane. And there have been a number of near misses."

Garcia took a deep breath. "I didn't know about all of those problems."

"These are not error-free aircraft." Harding turned to Nabhas. "What do you think, Zamir."

"I've been impressed with David Garcia and the staff I've met at Sterling. Their assistant project manager, Megan Alcott, has taken over temporarily. She seems very talented. I know she's been traveling to Shelby on a regular basis to coordinate the program. The economic impact of this project is immense."

"I've met Ms. Alcott," Harding said, "and I believe she's competent. In any event, Zamir, I'd like for you to put together a small team and review out computer security. Do it as quietly as you can, obviously without alerting Sterling." She turned back to Garcia. "Admiral Steele told me this was important and I agree. Thank you for coming in."

"Have you been working in the drone program long?"

Harding seemed to grit her teeth. "Yes."

Garcia had heard there were some problems between pilots and drone operators so she had to be careful. "That seems to bother you. May I ask why?"

Harding stared at Garcia for a moment.

"I'm sorry if I asked the wrong question."

Harding leaned back. "No, it's just a source of frustration in the air force. I entered the air force to fly jet planes and I flew the F-22 stealth fighter for the first part of my career. I had the fantasy of being the first female air force chief of staff. As a woman, you know how hard that would be."

Garcia nodded.

"But I was determined. Got good at flying jets, obtained a PhD, and was on my way when the drone issue hit around 2005. Guess what female officer ended up at Creech Air Force Base in nowhere, Nevada, working on the drone program. No more life in the wild blue yonder."

Garcia didn't know what to say.

"Don't try and figure out what to say. I made my two stars, but probably won't be chief of staff because there's some male F-22 pilot who will get the nod to do that. But, that's life in the 'Boys' Club.'"

Harding looked out her window for a moment. "And the other thing that wrangles me is all the problems with sexual abuse in the military. Every day, I see where some female officer or enlisted member ends up getting screwed, literally and it messes up her career. Well as my daddy used to say, 'can't fix it, gotta live with it'."

Garcia stood. "Thanks for your time, General. Please keep us advised on what you find out."

"I will." She turned to Nabhas. "Zamir, you're my point person. I expect you to track this and be sure to keep Colonel Garcia in the loop."

As Garcia walked out, the general called to her. "Did you say David is your brother?"

"Yes."

"Oh, I'm so sorry."

"So am I," Garcia muttered as she left.

16

Strathmere, NJ, Thursday, 7:30 p.m.

After they finished dinner, Max drove them back toward Sea Isle City along the narrow, two-lane road that paralleled the beaches. The sunset colored the heavens a deep crimson and the evening sky began to darken.

Zack periodically glanced at Max. She was fun and so damn good looking, a cross between the girl next door and a movie star. What did she think of him? She seemed to be enjoying herself. Or so he hoped.

Max looked up through the windshield. "A beautiful evening. Hey, there's the moon."

"Absolutely beautiful, just like my companion."

"Why, Zack, what a sweet thing to say. Are you one of those silver-tongued devils?"

"Nope. Just tell it the way I see it." He paused for a moment. "Is there someplace we can stop and walk along the beach? I'd like to relax a little before we get dumped back into the rat race."

"The beaches between Sea Isle City and Strathmere are always quiet. You know, private. I love to walk those beaches. Don't get jounced around by the mad hordes."

She pulled over and parked the car. "Come on, let's get our feet in the sand." Waiting for a couple of cars to pass, she jumped out and ran across the street, then up a short flight of wooden steps. "That's what beach lovers always talk about," she called. "Squish your toes in the sand."

Zack followed her up the stairs. At the top, his breath caught at the majesty beauty of the ocean. He enjoyed the sounds of the waves lapping up against the sand. His gaze shifted left. "What are all those lights over there?"

"Atlantic City. The place is in full swing around the clock. It's fun to drive up to the casinos. You know, work on your retirement plan." She put a hand on his arm for balance and kicked off her shoes. "All right, Mr. Colonel, off with your shoes. It's time you became a beach bum like the rest of us. If only for a few minutes."

The soft touch of her hand sent a small charge through his body. He kicked off his docksiders and bent down to pull off his socks, then wiggled his toes in the sand. "Not bad."

Max laughed. "Now you're getting it."

Zack walked next to her. The moon reflected on the water and the evening breeze blew warm against his skin. He worked to blank out the thoughts swirling around in his mind, but he couldn't. Too much didn't tie together.

Max spun left to dance in little circles, arms spread wide. "I love it," she called. "Summer evenings are a special time to be here. September and October are actually my favorite months at the shore. The water is still warm and the mobs of tourists have gone back to their slave labor. But I'll have to admit, this is pretty nice."

Zack watched her dance, admiring the curve of her hip and breast. "I'm surprised how empty it is. It's almost like we're alone on a deserted island."

"This part usually is. Beaches are busier as you get closer to Sea Isle City." She hummed a song. "I probably shouldn't have had that third glass of wine. I'm a little buzzed."

"Yeah, me too, but it feels good."

Their hands brushed and Zack connected his finger with hers. "I enjoy being here with you."

She gave Zack's hand a little squeeze. "I do too, Zack."

A boat passed them maybe a hundred feet from shore.

"Fishing boats going out or coming in," Max said. "They keep pretty odd hours."

Zack watched the water lapping the beach, the constant sound of the waves relaxing him. He became aware, very aware of the brush of her hip against his. "What's that? Sounds like another boat."

"I hear it, too."

It cut through the water, the running lights out so all they could see was an outline.

"Over there," Zack whispered. "Looks like it's coming closer to shore. Maybe looking for someone? It could be dangerous running without lights."

"Whatever," Max said. "Looks like they're gone."

They strolled along the still-warm beach sand, stars twinkling above them, and the crunching sand music to his ears. Zack decided to venture into new territory. "What do you think of Sprite?"

"A little rough, but not a bad sort."

"Why is he such a prick during interviews? I almost slugged him when he was so hard on Linda in that first interview. Hell of a tough time for her."

"He lost his wife about a year ago. I don't think he's recovered yet."

"Okay."

Zack reached down and picked some sand, letting it slip through his fingers. "Maybe we could come back later and take a swim."

Max glanced up and down the quiet beach. "Why wait till later? A little wine and it's time to do something crazy." She shucked her jacket, then pulled her shirt over her head and pushed down her slacks. She wore a light-colored bra and panties.

The light from the moon caught and framed her silvery skin accented by her long black hair, almost mesmerizing Zack.

She unhooked the bra, pushed her panties down and kicked them free. Running toward the water she called, "Last one in is an old shoe."

Zack stood there for a moment, his breathing quickening. Holy shit. He came to life, yanked off his shirt, slacks and underwear, then ran after her into the surf.

Max surfaced and turned to face him, the water dripping from her breasts. Looking him over she said, "Quit pointing that damn thing at me. All I want to do is take a swim. Nothing else."

Zack laughed. "I meant it as a compliment. Sometimes it has a mind of its own."

"I've heard that happens. Well, I accept your compliment. Thank you."

They swam for a few minutes, Max showing no hesitancy about her nakedness. They played in the water, splashing one another.

Max stood. "Time to leave our little paradise. She ran back toward the beach, Zack watching the sway of her hips.

 She pulled on her panties and struggled with fitting her shirt. "Wet skin. Hard to get dressed."

Zack picked up his underwear and started to dress. He heard a noise. "Is that your phone?"

"Oh, damn, I hope no one else hears it." She reached down and pulled it out of her jacket pocket. "Powell."

She listened, then disconnected. "Shit. They found another body. Sixty-third Street beach in Sea Isle City. Get dressed. We gotta go."

———————

Lieutenant Scott walked over and adjusted the volume on the TV set in her office. "Can you hear that okay?"

Harper and Fairchild both nodded.

David Garcia's face popped up on the screen. A slender, young-looking man, his wide brown eyes and long black hair a striking combination. He wore a navy-blue suit and a red-striped tie. "Funny," Scott said, "still looks like a computer nerd with the hair."

"I wonder how they got a suit on him," Fairchild said. "He looked more like a college student the last time I saw him."

David opened his pitch by saying, "Normal anti-virus software can miss more than twenty percent of the Trojans attacking your computer. A recent study showed a computer attached to the Internet without protective software will, on average, be infected in about twenty minutes. Cyber-warfare is so complex that first, an intrusion team will breach your security system, then an ex-filtration team can retrieve the data. What can you do to prevent this from happening at your company?"

The music grew louder in the background. "Sterling Software has the answer. We've developed a new program that will protect your company. Red Dog has been field-tested across the spectrum of industry and it's blocked all hacking attempts."

A schematic of a barrier blocking electrical impulses flashed on the screen. "Believe me," he emphasized, "the risk is real to your company. A Carnegie Mellon study concluded most companies don't see themselves as vulnerable until it's too late."

David Garcia pointed at the screen behind him. "Cyber-spies have stolen the crown jewels from a number of American companies. Remember, exploration or bid materials are also at risk. In other words, a hacker can zero in on your new discovery, putting your company at a major competitive disadvantage."

The camera panned to the audience of probably thirty individuals, mostly well-dressed. A young woman asked, "How can we obtain more information?"

A phone number flashed across the bottom of the screen as David said, "Do what many of your competitors have already done. Call this number. We have experts who will come directly to your headquarters and answer all of your questions. Don't be that one company to fall behind. Call today and settle back, safe in the realization you have blocked future hacking threats. My company has been entrusted with some of the most vital government secrets. We can protect your secrets, too."

The music swelled again as the words "Red Dog" and a logo of a Saint Bernard protecting an office building appeared on the screen. An American flag fluttered from the doorway in the background, then the screen darkened.

Scott stopped the DVD and leaned back in her chair. She was impressed. "Pretty effective PR. I'd probably call. How do hackers do all this crap?"

"Let me take that one," Fairchild said. "I hope you're ready for all this. It's taken me awhile, but I think I've got it figured out. The hackers' main weapon is the botnet."

Scott wrinkled up her face. "Botnet?"

A smile spread across Fairchild's face. "I said the same thing. A bot is a remote-controlled software program placed on a computer without the owner's knowledge. Hackers use viruses, worms, or other automated programs to scan the Internet looking for potential zombies. These machines have literally been hijacked. Once that happens, the computers are called zombies."

Fairchild took a swallow of her coffee. "The bots connect zombies to a channel in a chat room. A herd of zombies is called a botnet. The herder issues orders to the zombies, telling them to send unsolicited emails, steal personal information, or launch attacks."

Scott thought about that. "Oh, man, this gives me a headache."

"Probably the biggest risk comes from hackers with ties to organized crime," Fairchild continued. "Defeating organized crime is where the FBI is focused. Spearheading this hacking effort is the Russian Mafia. They've infiltrated businesses in the former Soviet Union and are spreading their influence around the world. We estimate they're operating in approximately fifty countries."

"How does this tie in to what happened to David Garcia?" Scott asked.

Fairchild leaned in toward Scott. "I wish we knew. But, what's new and sobering, is not only the escalating scale of the attacks, but also the precision with which these programs can scan computers for specific information. Hackers look for corporate and personal data, then drain money from online banking and stock accounts."

Harper sipped his coffee. "The question is what would David Garcia have uncovered with his microphone? Is Sterling involved in some sort of illegal computer activity and is someone at Sterling responsible for what happened to him?"

"Wasn't any damn accident," Scott said. "Now, what you've said is great stuff, but I have no idea how it'll help me solve what I believe is the attempted murder of David Garcia."

"While you're stewing on that, we'd better get going." Harper stood and extended his hand. Thanks so much for the information and the coffee. I look forward to working with you."

"What do you know?" Scott said. "Smart Feds. Will wonders never cease."

As Harper and Fairchild walked out her door, Scott's intercom rang. She answered it.

"Lieutenant, there's a woman out here demanding to see you. She's Korean and says you stole her baby. The squad brought her over from the house."

Scott stepped out of her office and started down the hallway toward the front of the station, wondering what shit storm headed her way.

A short, slender Asian woman stomped toward Scott, calling, "Where my baby? Oh, please tell me where is she?"

"Wait a minute. There's no need to yell."

"Please give me baby." She started to cry. "Oh, I want my little baby."

How to best handle this woman. Why had she run off and left her baby? "Look, calm down and come with me. Let's see if we can sort this out." She led the woman into her office and left the door open. "Please sit down."

The woman sat in one of the chairs around the conference table. "Where my baby? I want her. Please. Now."

Scott pulled out a chair and sat. "First of all, do you have some identification?"

"What have to do with baby. You a thief. I expect more from police. In America, the police are supposed to protect people, not steal children."

Scott took a deep breath and swallowed her frustration, "Can you show me some identification? Please."

The woman pulled a card out of her wallet and showed it to Scott. "My name is Yun Hee Soon. I come to United States four year ago from South Korea. I work as a waitress for two years until I meet David. He a wonderful man. We had a baby four months ago. She sweet little girl."

"Why did you run off today when I arrived at your house?"

Yun Hee Soon wrapped a tissue around her fingers. She looked down at the floor, then back up at Scott. "When you show me badge, I panic."

"Come on," Scott said. "You're a grown woman. You have a baby. You know I'm not going to steal your baby. Why in the world would you run and leave your baby alone?"

Soon stared at her, then more tears came. Scott handed her another tissue."

"Now," Scott said. "Tell me the truth if you want your baby back."

"I," she stammered, "I was a changnyeo in Korea."

"A what? What in the world is that?"

"Ah, you call prostitute." Soon looked down at the floor, then up at Scott. "I smuggled into this country without papers by gang. Given to rich man."

Scott began to see the problem. "You have no green card?"

Soon shook her head and started to cry again. "David no know. My pimp awful man. Beat me. I escape, live on the street. Find work as waitress. David meet me at diner. Took me in and treat me with respect. First time anyone treat me with respect."

"All right," Scott replied. "I understand that."

"I fear if David find out, he leave me and the baby. I think if I run and disappear, David will care for little Lee An." She looked down at the floor again. "Lee An deserve a better future than me."

Scott reached over and touched her arm. "Don't worry. I will try and help you. Perhaps we can help you get a green card. I don't know all of the steps but maybe I can help. Believe me, I don't want your baby."

Soon smiled for the first time. She had a lovely smile. "Thank you. Thank you. You good person. Can I take her home? She be scared. Please?"

Scott wasn't sure what to do. She didn't want to keep the baby from her mother. On the other hand, she didn't want Soon to run again. "Did you know a truck hit David Garcia yesterday?"

Soon's eyes widened. "David hit by truck?" Tears formed again in her eyes. "When? Where? I think he work late. I walk. Stay with friend. Not have phone."

"A little before six o'clock Wednesday morning. About two blocks from your house."

"Where is he? I must go to him."

"He's at Fairfax Hospital." Scott shared with her what had happened. While Soon sobbed, Scott walked to her desk and retrieved another box of tissues.

When Soon settled down, Scott said, "The incident with David is why I came to your house. I'm investigating what happened. I found the baby in the house and turned her over to Social Services. That's where she is now."

"I must go to her. She be afraid."

"First, do you know why anyone would try and harm David?"

"No. He wonderful man. We have nice life. He work so hard. Sometimes all night. I must see him."

"Let me see if I can get Social Services to release your baby." Scott picked up the phone. As the phone rang she thought, *I hope I don't regret this.*

When the night supervisor at Social Services answered, she said, "This is Lieutenant Scott at the Fairfax Police Department. I have straightened out the problem with the mother that happened today and I need to pick up her baby. Would you prepare the necessary paperwork? I'll be over with the mother in a little while to sign the forms."

Scott hung up the phone. "Social Services will follow up with you. They'll want to make sure you are caring properly for the baby."

"I understand. Thank you. Thank you."

17

After dropping off Soon and her baby at their house, Lieutenant Scott drove home and pulled into her garage, and shut off the engine. She sat in the truck for a moment, almost too tired to move. Finally she pushed the door open, stepped out, and made her way through the laundry room and into the house.

When she opened the door to the kitchen, Brutus jumped up on her, his tail wagging. Brutus belonged to her grandmother and they all shared the house. Cute little guy. Scott watched Brutus whenever her grandmother traveled or stayed out late playing bridge.

Scott had labs when she was growing up so a young Westie like Brutus brought new challenges. Lots more barking.

She grabbed the leash and took the little guy out for a walk. Brutus spotted a neighbor's cat, Lennie, and started his barking routine, then he howled. Scott bent down to shush the dog. Never worked worth a damn, but it was too late at night for howling.

Back inside, she checked Brutus's water, fed him, opened a beer and sat down on a couch in the living room. Time to think her way through what had happened today.

First, a truck hit David Garcia. Probably not an accident. Only yesterday. Hell, it seemed like a week ago. The frustration built. Only a day and Scott had no leads.

Second, could someone at his work have tried to kill him? Another employee. Who?

Third, David Garcia lived with Yun Hee Soon. Note to self. Check to see if Soon is legal and they are married. What mother would leave a baby? Is her story true?

She took another sip of beer. The liquid slid down her throat and lubricated her thoughts. She had to connect the dots here and do it fast. Reaching down, Scott gathered Brutus up on her lap. "What do you think, pal? What's going on?" Brutus looked up at her, his big black eyes searching hers. "Well, you're not alone my friend, I don't know what's going on either."

Scott decided she needed to return to David Garcia's house and interview the rest of the neighbors. *That woman she'd talked to had seen a car. Was that somehow involved? Could it be someone with a grudge against him?*

The automatic garage door sounded, the back door opened. Brutus jumped down and ran into the kitchen, barking and howling like mad. In a minute, her grandmother popped her head into the living room, Brutus wrapped in her arms. A small woman, her personality packed a wallop. "I'm back from bridge and thought I might make something to eat. Can I get you a little snack, Pamela?"

As if on cue, Scott's stomach growled. "Not a bad idea, Gran. I forgot all about being hungry."

"Let's go in the kitchen," Gran said. "I bought a new kind of cheese at the store today. What say we try it out? Got some great crackers too."

Scott followed her into the kitchen. "How are you feeling? Did you get your EKG results today?"

Her grandmother had raised Scott and Scott's brother when they were abandoned by their father after the death of their mother. Pissed her off every time she thought about him.

"I've got a little flutter according to the doctor, but after checking it out, she said to just keep an eye on it." Gran opened the refrigerator and took out two packages of cheese. "I'm glad my doctor doesn't over treat me. So many of them do, you know." She spread cheese wedges on a plate, lifted a box of crackers out of the cupboard, opened them and arranged some in a small basket.

"You'd better take care of yourself. I need you and that's no shit."

"Pamela Scott, quit using that language. Haven't I taught you better?"

Scott laughed. "Yeah, you have, but I regress every once in a while. Occupational hazard, you know, being a cop and all. Got to show my masculine side once in a while."

"Speaking of masculine side, that nice young man, I forget his name, called for you this evening. He certainly is big."

Scott got a pleasant twinge. She'd met him on her last case. Nice guy. Little rough around the edges, but a nice guy.

"Yes, that's him. He beat around the bush and never came out and said it, but I think he wants to ask you out."

"Why doesn't he get on the ball and do it." They'd been out on a couple of dates but nothing in the past three or four weeks. *Why?*

Her grandmother looked at Scott over her glasses. "And you'd better go. You're not getting any younger. I miss having some little ones running around the house. Time to liven this place up."

"Gran, let me go out with the guy for a while before you start planning how many children I'm gonna have."

Gran laughed. "I guess we do need to keep everything in order."

They sat in silence, Scott enjoying her beer and a handful of cheese and cracker sandwiches. Her cell phone rang. *Eleven thirty. Now what?* She picked it up. "Scott."

"It's Rene Garcia."

Uh, oh, Scott thought, *this can't be good.* "Hey, what can I do for you?"

"I'm at the hospital with my brother. I think someone just tried to kill him."

"Don't move," Scott said. "I'll be there in fifteen minutes. And for damn sure, don't leave him alone till I get there."

"Okay, but hurry. I talked to the nurse and she called security."

"What's was that all about?" Gran asked as Scott hung up the phone.

"It's this case I'm working on. Someone is after this guy and it looks like they tried again at the hospital. Sorry, but I've got to run out on you."

Scott grabbed her coat, her trusty semi-automatic, ran out to the garage and climbed back into her truck. It roared to life. *We've got to protect David Garcia*, she thought. *Should have demanded security sooner. Oh, man, I hope I'm not too late.*

Seventeen minutes after she got the call, Scott hurried down the hallway toward David Garcia's room. Rene Garcia stood outside a door, talking to a red-haired man in a blue and white security uniform.

When she reached them, Scott gave the man the once over. "Who are you?"

"Officer Coats, security. Who are you?"

Scott pulled out her badge. "Lieutenant Scott, Homicide, Fairfax County."

He squinted at her through dark-framed glasses. "Delighted to meet you, Lieutenant. I've heard a great deal about you."

"What you've probably heard is I don't tolerate bullshit or inefficiency worth a damn."

"Yes, Lieutenant."

Scott turned to Garcia. "Now, what's going on?"

A nurse stepped out of David Garcia's room. "I'm sorry, but you'll have to move. You're making too much noise out here." She nodded toward a room across from David's room. "You can talk in there."

Coats and Garcia followed Scott into the room. Four bright orange chairs stood in a line against the far wall. Scott motioned toward the chairs. "Pull them into a circle so we can talk without shouting and angle them so we can see his doorway. No one gets in there again unless we know who it is."

Coats organized the chairs and they sat.

Scott got out her notebook. "Okay, tell me what happened."

Garcia took a deep breath. "I arrived at the hospital about ten o'clock after my meeting at the Pentagon with General Harding. First, I stopped by the nurses' station and talked to the nurse on duty . . . must have been for only a couple of minutes."

"Did she say if your brother had any visitors?" Scott asked.

"Apparently my parents left about eight o'clock, then Samuel Foster from David's work brought some flowers."

Scott made a note to talk to the nurse on duty. "Okay, go ahead."

"When I got to his room, a doctor stood by the bed, leaning over David."

"How did you know he was a doctor?" Coats asked.

"You know, when you see a guy in a long white coat in a hospital room, you kinda assume he's a doctor."

Coats swallowed, his Adams apple bobbing up and down. "Guess I ask some pretty dumb questions."

"Not really," Garcia replied. "He probably stole the coat out of the laundry. The guy didn't have an identification badge on his coat so I asked his name."

"No badge?" His eyes widened. "Hospital personnel are supposed to wear badges."

"I found that out from the nurse, but didn't realize it when I first saw him. He said his name was Pell."

Scott looked down at her notebook. "Damn, wish we could smoke in here."

"Sorry, Lieutenant," Garcia replied. "You're going to have to stay healthy for a little while longer."

"Swell. Was he holding anything in his hand, a needle, scissors, bottle of pills, anything at all?"

Garcia thought for a moment. "I don't remember anything in his hands, but he did have gloves on."

"Rubber gloves? Interesting." Scott looked up, chewing on the pencil eraser. "Okay, what happened next?"

"He told me his name and he was checking on David. He did use David's name."

Scott nodded. "He definitely knew your brother's name."

"Yes," Garcia replied. "He said David Garcia."

"Could you see what he was doing?" Scott asked

"Not exactly, but it looked like he worked with something on the IV stand."

"What?" A female voice echoed behind Scott. Scott whirled to see the nurse standing in the doorway.

"I stopped for a moment to hear what happened. You said he touched the IV?" The nurse turned and her footsteps echoed down the hall. In a moment, a recording came over the loud speaker announcing an emergency.

More footsteps sounded in the hall. The nurse called, "We need a full work up on David Garcia, stat. I'll explain later."

Coats moved to the door, watching all the activity. "Do you think he's all right?"

"The nurse said she'd keep me updated," Garcia replied.

Scott looked at Garcia. "Okay, give me a description, everything you can remember about him."

Garcia closed her eyes. The chair squeaked when she shifted positions. "This Doctor Pell stood about six feet tall and had long, sandy brown hair trailing down in back to his shirt collar. He wore what looked to me like the standard doc white coat with a maroon shirt and black pants underneath. Can't remember the color of his shoes, but they were dark."

"Wait." The pencil scratched on the pad as Scott scribbled notes. "Let me get all this down. I don't write that fast."

Garcia paused. "I'm beginning to understand. . ."

"Understand what?" Scott asked.

"He wore a white mask, pulled up under his nose. You know, it seemed funny to me at the time. I'm thinking he covered part of his face so I couldn't describe him. I should have reacted quicker."

"Anything else?" Scott asked. "Eye color, tattoos, distinguishing marks?"

"He had brown eyes." Garcia tapped her cheek. "Yes, brown, I'm sure of it."

"What about his hands?" Scott asked. "That can be key to what he does for a living."

"Good point. Large hands. I remember thinking, the guy's hands are big for a doctor."

Scott smiled. "Thank heavens you've got a great memory. Your description is very important. I think I've got it all."

"Advantage of being a cop." Garcia looked at Officer Coats. "Any chance of finding some coffee? I'm fading."

"You bet. I'll get on it." Coats hustled toward the door, then turned back. "Cream and sugar?"

Garcia shook her head. "Take it straight."

"Any distinguishing marks on what you could see of his face?" Scott asked.

Garcia closed her eyes again. "His eyes were set close together. I think he may have had a small birthmark on the right side of his forehead."

Scott patted her knee with the tablet. "He told you his name was Pell. Did he tell you his first name?"

"Doctor."

Scott chuckled to herself. "Yeah, guess we've got lots of those around here."

Coates arrived, juggling three cups of coffee and handed them around.

"Thanks." Scott took a sip. "Not bad. Do you know if anyone else saw this Doctor Pell?"

"We can ask the nurse on duty, but she seemed surprised when I told her." Garcia blew on the coffee and took a sip. "Man. That's good. Once I arrived in the room, Pell only stayed a couple of minutes. Then he hurried out, pushing past me. I thought to myself, the guy's not very courteous." Garcia snapped her fingers. "Oh, yeah, Pell said he was consulting from the Department of Radiology."

"Radiology?" Scott made another note.

"I figured he was preparing David for some sort of procedure. You know, the mask and all."

"Makes sense," Coats replied.

Garcia blew on the coffee and took another sip. "Not bad for hospital coffee."

"How long after this Doctor Pell left before you went out to find the nurse and ask her about him?" Scott asked.

"It couldn't have been more than ten minutes, fifteen tops. When I got to thinking about it, the guy bothered me. Something didn't ring true. I went out to the desk and mentioned Doctor Pell to the nurse on duty. When she couldn't find his name on the roster, I called you. I'm going to recommend to security they review all of their procedures. There's a hole somewhere in the system."

Coats scratched out a note. "I'll check the logs. Anyone who arrives after visiting hours should be logged in at the ER. It's the only door open after our visitors have left for the evening."

"I wonder if this hospital often has problems with security?" Garcia asked.

Coats shook his head. "First I can remember."

"This guy specifically looked for David," Garcia said. "It wasn't some random clown wandering around the hospital. What's next?"

"Can you come to the office in the morning?" Scott asked. "I'll set up an appointment for our artist to do a composite drawing. We've got a lead on this guy and I don't want to lose it."

"No problem, Lieutenant," Garcia replied. "I can be there first thing."

Scott turned to Coats. "I want a twenty-four-hour guard on this room. If your staff can't handle it, call the station and I'll provide officers to help out. I don't want anything else to happen to David Garcia. We must protect him. Someone is definitely after him."

"Right, Lieutenant," Coats said. "I'll get on it right away."

After Coats left to use the phone, Garcia whispered to Scott, "Tell me a little more about your visit to my brother's house this afternoon."

Scott knew how difficult this must be for Garcia, so she repeated much of what happened during the incident with Yun Hee Soon. "She came to my office this evening, told me she panicked and ran away. I didn't believe her so she finally told me her whole story. She's had a tough life. After our discussion, Soon seemed okay when we talked so I went with her to pick up the baby. Social Services checked her out, cleared her to take the baby, then I drove the two of them to her house."

Garcia shook her head. "I can't believe it. My folks are gonna freak when they hear about this. Are they married? Is the baby David's?"

"I'm not sure about marriage, but she said the baby is his. I will check a little more and let you know for sure."

Garcia slumped in the chair. Put her head in her hands. "My god, my brother has a baby girl. Makes me an aunt. This is too much." Garcia stood. "I gotta go. See you in the morning."

After Garcia left, Scott started down the hallway. The nurse motioned for her to stop.

Scott walked over. "Can I help you?"

"I don't know if this is important or not, Lieutenant. It's just a feeling I have."

"Go on." Scott reached for her notebook.

"Colonel Garcia seems like such a nice person."

"I think so, too," Scott replied.

"But you know what, I never saw that doctor and I could tell someone had touched the equipment in David Garcia's room. One of the nurses on the earlier shift told me Colonel Garcia had a big fight with her parents. I don't want to say anymore, but I think you need to keep an eye on her."

18

Naval War College, Newport, Rhode Island, Friday, 7:00 a.m.

Petty Officer Rosemary Edelman drove along Route 138 East toward her destiny. She'd left Sea Isle City at five o'clock that morning and caught Interstate 95 outside of Philadelphia She'd driven it often enough. But this would be her last time. Her mind kept moving, each memory hitting her again and again. *The rape, the awful rape. Then the pictures. Those awful nude pictures. The officers passed them around. Laughed at her when she asked them to stop.*

She crossed the Jamestown Bridge, then the Newport Bridge. This would be the last time she used her EZ Pass and she knew the investigators would be checking that. She reached the rotary exit, the one she'd driven so many times and almost had to pull over because of the tears. *Why had the bastards done that to her? So unfair.*

Most visitors stopped at the ID office prior to driving to Gate One, but she had her post sticker so she drove right up to the gate and got waved through. She checked her watch. Seven thirty-five. Right on time. She followed Training Station Road past the Naval War College museum and turned right on Cushing Road.

Why didn't she run into a nice guy like her sister had? Why did she have to run into that asshole Butler who'd ruined her life? But the

Dark Angel had seen to it that Butler paid. Paid for what he did to her. Now, the others would pay for those naked pictures.

Edelman stopped her car and turned off the motor. She fingered the briefcase next to her. *Could she do this? Did she have the nerve? Yes. People wouldn't ignore her anymore.*

She got out of the car. *Don't forget to lock it.* Then she had to smile. *Why lock it?* She didn't need it anymore. She walked up the front steps and followed the rush of officers into the building, everyone talking to each another. She no longer belonged.

She started to cry again. *The rape. The pictures. Why her? The Dark Angel had said the bombing had to be done at eight o'clock. Twenty-four hours between each bombing. She couldn't let the Dark Angel down. Couldn't let her sisters down. They wouldn't let her down.*

Walking into the classroom, she called, "My name is Petty Officer Rosemary Edelman. I was raped by a marine officer. Two of the officers in this class passed around nude pictures of me and posted them on the Internet. I tried to stop you bastards, but no one would help me. No one would do anything about it. Well I'm doing something about it now."

With that, she opened the briefcase and pushed the red button. A bright flash, then nothing.

The shrill ring of the alarm clock rousted Scott from a deep sleep. She had dreamed about a doctor strangling her. In her dream, she couldn't move. Beat her fists against his arms. Hard to breathe. Couldn't stop it.

She shook her head again. Came around. *She needed to get a life. Pull in better dreams. Maybe dream about her prince. Whole lot better than getting strangled.*

As she readied for work, she thought she'd better give Agent Harper a call and tell him about the events of last night. She punched in his cell phone number.

"Harper."

"It's Lieutenant Scott."

"Yes, Scott, what's up?"

"I thought you'd want to know about an intruder at Fairfax Hospital last night. Colonel Garcia caught him in her brother's room."

"Give me a minute." A rustling of paper. "Why didn't you call me last night?"

Why indeed, Scott thought? *Maybe she wanted to keep some things to herself until she could think them through.* She related the events. When she finished she added, "It may be this Doctor Pell is on the up and up, but I don't think so."

"Does the hospital have any record of him?" Harper asked.

"So far nothing in the Department of Radiology or as a private physician on consulting status to the hospital."

"We need to place a guard on David Garcia's room."

"The security guys at the hospital have someone outside his door. I've alerted the nursing staff to watch for anything unusual."

"Maybe a private room where we can seal him off. What do you think?"

"Already done. Garcia's coming in this morning to work with our artist. The problem is the guy had a mask over his lower face. You know, like doctors wear in the operating room."

"Garcia didn't think the mask seemed funny?" Harper asked.

"Pell told Garcia he worked in Radiology. She assumed the guy was preparing her brother for some test. Figured the mask must be standard procedure."

"We've got artists if you need backup."

"We'll be fine." Scott paused. "Something else you might be interested in."

"What's that?"

"David Garcia's neighbor saw a late model blue Toyota drive up and down in front of his house Tuesday night. Unfortunately, she didn't get a license number. Didn't think much about it until I talked to her."

"Worth checking out."

"I'm running late model Toyota's through our database. There's a gazillion of them. And it could be stolen. We'll screen the list against known slime balls. See who falls out."

"Have you uncovered anything on the maroon truck yet?" Harper asked.

"The D.C. cops found it yesterday afternoon, abandoned behind an empty warehouse in southeast D.C. The truck had a dent in the right front fender with blood stains on the fender. We're running a check on the stains, but not much doubt in my mind it's the truck. The D.C. guys couldn't come up with any prints. I'm not surprised, the guy's probably a pro." Scott paused. "Another thing."

"Yes."

"When I met with Foster at Sterling Software, I did learn one interesting detail. He got his position at Sterling by marrying the boss's daughter."

"Not a bad way to do it."

"But get this," Scott added, "Foster became president when old man Sterling died."

"How did he die?"

"I checked it out with the Virginia State Police. He died in an accident. His brakes failed when he was taking a trip along the Skyline Drive in the Shenandoah Valley. Poor bastard ended up in a ravine."

"Was anyone else hurt?"

"No, Sterling had been traveling alone. His wife died several years before."

"I don't imagine you believe all of this is a coincidence."

"Absolutely not." Scott paused. "Now, I've shared with you. What else can you tell me? I know you guys aren't doing this for your health."

"I can tell you're a detective. Smart, with the clues."

Scott laughed. "Even a blind squirrel finds a nut once in a while."

Harper chuckled. "How about if I plan to stop by your office later this morning? What time will the sketch be ready?"

"If Garcia gets in early enough, by noon at the latest."

"I'll pop for lunch," Harper replied. "My treat."

"I've got just the place." She gave him the address. "See you then."

She hung up. *Why didn't I tell him about the baby?* Best to keep something to herself until she got a better feel for him. Still not sure she could trust him. Besides, this might be good trading material.

Garcia stared at the phone. She needed to call her parents before she left to see Lieutenant Scott and let them know what happened the night before. She hoped her mother would answer. No way did she want to talk this over with her father. She definitely did not need another lecture.

She dialed her mother's cell. "Hello, Mother, it's me."

"Oh, my dear, I'm so glad you called. I wanted to tell you I'm sorry about the other day. Your father can be so stubborn and I don't know what to do about it."

Tell him off, Garcia thought, *before I do.* "I know, Mother. He really upset me. I didn't even know David lived here. He knew I worked at the Pentagon and never bothered to contact me. How does father think that makes me feel?"

"I know, but I believe he means well. I'll try to talk some sense into him."

"Thank you, Mother. I called because someone sneaked into David's room last night."

"What? Why would they do that?"

"I think they meant to kill him."

Her mother didn't reply. Garcia realized she had never told her mother the police believed the truck meant to hit her brother.

"What is David into?" her mother asked.

"I don't know. The police believe the truck driver hit David on purpose. Like someone tried to kill him. Now, that someone's trying to finish the job."

"What? How? Why?" Garcia's mother snuffled. "He's such a sweet boy."

There's that sweet-boy crap again, Garcia thought. "The reason I called is to let you know about the incident last night, plus to make sure you realize you'll have to sign in with security when you arrive. They're being very careful now."

"Oh, my, how will I tell your father?"

"It's time to be honest with him, Mother. Quit trying to protect him. I have to go. I'll call you later."

She disconnected. *Why hadn't she said anything to her mother about the baby? Because her mother would panic and want to run to his house. Probably wouldn't be productive. At least not yet. And her father would go nuts. David hooked up with a Korean woman. Not a nice Hispanic lady. Imagine that.*

19

Fairfax Police Station, Friday, 8:30 a.m.

When Garcia entered the office, Scott sat behind her desk in a navy-blue pants suit with a red-and-gold-striped scarf around her neck. A pudgy detective sat at the desk next to her, cleaning his fingernails with a pen knife and talking to his partner. Cigar smoke hung in the air.

Scott waved her over. "Morning, Colonel. Thanks for coming in so early. Coffee?"

"Sounds great," Garcia replied. "And why don't you call me Garcia? Everyone else does. Hey, great looking scarf. Hot."

"I'm the fashion guru for the office. Course, that's not saying much." Scott walked to a Mr. Coffee and poured a cup for each of them, then motioned Garcia to a chair next to her gunmetal gray desk. "Hey, you jug heads, hold down the damn noise."

The conversation level dropped.

Garcia laughed. "Wow, you've got some pull. I'm impressed."

"Don't be. All these clowns work for me. They're still arguing about the football draft. Simmons felt the Skins should have drafted another linebacker rather than a defensive end. You know, top drawer stuff like that."

She pulled out a Philly Cheroot and stuck it in her mouth. "Hope you're not allergic to smoke."

Garcia waved her hand. "Isn't it illegal to smoke inside a public building?"

"That's what they tell me, but no one has turned me in yet. One of these days I'll probably get nailed. Then I'll have to go outside and smoke." She lit her Cheroot and took a deep drag. Sighed. "We've heard no more from the hospital. They placed a security officer outside your brother's room last night. I don't know what the deal is with this guy, Pell, but until we can sort it out, I don't want to take any more chances."

One of the detectives started pecking away with two fingers on a typewriter, the clicking sound echoing in the room. The typewriter sat next to a computer, but no twenty-first century technology for him.

"We may find it was a damn good thing you were there," Scott said. "I'm becoming more and more …. Well, let's see what happens."

Garcia leaned forward. "No, finish what you were saying."

Scott moved some papers around on her desk. "I don't believe in coincidences. First, we have a witness who claims the driver meant to hit your brother. Second, we have the report from his neighbor about the blue Toyota. And now this."

Her chair squeaked every time she moved. "Damn chair. One of these days I'm going to throw it out the window."

Garcia laughed. "Wouldn't it be easier to oil it?"

Scott watched her for a moment, thinking, then she laughed, too. "Yeah, I guess it would." She pushed up from the chair. It squeaked again. "Come on, I'll introduce you to our artist."

"Wait a minute," Garcia said. "Did you ask my brother's girlfriend about any threats on his life? You know, anyone after him. Something like that?"

Scott shook her head. "Not yet, but I will. Come on." She led Garcia down the tiled hallway and knocked on a door. A dark-skinned woman, dressed in a beige dress with a necklace of twisted wire and beads, opened the door and stood in the doorway.

"Hi, Dorothy, let me introduce Colonel Rene Garcia."

Dorothy's round face broke into a smile and her eyes glistened. "Colonel, I've been expecting you. Please come in and sit down."

Scott stepped back and Garcia entered the room. "Would you bring her back to my office when you finish here?"

"Will do, Lieutenant."

"Thanks." Scott started back down the hall. Two officers moved to the opposite side of the hallway as she passed. *That's good*, she thought. *Keep them wondering about me. On edge about what I might do next.*

———————

Megan Alcott sat across the desk from Samuel Foster in his office. The morning sunshine reflected off the mirror on the inside wall. A photo of Foster's wife and kids sat on the corner of his desk.

"When are you going to get rid of that damn picture, Sam?" she asked. "Better yet, when are you going to dump your wife? For the past six months, you've promised me we'll be together, yet I still see her everywhere I look."

"It's complicated, Megan, you know that. I need to think of the kids. They can't be put out on the street." Foster turned the picture over with a clunk. "Ah, how did your meetings go with General Harding's people at the Pentagon yesterday afternoon?"

"I met with the staff and assured them that in spite the incident with David, we'd still be able to provide the support they need. Most of them have gotten to know me over time, so it'll be okay. I heard Harding met with that Colonel Garcia and Zamir Nabhas last night. I need to find out about their conversation. Maybe David told his sister something. Could be a problem."

"Is Harding all right with you taking over?" Foster asked.

Alcott nodded. "Seems like she is so far. I'll be interested to talk to Nabhas again today. He doesn't keep eying me because I think he's gay." She winked at Foster. "I have to keep diverting looks from the rest of the male staff back up to my face."

Foster leaned forward, wiping his forehead with a handkerchief. "Do you think they suspect anything?"

"Most of those guys are too busy looking at my boobs. But if they start working with this Garcia bitch, that would ratchet up my concerns. I understand she's with some troubleshooting team that works for the president's national security advisor."

"Oh, no. I argued with the boss we shouldn't have moved as fast as we did, but she told me we didn't have any choice."

"Why, Sam? What would you have done differently? We have a failsafe system. No one is going to stop the launch until it's too late. I'll keep meeting with the staff and see if I can keep them calm. Maybe I'll have to drop my drawers for a couple of the guys."

"No, no, don't do that . . .."

"Don't worry, Sam, I've got the codes to get into their system. I'm in charge and know how to run Red Dog. What will work and what won't. They can't do anything to stop me."

"When we hack in, can they trace it?" Foster asked. "Maybe backtrack the codes to us?"

"Give me some credit, Sam. It's simple to fake an IP address so they don't know. I used one of the sites on the Net. No one will figure out who we are."

Foster tapped his finger on his desk. "I don't like to move this fast."

Megan took another sip of her coffee. "Once we complete this action, maybe it'll be time for another one. The boss can jack up the price and make millions. By the way, I think it's time I met whoever it is."

Foster folded his hands in his lap. "Nice try, Megan. But this could be a one-time thing. I'm going to keep that name to myself for a while longer."

Damn Foster. She needed to get more information out of him. Make him hungry for her. That always worked. She kicked off her shoes and walked around his desk. Wiggling her butt onto a corner of the desk, she raised her foot to the arm of his chair.

Foster's eyes widened. "I like it when you do that."

She placed her foot in his lap and moved it around. Her skirt fell back so he could watch her legs. "Don't you trust me, Sam?" She was sick and tired of Foster and all his groping, but she needed him a while longer.

"Ah, God, that feels good." He shut his eyes for a moment, his breathing picking up. "I trust you, baby, but my client told me not to give a name to anyone. You're the key to this whole operation." Foster reached up and massaged her leg. "Don't worry, I'll introduce you soon."

Megan hoped his contact wasn't some overweight slob who'd drool all over her like Uncle Jasper back in West Virginia. She kept sliding her foot around in his lap and could feel Foster getting aroused.

"Oh, don't leave me like this," he groaned.

The wind blew against the window, seeming to keep time with Foster's heavy breathing.

"Come on, Sam, we're partners. Maybe I should be appointed vice president."

Foster straightened. "Are you kidding? I only named you project director yesterday." He paused. "Are you sure there's no way the authorities can trace the incident back to us?"

"Sam, don't worry so much. Let me do it. I'll take care of the system. I'll take care of everything." She had the ability. Now she needed the boss, whoever that was, to depend on her not Foster.

"You know," she said as she put her finger to her lips and licked it, "things like this really get me excited. I don't suppose they have the same effect on you."

"No, but you do."

She slid off the desk and slipped into her shoes. Leave him hanging. He'd learn to keep her in the loop. Besides, if she could get rid of him, she'd be in charge of everything.

———

Scott returned to her desk and set about doing paperwork. She wasn't a big fan of paper, but it seemed that every year police work got more complicated and everything had to be papered. Hell, why couldn't she nab bad guys and throw them in the slammer for life? Make it easy.

She worked for a while, then looked at her watch. Forty-five minutes had passed, should have been plenty of time for Dorothy to finish the sketch. She wandered down the hall and knocked on the door.

When Scott pushed the door open, Dorothy stood at the easel. The sound of her pen blended with the ticking of the clock on her desk. A jackhammer outside shattered the silence every two or three minutes.

"Goddamn jackhammer," Scott said, "when will they be done with this construction? Drives me nutzo."

Dorothy shrugged, then turned her easel toward Garcia. "How's this?"

"Yep, you've got it," Garcia said. "Too bad he had that mask covering half his face."

"Why don't you look at our Doctor Pell for a moment? I'll pour us a couple of cups of coffee."

Dorothy stood and wiggled her way past Scott to the small table that held the coffee machine. "Take your time. The memory is quite a tool. Things will come back if you close your mind to everything else and focus on the picture."

Scott watched her. "Think it's him?"

Garcia nodded. "Dorothy's been very helpful."

"She's good."

A streak of red flushed over Dorothy's face. "Good luck, Colonel. If you need to revise anything, let me know. In the meantime, I'll scan this into the computer."

Scott led Garcia down the hallway to her office. The noise level and talking had picked up again. "All right, shut the hell up so I can concentrate."

The room lapsed into silence, each detective looking down at his desk.

Scott lit her cigar again, took a puff, then blew the smoke in the air. "We'll compare the sketch against known suspects in the area and see if we can get a match. Also I'll screen it against names we came up with on the blue Toyota database. The guy's smart enough to wear gloves at the hospital, so there'll be no fingerprints."

"How did Pell get in and out of the hospital after hours?" Garcia asked.

"I'm surprised no one else saw him." Scott remembered what the nurse had said about Garcia.

Unless he doesn't exist.

20

FBI Headquarters, Washington D.C., Friday, 11:30 a.m.

Zack sat with Gracia and Agent Harper in Director Burnside's outer office on the ninth floor of the Hoover Building, the FBI's Mecca. He'd caught a National Guard helicopter back from Sea Isle City that morning and briefed Admiral Steele. He had to smile every time he thought about Max.

Garcia had told him she thought the plot to hack into the DOD data base should be considered along with the bombings. Too big a coincidence, both starting at the same time. Harper agreed so Admiral Steele wanted Burnside brought in on their thinking. *Who the hell pulled those strings?*

The executive assistant's voice interrupted Zack's thoughts. "Let me check with the Director. He's expecting you and I think he's ready."

Two secretaries answered ringing phones. They both used operator headsets so they could keep typing on their computers. The events of the past two days kept things moving at a frantic pace. Steele told Zack not to keep the director long. Move it along.

Zack ran through the briefing in his mind for what seemed like the hundredth time. He wanted it to go perfectly.

The assistant's voice brought him back to the present. "Mr. Burnside will see you now."

Zack followed Harper and Garcia into the director's office. Ambrose Burnside's corner office, generous enough to play a half-court basketball game, had a magnificent view overlooking downtown Washington. The sun glistened from the Washington Monument, it's shadow falling across the mall and pointing at the White House.

Burnside looked up from his desk. "Agent Harper, you're getting an orientation on the fast track. I understand from Admiral Steele you'd like to discuss these bombings and this Dark Angel."

Zack noticed a pronounced Southern drawl when Burnside spoke. The director hailed from Savannah, Georgia, and Zack remembered how much he'd enjoyed his tours with the army rangers at Fort Stewart. That seemed so far away now. Much simpler time.

Harper opened the discussion by introducing Zack and Garcia. They shook hands, then took seats at the conference table, Burnside at the head. Zack and Garcia on one side, Harper on the other.

Harper cleared his throat. "Colonel Kelly and Lieutenant Colonel Garcia are members of Admiral Steel's special task force. You're well aware of the bombings and the hacking efforts, but probably not aware of the possible synergy we see between them. So we don't waste your time, I'll ask Zack to provide you a short overview."

"Sir," Zack began, "five days ago Colonel Garcia and I met with her brother, David. He's with Sterling Software in Fairfax. They have the contract to protect the data base for this new FAA initiative with the unmanned air initiative at Fort Shelby, Mississippi. Her brother claimed Sterling planned to hack into that data base."

"What did we find out?"

"David Garcia was hit by a truck. He's in Fairfax Hospital in a coma."

Burnside looked at Garcia. "I'm so sorry to hear that. How is he?"

"The doctors aren't sure when he may come out of the coma."

"I've been working with the Cape May County police in an effort to uncover why someone is killing military officers," Zack said. "It appears the same individuals may be involved with the bombings. We have to consider the possibility of another bombing tomorrow."

Burnside tapped his fingers on the table. "Sounds to me as if this is all working. What do you need from me?"

Zack took a deep breath. "Sir, it's possible someone in the Executive Branch may be the mastermind."

Burnside loosened his dark blue tie and opened the button at the neck of his shirt. "What do you base this on?"

"This Dark Angel always seems to be one step ahead of us."

Burnside sat in his chair, elbows on the arms, fingers pointing at his chin. Then he reached down and pulled out a basketball from under his desk, shooting at the hoop in the corner of his office, startling each of them. "Sorry, but it helps me to think."

Harper laughed. "The director was quite a basketball player at North Carolina State University. I should have warned you. The staff has learned to be ready for a couple of shots to break the stress."

After Harper finished talking, Burnside sat for a minute or so, eyes straight ahead. "So you see synergy between these two incidents?"

"To be honest sir, I believe there could be. The woman raped by Toomey is the one who set off the bomb at the Army War College. I plan to return to Cape May and see what else I can unearth about the Dark Angel. Agent Harper and Colonel Garcia will be here trying to uncover more about the hacking efforts and whatever they can find out about the bombings."

Burnside turned and looked out the window. "All right, I'll do what I can. Agent Harper will be the point of contact with your task force on the bombings. Can you have an information paper on my desk in an hour?"

"Yes sir."

"I'll bring it up with the president at my normal briefing for him. If he wants to hear more, have your people on call."

The three stood. Harper nodded. "Thank you, sir."

As Zack walked out of the office, his cell phone rang. He touched Garcia's arm. "Excuse me, I'd better take this. It's Laura."

He answered, "Hi."

"Dad?" Her voice sounded strained.

His heartbeat shot up. "What's wrong?"

"It's mom. She wants me to travel back to Minneapolis."

Wait a minute, he thought. *She's still in jail.* "Tell her, when she gets out of jail, we'll talk it over."

"Dad, she's here."

"Where?"

"At your house."

"What?"

"Yeah, what. She arrived about an hour ago. I tried to call you, but your phone was turned off."

Zack couldn't believe it. He had to calm down. *Think.* "She's there? Didn't call first?"

"Yeah, she's here. Wants me to come back to Minneapolis with her."

"Okay. Stay tight. I'll be home as soon as I can." Zack disconnected.

"Something wrong?" Garcia asked.

"Yeah. You might say that."

———

When Garcia entered, people carrying flowers crowded the hospital lobby, talking quietly to one another and even a few sniffling into tissues. A clerk waved to her from behind the information desk. "Hello, Colonel. I understand there may have been a problem last night. How's your brother doing?"

"I'm afraid there's no change."

"I'll keep my fingers crossed that he comes out of his coma today."

"Thanks." Garcia hurried toward the elevator, but the sign for the cafeteria and the smell of fresh coffee caught her attention. She hadn't eaten breakfast yet. Her parents wouldn't arrive for a little while, so what the heck, take a break.

Sunlight flooded the cafeteria. The blue sky and white clouds outside the window lifted her spirits. Leaves fluttered in the gentle

breeze. Summer, her favorite time of the year. A time for new begin-
nings. Maybe with her parents? With David? Who knew?

She inserted change into the machine near the door and pulled
out a *Washington Post*. Grabbing a couple of Krispy Kreme donuts
off the cafeteria line, she drew a cup of coffee from the silver urn and
paid the cashier. The smell of barbecue wafted from the kitchen.
Lunch time. Maybe she should take time to eat a good lunch. Meals
kept getting away from her.

Garcia glanced around the coffee shop. It contained about
twenty round tables, most with seating for four people. She picked a
table and sat. At the next table, two nurses huddled in whispered
conversation. Three young doctors, probably interns, sat at the table
near a window, one of them, his head bobbing, looked about ready
to fall asleep. Guys must work pretty long hours.

A noise startled her. She turned. An Asian man cleared dishes
from the table behind her, tossing them into a gray plastic container
with a clatter. He took a towel off his cart and swished it around the
table.

Garcia almost burned her tongue when she sipped the coffee.
She gobbled down the donuts and perused the paper. A headline
caught her attention, "Air War College Hacked." *Uh, oh,* she thought,
*another hacking scandal. Busy time for the FBI. What would she
find out about Sterling?*

She stood and stretched, slipped the *Post* under her arm and
started toward the door. Stopped. The guy who had called himself
Doctor Pell stood in the hallway looking in the other direction. Dressed
in a UPS uniform, he'd tucked a brown package under his arm. No
doubt in her mind. Even without the mask, the thin face and long
sandy hair gave him away.

She turned and slipped back to the cashier, pulling out her badge.
"I'm Colonel Garcia, a military police officer. Call security. Tell them
I need backup."

The cashier's eyes widened. "What?"

"Don't act surprised. Just call security and don't look over toward the door. It'll be fine."

The woman walked to the phone hanging from a wall and picked it up.

Pell looked up at that minute and spotted Garcia. His eyes widened. Turning, he ran down the hallway, nearly knocking down a woman.

Garcia dropped her paper and started after him, bumping into the Asian man clearing a table and causing him to spill coffee on the floor. "Police," she yelled. "Stop."

21

Arlington, VA, Friday, 1:00 p.m.

Zack's mind raced as he pulled onto his street. *What was Ellen doing here?* They'd been married during his first year in college, but after his third tour in Afghanistan she'd had enough of his being gone all the time and demanded a divorce. Laura stayed with her mother in Minneapolis until the DEA caught Ellen selling prescription drugs and she ended up in prison.

Initially things were pretty rocky when Laura moved in with Zack, but they'd gotten past that. Laura had qualified for a soccer scholarship her freshman year at GW University, then who shows up but fucking Ellen.

He pulled into his driveway and hit the brakes. *Well, no way was Laura going back to Minneapolis.* He had the custody agreement in writing, although he wasn't sure how her being college age would affect that. Better check with an attorney.

Zack jumped out of the staff car he'd signed out from the Pentagon motor pool and hustled up the sidewalk. *Okay. Go inside and reason with Ellen,* he thought as he pulled the front door open.

"Hello, Zack."

There she sat, her brown hair pulled back in a ponytail. She looked as if she'd lost a lot of weight.

"What are you doing here?"

Laura came out of the kitchen, two glasses of ice tea in her hands. "Hi, Dad."

Zack struggled to keep his anger under control. He thought of what his shrink had said. *Take a deep breath, don't let your temper get away from you. You can't go around punching people out.* "Why didn't you say something? I thought you were still in prison."

Ellen twisted a handkerchief in her lap. "If I had called and said I wanted to come out and see Laura, what would you have said?"

Goddamn, what would he have said? But now he had to think of Laura. She was an adult. He managed to stammer out, "I probably would have told you to go to hell, but Laura has a voice in that decision."

"Thank you," Laura said. "I don't know what I would have said. I would have probably been interested in why you wanted to come out and see me."

"Isn't that obvious?" Ellen replied. "You're my daughter. I love you and want to spend time with you."

Zack had about enough. "Too bad you didn't think about that when you were dealing drugs."

"Well, that's true," Ellen said. "But, you played a role in that. You were busy running all over the world and left me alone to raise our daughter. The depression set in and started me on a downhill spiral I couldn't seem to stop."

Zack bundled his hands into fists. "Don't you dare put that off on me. That's the same thing you threw at me all those years. It's my job. I did the best I could."

"Ah, the martyr," she said with a sneer, "always the martyr."

"Stop it, both of you," Laura screamed. "You two sound like a couple of two-year-olds. This is now and she's here. What are we going to do about it?"

Zack glanced over at Laura, his respect for her building by the minute. "Laura's right. As much as I don't like it, you're here." He struggled to think. "Ah, where are you staying? For how long? And where the hell did you get the money to come out here?"

Ellen smiled again, that self-satisfying smile that frustrated Zack. "Thank you, Laura, for being the adult here. My parents advanced me the money to fly out here, rent a car, and stay in a motel for three days."

Zack's mind spun various scenarios. *He had to leave shortly. Get back to Sea Isle City. Ellen would probably use that to her advantage. But he had to play nice.* Swallowed hard and said to Ellen, "What do you think we should do?"

"I'd like to spend some time with Laura. I've made a huge mistake and I'd like to try and make it up to her."

Zack couldn't shut her out of Laura's life unless Laura wanted it that way. He glanced at Laura. "What do you think?"

She sat quietly for a moment, then said, "Since mom is here, I would like to spend some time with her. See how it goes."

Shit, but Zack smiled and nodded.

"But," Laura continued, "this is my life now. I'm enrolled at GW and will be on the varsity soccer team. There's nothing for me in Minneapolis. My life is here."

Laura walked over and put her hand on her mother's arm. "I would like to get to know you again, but you need to understand that I am not moving."

"All I want is time with you," Ellen said. "I can't take back what happened, but I'd like a chance to prove I've grown from those awful years in prison."

Okay, Zack thought. *Maybe this will work.*

"You know, your grandfather played football for Carlton College," Ellen said. "One of his classmates is the new athletic director. I bet grandpa would introduce you to his friend if you wanted to check it out."

"Carlton?" Laura asked.

"Yes. Carlton is a great school about ninety miles south of Minneapolis."

Laura sat back down and looked at her dad. "It's too early to even think about that."

"Laura's right," Zack said. "Okay, we have a plan. Why don't you stay for dinner and the two of you can catch up." *And I need to get back to work but no need to say that now.*

"Please join us, Dad."

"I'm afraid I can't. I'm supposed to be back at the Pentagon."

Ellen smiled. "Oh my, I guess some things never change."

Jose Garcia sat in a wooden rocker, still in his pajamas and robe, reading one of his student's papers. Magnolia trees bloomed outside and the forsythia bushes added their bright yellow to the landscape.

He'd spent the morning reading and just finished lunch. Now he needed to get ready to go to the hospital and see to his son. Each time he took a break from his reading, he thought about David and Rene. The frustration hit him and built up to anger at the two of them. *Why didn't they get along, take care of one another?* How much easier that would be for him. Rene should know better.

The pain seemed more intense today. It radiated up his left arm to his shoulder. He couldn't remember it ever being this bad. It spread to his chest. He began to sweat and had trouble breathing.

He yelled and tried to stand, but toppled from his chair. He grabbed for a lamp on the end table. It fell, hitting the floor with a crash.

"Help me," he cried, before the unrelenting pain sucked the air from his lungs, then . . . blackness.

Garcia raced through the open cafeteria door and down the hallway toward the emergency room, slipping on a portion of the tiled floor. "Stop. Police. Stop."

A nurse standing next to the door glanced at Garcia, her eyes big. "What's going on? I told that man not to run in a hospital."

"Call security," Garcia yelled. "He's dangerous."

Pell ducked toward the elevators and skirted left around another corner.

Garcia ran hard and gained on him.

A gray-haired woman in a blue coat walked out of a room in front of Garcia. Garcia pushed into her, almost knocking the woman over. Stopping, she grabbed for the woman's arm and steadied her. "Sorry."

The woman regained her balance, adjusting her hat. "What do you think you're doing?"

Garcia pointed after Pell. "I'm a police officer and that man's a security risk." She started down the hallway again, shoving a laundry cart out of the way and tripping over a mop. She caught herself in time to bump into a slender Hispanic woman in a gray uniform.

Grabbing the woman's hand before she fell, Garcia yelled, "Call security."

When she reached the intersection of two hallways, a crowd of people approached from the left, none of them Pell.

Where did he go? Garcia chose the hallway to the right. As she passed a nurse, she called, "Did you see a man in a UPS uniform running this way?"

"He almost knocked me down. What's going on?"

Garcia stopped. "Which way did he go?"

The nurse bent over to brush off the front of her scrubs. "The clown ran into the men's room while I was coming out of the lady's room. He told me he was from maintenance. Seems someone called to report a plumbing problem."

Garcia pointed. "In that bathroom?"

"As far as I know, he's still in there. Funny he didn't put a closed sign on the door."

Garcia flashed her badge. "I'm a police officer. You think he's still in that bathroom?"

She nodded and took out her cell phone. "I'm going to call security."

"Tell them an officer needs assistance in a first floor bathroom." Garcia banged the door open to the men's room. It looked empty. She stepped inside, the door slamming shut behind her. "Hey, Pell, I want to talk to you."

The door to the hallway opened and a young man in a tan sport coat walked in. He saw Garcia and stopped, his hand up to his mouth. "What are you doing in here?"

"Police. I'm looking for a guy who ran in here."

The man stepped backward toward the door. "Are you some kind of pervert?" He turned and hurried out of the bathroom yelling, "A woman's hanging around in the men's room."

Garcia pushed open a stall door.

The door to the hallway opened again. A security guard ran in, face red and puffing slightly. "Are you the officer needing assistance?"

"I'm Colonel Garcia, a military police officer with the army. I think the man who tried to kill David Garcia in the ICU last night ran in here. Help me look."

Garcia checked the rest of the bathroom, windows still locked from the inside. "He's not here. Where did he go?"

She hurried back out into the hallway. A group of people had gathered, pulled in by the man in the sport coat who yelled about Garcia being in the men's room.

Garcia held up her arms to quiet the crowd. "It's all right, police business." Another security guard came running down the hall. "Have you got the composite I did on the suspect?" Garcia asked. "Lieutenant Scott should have forwarded it to you earlier today."

"Roger. It's been distributed to all departments."

Garcia pointed. "Check that hallway. He's close by. Don't let him get away."

"Will do."

As he started away, Garcia pulled on his arm. "Wait a minute. Give me your radio." She pushed the on switch. "This is Colonel Garcia. I'm at the first floor bathroom in the rear of the hospital. We lost the suspect. Double check David Garcia's room to make sure the guard is alerted to the problem."

A male voice answered. "This is the chief of security. Will do."

"Your men at the various points around the hospital need to check for this guy. He's wearing a UPS uniform and he's smart and dangerous. What's your location?"

"To get to my office, head down the hallway where you are," the voice replied. "Turn right at the next corridor. Third door on the left."

Garcia ran in that direction. She burst through the door, startling the man checking the monitors. "See anything?"

The officer shook his head. "Nothing out of the ordinary."

"Did you double-check with the guard on David Garcia's room?"

The man at the monitor nodded.

"Keep at it." Garcia walked out and stared up and down the hallway. *Where would Pell go? Where would she run if she were Pell? Probably out through logistics and the loading dock.*

She saw a sign for the laundry and ran down that hallway. Nothing. All quiet in maintenance. She decided to check on David so rode the elevator to the fourth floor. Things were hopping in the ICU, but the guard on David's room said no one had attempted to get past him.

Garcia peeked in just to make sure. Saw a nurse she hadn't met. "I'm David Garcia's sister. Is everything okay in here?"

"Yes, why?" the nurse responded.

"I spotted the guy who impersonated the doctor last night. He got away."

The nurse grimaced. "Do you think he was after Mr. Garcia?"

"I'm afraid so. Be sure to check with security if anything looks suspicious."

"Thanks. It makes me feel better to know security is involved."

As she left the room and turned to walk down the hall, it dawned on her. Where were her parents? They should be here visiting David by now.

22

Fairfax County, Friday, 2:00 p.m.

Lieutenant Scott sat in the front passenger seat of the police cruiser behind the rusting white laundry van, waiting. Her new partner, Detective Morrow, sat next to her tapping his fingers on the wheel and humming some county-western tune. One of her favorites, but she couldn't remember the name. She started humming it herself.

An eager kid, Morrow had joined the force only a couple of years before. Done well on patrol. He drove Scott nuts with all his questions, but he meant well. Tried like hell to do a good job and that counted big points with Scott.

She watched a half-dozen kids playing soccer in front of the apartment building and hated to break up their game, remembering how much she enjoyed soccer. She'd enjoyed playing football too, although the boys always seemed to spend extra time tackling her. *Hmmm … kinda fun.*

This was it. They'd gotten a positive ID from Garcia's picture and the car. A small time hood by the name of Homer Jensen. She shared what she knew with Harper on the phone before she left for the house. *Another damn day with no time for lunch.*

If she could nail Jensen, maybe finally she could get some answers to this whole mess. Why was he after David Garcia? How did the attack relate to the Korean woman and to the baby, if at all? So many questions.

She climbed out of the cruiser and walked up to the back of the van. Knocking, then whispering her name, she opened the door. Computers and other electronic equipment lined the walls of the van. Five SWAT Team members sat on benches, dressed in black uniforms, AR-15s stretched across their laps.

Lieutenant Tom Packer, leader of the Fairfax County SWAT Team for the past four years, glanced at her. "Hi, Lieutenant. Do you have the warrant?"

"You bet. Ready when you are."

Packer motioned for Scott to lean into the van and pointed at the computer screen. "You can see the front door of the house on this screen and that one shows the back. We'll use those doors as entry points. The subject's apartment is on the third floor."

He handed her a picture of the roof. "Our chopper took this photo a couple of hours ago. I've got two guys ready to rappel down a rope and land on the roof if the subject makes a break up the stairs. Clown won't be going anywhere."

"Jensen has shown he doesn't mind killing people, so be careful."

"Don't worry," Packer replied. "We always are."

Checking her watch, Scott made a note of the time. "All right, let's go." She hurried back to the squad car and climbed inside.

Morrow hit the gas and followed the truck around the corner, stopping in front of Jensen's apartment building, red light circling on top of the car. They jumped out of the cruiser and Morrow moved the kids down the street to safety.

The team launched out of the van. Three men hit the front door and two went around to the back. The helicopter hovered above the building awaiting Packer's signal.

Trash littered the crumbling sidewalk and paint had peeled in strips from the walls of the building. A broken doll buggy lay discarded next to the front door. The screen door clung to the wooden frame by one of two hinges and swung easily in the afternoon breeze.

Scott didn't see the blue Toyota parked in front of the house nor by the garage. Not a good sign. Looked as if Jensen had beat it out of there.

In a moment, Packer's voice sounded through her earphone. "Apartment's a mess but appears to be empty."

Scott spoke into the portable microphone to her own backup. "Squad One, stay in position behind the building. Don't let anyone out the back. Morrow and I are going in the front."

Scott picked her way around the cracked cement and up to the door, Morrow a step behind her. Pulling the warrant out of her pocket, she nudged the front door open. "Some security system."

"Yeah," Morrow replied. "Course I'm not sure what these folks are trying to secure in this rat trap."

Scott pulled out her .45 and ducked inside. She led Morrow up the three flights of stairs, the smell of urine assaulting her nostrils. A couple yelled from inside one of the rooms on the second floor. Suddenly a thud sounded against a wall. A baby cried from behind another door.

When Scott reached the third floor, the scarred door to apartment 3B on the right side of the hall hung open.

The door had split away from the frame and Packer stood in front of it, his own AR-15 cradled in his arms. "We did a thorough check. No one inside."

"Thanks," Scott replied. "Will you guys hang around for a few minutes till I go through the apartment?"

"Will do, Lieutenant."

She slipped inside, scanning the room. Dirty plates and a stack of men's magazines littered a coffee table, one leg missing and supported by four phone books. Empty beer bottles lay scattered around the room. Burn marks scarred the tattered rug. Shades were drawn over two windows and shades for the other two had been pulled off and lay on the floor under the window in a heap.

Scott motioned to Morrow. "You take the bedroom, I'll look around in here." A dresser next to the bedroom door stood empty except for a few T-shirts and shorts. Jeans, three long-sleeve shirts, and two pairs of work boots littered the floor of the closet.

Scott moved into the kitchen, the smell of rancid food sticking in her nostrils. The cupboard contained plates, cups and a half full can of coffee. She called out to Morrow, "Jensen's not much of a housekeeper. Damn place is messier than mine."

"Right, Lieutenant, I don't think Jensen would qualify for an award in *Better Homes and Gardens.*"

When she returned to the living room, Morrow walked out of the bedroom. "You don't want to go in there, Lieutenant, it's a mess. He must be an orgy guy and doesn't bother to clean up after his parties."

Scott laughed. "Shouldn't have any problems getting DNA."

Morrow pulled open a storage room door and peeked inside. "Jensen's not here."

"Somehow I didn't think he would be." She turned to Packer. "Thanks again. Your guys can take off."

"Okay, Lieutenant."

Scott glanced at Morrow. "Contact the squad outside. One the guys stays in the back, the other goes up floor by floor interviewing all the tenants in this picturesque building. When he finishes in this building, I want everyone in the buildings on either side interviewed. Somebody's got to know something about Jensen."

"Okay, Lieutenant, I'll get right on it."

"Oh, and call the lab guys. I want fingerprints and DNA on this guy. From what you say, DNA shouldn't be a problem, but we need to make sure who he is. It'll be nice to know who his friends are, too. We can bring them in for questioning."

"You got it, Lieutenant."

Something deep in her gut told her one day he'd make a great cop. "Meantime, you and I are going through this place brick by brick. Everything gets turned. Maybe we can get a lead on where the bum's gone."

Morrow pushed the button on his microphone. "Jensen's not here. One of you stay out back, the other interviews tenants starting on the first floor. No one gets outside without being checked."

Scott stepped over to the desk and pulled open the cover. It fell off. Inside lay a stack of pencils, three decks of cards, and a batch of comic books.

Several travel brochures littered the writing board. "Ah, ha," Scott said, "it looks like the good Mr. Jensen is planning on a trip. Maybe we can ask the FBI to form a welcoming committee to greet him at his destination."

23

Strathmere, NJ. Friday, 7:00 p.m.

The song, "Country Roads," greeted Zack and T.J. Wilson as they entered the Strathmere Inn. After a late lunch with Laura and Ellen, Zack had called Wilson who set up a helicopter to fly them back to Sea Isle City. They picked up Zack's truck at the heliport and drove to the inn.

A warm, sunny evening, and people in all types of dress sat around the white tables on the deck enjoying drinks and dinner. A man with his guitar and a tall woman with a sultry alto voice provided background music. The normalcy threatened to overwhelm Zack. Laura would enjoy being here with him. *How was she getting along with her mother?*

A low buzz of conversation radiated throughout the deck. Two couples rose from their table and headed along the short pier to a cabin cruiser. *Man*, he thought, *must be nice.*

Returning here made him think of Max and their evening together. He looked forward to seeing her again.

"Come on," Wilson said, "let's go back inside and check out the bar."

Zack followed him. "We'd better look like a couple of guys on the prowl. Don't want anyone to know our actual motives."

"I can do that," Wilson said. "Not a problem."

They each pulled out a stool. The multi-colored sign on the wall behind the bar advertised Alisha Spadafini, "The Blue Jeans Lady," entertaining on Saturday night, then Brett Holmes would be playing on Sunday from noon to five.

The bartender looked as if he should be playing right tackle for the Philadelphia Eagles. A tattoo, with the lettering, "Ginger," stretched across his right bicep. His brown eyes watched Zack above a friendly smile. "Can I help you?"

"How about some dinner?" Zack asked. "I'm starved."

The bartender glanced at Wilson, one big man measuring another. "I can see that." He produced a couple of menus which Zack and Wilson surveyed. The tantalizing aroma of French fries and deep fried shrimp smelled good.

"I'd like the crab cake sandwich and coffee, strong and black," Zack said. "And throw in an order of home fries."

Wilson looked up from his menu. "Make that two of everything, but drop the coffee and add a Bud."

When the bartender returned with the coffee and beer, Zack asked, "Things look like they're hopping. Is it always like this?"

"Next six weeks is the busiest time of the year. Business picks up when the summer folks arrive, then stays frantic through the summer. Sunday is the Fourth of July. Will be big."

"Are there many people who live here year around?" Zack asked.

"A few. Most work in Ocean City or depend on the summer trade, you know, real estate, fishing, restaurants, then hibernate during the winter." The bartender sauntered off to take care of another customer.

Zack looked out at the boats, leaned over and whispered, "You know, it'd be easy to smuggle people in here. Just wait until dark then bring 'em on."

"No shit, Colonel, piece of cake."

Zack waved at the bartender who walked back toward him. Time to stir things up. "How about the ladies? Are there many singles who come in?"

The bartender stared at him for a minute. "I'm only here part time. Let me check with the manager."

Did he tense up? Could he be hiding something. Wait a minute, Zack thought, *don't be so paranoid. You'll drive yourself nuts.*

The bartender raised his hand and waved. "She's over there, talking to that group by the dock. Say, Audrey," he called, "can you come over here for a minute?"

Zack turned on the barstool. A group of women sat at one of the tables. One wore an old fishing hat pulled down over her eyes so it was hard for Zack to tell if he'd seen her before. Large. Muscular. Something about the way she moved. Probably just reminded him of somebody.

The manager, a short, dark-haired woman in a pair of shorts and a brightly colored shirt, walked over to where they sat. An attractive woman, Zack judged to be in her early forties, her inquisitive green eyes looked him over. "Hi, my name's Audrey. Didn't I see you in here the other night?"

"Yep, that was me. Name's Zack Kelly. This is T.J. Wilson."

She looked at Wilson's arms. "You looking for a job as a bouncer? I could use the help if you are. The drunks never stop coming in. Only a few of them stir up trouble, but that's enough."

Wilson laughed. "I don't think so, but thanks for the offer."

Zack sipped his coffee. "We're new here and just checking around."

She leaned against the bar. "When two guys like you two are looking around in a little town like this, I get uncomfortable."

"No, nothing like that," Zack replied. "Only visiting for a few days."

"I see." She hopped onto the stool next to Zack. "To be honest, not much happens that I don't know about. Most folks have lived here for a long time and renters tend to return each year."

Zack risked another look at the woman in the corner. She took a drag on her cigarette, then a long pull on a beer.

When Zack turned back, Audrey stared at him.

"Is everything all right?" she asked. "You seem uneasy."

Zack took another sip of his coffee. "I'm fine."

"Okay. You probably drove across the bridge from Ocean City," Audrey said. "If we get a northeaster, the causeway from Ocean City floods and the road into Sea Isle City floods out too. We stock extra food people can buy. So like I say, not much goes on I don't know about."

Zack turned to look at the woman again. Still drinking her beer.

She cocked her head. "We're having an open house this weekend. Should be fun. Hope you can join us."

"Hey, sounds great," Wilson said. "Lots of brews."

"Is there someone over there you recognize?" Audrey asked.

"That woman looks a little familiar." Zack rubbed the back of his neck. "Do you know her?"

Audrey shook her head. "She comes in with other women a few times a week. Quiet. Doesn't make a fuss. I think former military types. All are good customers."

The band struck up, "Yellow Bird." Zack hummed along, tapping his fingers on the bar. He watched a large boat pull in. A woman jumped down and tied the boat to the dock. "Some of these boats are pretty big. Do they travel very far out into the ocean?"

"Oh, yeah," Audrey replied. "The people who just tied up head down to the islands about twice each year."

Zack turned again The woman he'd been watching took off the hat. Her hair cut short, she could be ex-military. Could he and Wilson have stumbled on something?

Suddenly, she stood and walked toward the door, pushed it open and stepped outside.

Zack slid off his stool. "Excuse me for a moment?" He motioned to Wilson. "I'll be right back."

Three cars moved in the lot. Zack wasn't sure which one held the woman he'd been watching. What was it about her? Something. Maybe the military look.

Ducking back into a corner, he tried to check out each of the drivers. No luck, they were already moving toward the street. "Shit, lost her."

The warmth of the summer evening made Zack sweat as he walked across the deck. Back in the restaurant, Audrey sat on the barstool, talking to Wilson.

He reached for his coffee. "Thought I recognized a woman. . . couldn't catch up with her."

"Like I said, she's part of a group that's new in town. Nice ladies. No trouble."

The bartender refilled Zack's cup. He looked at Wilson. "Another beer?"

"You bet. Always room for one more."

"Do they own a house around here?" Zack asked.

"I'm not sure if they're renting or if they own the house. Really none of my business. But, you can't miss it. It's the last one on the right, set off by itself. Located on the bay, about half a block before the fishing wharf. Big house with a tall fence around it."

Bingo, Zack thought. "She likes her privacy."

The bartender placed a sandwich in front of Zack with the home fries. "Coffee still okay?"

"Yeah, thanks." Zack took a bite of the sandwich, licked his lips. "This crab cake sandwich is outstanding."

Wilson had demolished his in about three bites. "Yeah, great."

"Thanks," Audrey replied. "People love to sit outside and eat on our deck. We have musical entertainment on the weekends year around and out on the deck during the summer."

Zack took another bite. "I enjoy the music. They're really good."

"Glad you do. Check with the folks at Strathmere Realty. They have a number of places to rent. Prices are high, but there are some good deals if you're careful."

"Thanks for the tip."

Zack and Wilson finished their food, then Zack paid the bill, leaving a healthy tip for the bartender. He walked across the patio to gaze once more at the bay. The tide rolled in and the herons and egrets looked to be heading to their roosting areas. Zack loved to fish and wished he had the time to make a few casts. Probably catch a bunch of flounder in a matter of minutes. He turned and walked back toward his truck.

Closing the door, he tapped his fingers on the steering wheel.

Wilson sat next to him. "What do you think, boss?"

"We need to check out that house where the women live. Military types. Best lead we've had so far."

He looked at his watch. "Still early to call in. Let's check it out first."

Putting the truck in gear, he pulled out of the lot. Laura's face popped into his mind. He wondered again how she was doing with her mother.

24

Rene Garcia picked her way down the neighborhood street, pissed that her Harley sounded so loud. No cars coming or going, no one out walking their dogs. All quiet. She looked up at the houses. *Did someone have it in for David, maybe enough to try and kill him?* She needed to find the key to the mystery and maybe she'd find it here in the neighborhood.

What about Yun Hee Soon? How long had she known David? Why didn't David tell anyone about her? Maybe he'd told his parents, but she didn't think so. She'd have to figure a way to break all this to her mother. Her father would freak when he found out about the baby.

And what about David's job at Sterling? Some tie there? So many questions. But she'd get answers. She always did. She'd find whoever tried to kill her brother and put his ass in jail.

Garcia stopped in front of David's house, cut the engine, and sat for a moment straddling her Harley and scanning the street. Nice houses with fairly expensive cars, but not many garages. Swing sets decorated a couple of the yards. Looked like a bunch of commuter families watching the tube tonight, then preparing for the unnerving log jam run into downtown Washington on Monday.

A light shone from the front window of her brother's rancher. She sat for a moment, letting the surroundings sink in. Garcia liked to sit and listen before taking any action. Size things up. It had saved her ass a number of times in the past. Pulling out her cell phone, she punched in David's number. The phone rang four times before the answering machine kicked in. She left a short message.

Vehicle traffic sounded from Columbia Pike only a block behind her, a surprising amount at this time of night. Trucks, cars, all in a hurry to go somewhere.

She climbed off her Harley and reached down to lock it. Yun Hee Soon had probably gotten ready for bed. *Was she a night owl like Garcia?* Something pushed Garcia toward the house. She'd learned over the years to follow her intuition.

Garcia walked up the front sidewalk to the house, her gaze sweeping the yard. Trees, plants, mowed grass. Typical spot in suburbia. Nothing out of the ordinary. The small garden in the front could use some weeding.

She needed to get to know this Yun Hee Soon. *What was she like? Could she be a suspect?* Soon hailed from Korea. David's outfit provided security for a DOD computer network and might be hacking into those computers. *North Korea stayed on the top of DOD's list for computer hacking. Coincidence?*

When Garcia reached the front door, she leaned over and peeked in one of the windows. Only a night light. Hard to see much. She wondered if they had a dog. Scott hadn't said anything about a dog. Don't want to stumble in on some big-ass brute.

As she reached forward to knock, she recoiled in surprise. Someone had left the door to the house cracked open about four inches. She pushed on it. The door swung open further with a slight creaking sound.

Could Soon be so out of it she had forgotten to close and lock the door? Any fool could walk in and rob her. Soon was a mother. Didn't seem like she'd forget something as basic as locking up.

Garcia took a deep breath and peeked inside. The night light in the corner of the living room cast a shadow across the walls. Didn't hear any dog.

She called, "Yun Hee Soon, are you here?" Took another step inside. "Ms. Soon, it's Lieutenant Colonel Rene Garcia. I'm David's sister. Are you all right?"

Nothing. She bumped the front door closed with her hip and surveyed the area. The kitchen lay straight ahead, the dining room angled to the right and back of the living room. Both dark.

She walked over to the end table closest to the door and turned on another light. "Ms. Soon, it's Rene Garcia. Are you here? Are you all right?"

Garcia wished she had brought her trusty Glock with her, but she didn't want to carry it at the hospital. She crept down the short hallway separating what looked like two bedrooms from the living room. "Ms. Soon, are you here? It's David's sister, Rene Garcia."

Light from the room on the right reflected from under the closed door. Only a night light in the bedroom on the left shining out through the partially open door. *Why doesn't Soon answer?*

She edged open the door to the master bedroom. The empty room had a made bed, two dressers and a couple of chairs. Looked neat, no clothes strewn around.

An uneasy feeling swept over her as she crept across the small hallway. Garcia turned the knob, pushed open the door and took one step inside. A slender Asian woman sat hunched over the computer. "Ms. Soon, it's Rene Garcia, David's sister. Are you all right . . .?"

The door slammed in her face with a force that bounced her across the hallway and into the other bedroom. She landed on her rear with a thud.

The den door flew open. A figure broke down the hallway.

Garcia pivoted on her back. She reached over to catch the person's right leg. The figure tripped and fell down the hallway, cursing when he bounced against the wall. Rolled on toward the living room. A man's voice.

Garcia jumped up, her hands spread in front of her in a fighting position.

The man rolled over to face her and bounded up. A flash of metal reflected the light. *Bastard's got a knife.*

She saw his face in the light. "Pell, it's you."

"A fucking broad." He turned to run. "Get out of my way before you get hurt."

"Don't you believe that for a second." Garcia launched after Pell and tackled him as he turned.

Pell went down with a loud thud. Another curse. He rotated back toward her.

Garcia jumped on him, slammed a karate chop to his nose. Blood spurted.

Pell's hand came up, the knife blade pointed at Garcia.

She raised her left arm to block the knife, but it slashed her arm. Pain radiated from the cut. "Shit." She pulled back, giving him enough time to roll and push to his feet again.

He kicked at Garcia. Started to run toward the front door.

"All right, asshole, now you're really pissing me off." Garcia sprang after Pell, catching him halfway across the living room. She chopped Pell to the back of the neck, sending him crashing to the floor again. The end table by the couch toppled over, a lamp fell, smashing a light bulb on the floor.

He tried to push up.

Garcia grabbed a dining room chair and brought it down over Pell's head. He collapsed with a groan. Turned toward her again.

The two glared at one another, breathing heavily. Garcia's heart pounded. Pell's nose oozed blood, as did Garcia's arm. The scene rolled through Garcia's brain like an old movie in slow motion. *Be ready,* she thought, *he'll move at me from the left.*

He raised the knife again, poised to strike.

She grabbed another chair. "Come on, I'm ready for you this time. This is payback for all the crap you've pulled." She raised the chair to smack Pell when a whispered cry sounded from behind her. "Help me."

Garcia turned. An Asian woman, framed in the light from the den, stood in the hallway. She leaned against a wall, the front of her shirt bathed in red. "Soon, my god, you're hurt."

Pell straightened and ran toward the kitchen. Garcia had to make a quick decision. Soon fell forward. Garcia caught her. The back door slammed.

The two collapsed to the floor, Garcia cushioning Soon's body with her own. She looked down at her own arm, the shirt ripped and blood seeping down her arm.

Soon lay face up in Garcia's lap, her face white. Her head fell against Garcia's leg. "Help me."

"Hang on, Soon," Garcia yelled, "stay with me. Stay with me, dammit."

She pulled out her cell phone and dialed 911, balancing Soon with her leg. "This is Colonel Garcia. Need an ambulance 3428 Hickory Drive in Fairfax. Hurry. A woman's in critical condition. Notify Lieutenant Scott, Fairfax County police. Need help looking for a white male named Pell. Hurry, dammit, hurry."

Garcia dropped the phone to one side. Felt for a pulse in Soon's neck. Nothing. She ripped Soon's shirt sleeve and tried to stuff the material into the wound to stem the bleeding.

Angling up on her knees, Garcia started mouth to mouth resuscitation. After about five minutes, she realized it was useless. Sat back down on the floor.

Garcia took Soon's head in her lap. Soon's eyes were locked open, but they would never see anything again. Garcia first thought about her brother. Then she realized the little baby girl would be without a mother now.

She teared up. These poor people. All because of Pell. *Well, she vowed, I'm coming after you, Pell. And when I catch up with you, it won't be pretty.*

Garcia laid Soon's head on the rug, then pushed up from the floor and stumbled toward the nursery. The baby was crying. It hurt to hear that little one cry.

———

Zack edged his truck down the side street, the crowds flowing back and forth along the sidewalks from a day at the beach, most of the walkers sunburned.

"Cool looking chicks," Wilson said. "Too bad we're so late."

"Come on, buddy, stay focused."

"You're right." He glanced out the window toward the water. "Must be the house."

They drove past it slowly. An eight-foot high fence surrounded the double lot, a gate in front. The gate appeared to be locked by a deadbolt.

"Place is right on the bay," Zack said. "It would be easy to launch a boat out to the ocean."

"Fucking place must have cost a bundle."

"Yeah." Zack drove to the end of the street and turned around. He parked in a space between two SUVs with attached boat trailers, their owners apparently still out on the bay fishing.

Good cover, Zack thought. "I'm going to walk past the house. Why don't you stay in the truck and keep watch."

"Roger that."

Zack stepped out of the truck. He nodded to a young couple, the man pushing a stroller with a youngster inside who looked to be sound asleep. "Musta worn the little guy out."

The woman smiled at Zack. "His first day at the beach. Oh, my, the waves fascinated him. He kept us on guard duty at the water line all day."

The couple cut right toward the main drag as Zack continued along the street on the bay side. The house loomed large on his left.

A truck horn blared and tires squealed from the main street one block over. The wind whistled down the street, carrying with it the sound of yelling children. Two young women strolled by, laughing, reminding him of Laura. Zack made a mental note to call Laura and see if everything was going all right with her mother.

Zack figured he could keep an eye on the house, but time worked against him. *The key to all this might be the women behind that fence. Did the owner have dogs or security cameras? Had the bartender been suspicious and called the owner?*

Zack hustled back to the truck and climbed in.

"What did you find?" Wilson asked.

"Didn't see anybody in the yard, but I think this place is worth checking out."

"Let's call Garcia for reinforcements. She can hit up a judge for a warrant to bust in and kick some ass. Grab whoever is in there."

Zack shook his head. "I don't think we can wait. If they know we're out here, they may be able to kill another officer before we can get to him. Or alert whoever is doing the damn bombings. We need the element of surprise to check things out."

"Okay, what do you think we otta do?"

"We know the bodies have been found only a couple of miles from here on the beach in Sea Isle City. Whoever did the killing must have had a place to do it. Where? We know the murdered officers have committed rapes against military women. This could all be a coincidence, but it's the best lead we've got. I'd like to sneak up to the house. Check it out first."

"Probably got sensors all over the fucking place."

"Here's what I think we should do. I'll walk down to the wharf behind us and see if I can gain access to the backyard from the bay side. You wait here."

"I don't like it, Colonel. Could be a setup and you'd get your ass kicked. I really think we need some fucking backup."

"I might get my ass kicked, but right now this seems to be our best bet." Zack pulled out the M-9, racked it, then slipped it back into his belt and pulled his shirt down over it again. "Besides, I've got my best friend with me."

"Okay, you're the boss."

Zack stepped out of the truck and shut the door. "Give me an hour. If I'm not back, call Garcia. Tell her to get the cavalry up here."

As Zack walked across the street and headed toward the wharf to see if he could sneak in behind the house from the water side, a shudder passed through him. *What if he were wrong?*

25

Fairfax, VA, Friday, 10:30 p.m.

Rene Garcia sat on a couch in the living room, holding the sleeping baby in her arms. *Cute little kid.* Garcia didn't know crap about babies, but she held tight to this one, thankful she slept.

Sirens sounded outside. Garcia walked to the front door and pulled it all the way open. Spotted the ambulance coming down the street. The baby opened her eyes and looked up at Garcia, then started to cry. *What the hell do I do with a crying baby?*

Out front, a police car pulled in and squealed to a stop behind the ambulance. A female orderly, wearing a white shirt and pants, hurried up the sidewalk and into the living room, carrying a black bag.

Garcia pointed toward Soon stretched out on the floor. "I tried resuscitation on Ms. Soon, but it was too late. She died in my arms."

The attendant hurried over to the body and knelt down, putting her hand on Soon's neck to check for a pulse. She looked up. "You're right. She's dead. The medical examiner will have to call it officially."

A police officer hurried into the room, gun drawn. "What's going on in here?"

Garcia turned the baby away from the policeman. "My name is Rene Garcia. I'm a military police officer. This is my brother's house and that's his wife on the floor. I've been working with Lieutenant Scott trying to find out who tried to murder my brother on Monday. If you point that gun away from me, I'll be glad to show you identification."

The baby kept screaming, further shattering Garcia's nerves. The orderly stepped over, arms outstretched. "Let me hold the baby so you can talk to the officer."

"Thanks." Garcia handed the baby to the orderly, pulled out her ID and showed it to the officer.

He checked Garcia's ID and holstered his weapon. "Okay, Colonel, what happened here?"

"First of all, has Lieutenant Scott been notified? She's working this case."

He nodded. "I'm told the lieutenant is on the way."

Garcia summarized the details of what happened. "The killer ran out the back door maybe fifteen, twenty minutes ago. You've got a sheet on him. Maybe you can get some cars out looking. I hope you can get that son-of-a-bitch."

The officer called in the information on his portable radio, then stepped outside.

Garcia followed him out the front door. She needed air. Three patrol cars with flashing lights had closed off the street. A fire truck stood at the end of the driveway, red lights still flashing, and its spotlight shinning in the direction of the woods behind the house.

People stood behind the yellow, crime-scene tape. Garcia ran a quick visual check of the crowd but didn't see Pell. Never hurts to check. Dumb shits did funny things. No one else in the crowd stuck out.

Lieutenant Scott pulled up in her truck and after talking briefly to one of the officers, hurried up the front sidewalk. She glanced at Garcia's arm. "You're bleeding."

"Don't worry about that now. Pell stabbed Soon, killed her. I tried to stop him, but he got away. One of the uniforms is supposed to be organizing a search for Pell." She looked down at her arm. "I guess I am bleeding. Better get one of the EMTs to check it out."

"Come on," Scott said, "let's go inside."

Garcia heard the baby crying from the bedroom. Her heart nearly burst with emotion. Little lady might be an orphan. All because of that bastard. "Let me check on her."

When she reached the bedroom, the EMT had just finished changing the baby and began pacing the floor, trying to calm the baby in her arms. It hit Garcia. She had a niece, crying her eyes out.

Garcia returned to the living room and sat down next to Lieutenant Scott on the couch. The other ambulance orderly came over to Garcia. "Let me take a look at your arm."

While they talked, the orderly cleaned and bandaged the wound. "We can get a doc to double check, but I think it'll be fine. You may need a tetanus shot just to be safe."

"Okay, thanks." Garcia turned to Scott. "Pell must have knifed Soon at the computer in that bedroom." She stopped to compose herself. "I had that clown down, but he got away when I turned to help Soon. Tried and tried to get her breathing again, but I was too late. Too late."

Scott put her hand on Garcia's good arm. "I found out the guy's name is Jensen. He's a half-ass thief who I guess has hit the big time. Don't beat yourself up. You did your best."

"Did I? Then why do I feel like shit that she's dead? I didn't even know her. My own sister-in-law."

Scott bit her lip. "I believe Soon is an illegal immigrant from Korea. David will need to sort that out when he is better."

"Okay. I'll check it out for him." Garcia pulled another tissue out of her pocket and dabbed at her eyes. "I wish I could have stopped it. And that damn Pell, ah, Jensen got away again."

"Are you sure it was him?" Scott asked.

"Hell yeah." Garcia shook her head to stop the tears. "She died in my arms. Couldn't help her in time. I hate crying."

Scott put her arm around Garcia's shoulder. "That's all right. Let 'em flow. Actually, let's go outside and get you some fresh air. We're in the way sitting here. Are you okay?"

"Yeah, just fucking beautiful." Her voice came out in a whisper. "Jensen, he's going down."

The uniform Garcia had talked to earlier came back into the room and leaned toward Scott. "The chopper is running quadrants in coordination with three cars. Gonna be tough to spot him at night. Lots of woods behind the house."

"No kidding," Scott said, "but we've gotta try. I want to get Jensen and I want him bad."

A young officer standing in the doorway glanced at Scott's chest. Scott walked over to the officer. "What do you want?"

"Ah, the medical examiner has released the body. Do you want to look around before they take it?"

Scott tapped her foot. "How many homicides you seen me at?"

"Quite a few."

"And how many times have I wanted to look over the crime scene before I release the body?"

"All of them."

"Any reason I should change now?"

"No."

"No, what?"

"No, Lieutenant."

She pointed toward the bedroom. "Get back in there and watch over things until I finish with Colonel Garcia and tell you what else to do."

"Yes, Lieutenant." The officer slouched out of the living room.

Scott walked back toward Garcia, shook her head and whispered, "Men can be such a pain in the ass."

Garcia tried to smile but couldn't. She stopped in the doorway and took one long, last look at Soon's body under the sheet, then she followed Scott into the cool night air.

A police officer held back the small crowd standing behind the yellow tape stretched across the front yard.

A man stood next to the TV news van, pointing his camera at Scott. "What happened? What's going on?"

"Just a minute," Scott said. "This won't take long." She walked over to the reporter. "There's been an incident here and I'll be investigating the circumstances. When I have more information, I'll let you know."

"What's the name?" the reporter called. "What happened?"

"For the benefit of those who weren't listening, I can't release any more information yet."

"Wait a minute," the voice called. "Tell us what you know."

The twirling red lights reflected an eerie glint on the Scott's face. "I just did." She turned and walked back to Garcia, motioning her back inside. "I'll get us some coffee. This is going to take a while."

26

George Washington Parkway, Friday, Midnight.

Homer Jensen drove along the George Washington Parkway and at two miles inside the beltway turned off at the sign for Turkey Run Park. He circled around to Area C1, pulled into the overlook and shut off the engine.

Leaning back in the seat, he shut his eyes. It wouldn't be long before he could get the hell out of this dump, fly down to the islands, find him some broads. He had money and they liked money, lots of money. And he loved broads. Lots of broads.

Headlights swung into the parking lot, tattooing a pattern across his back window in the darkness. He glanced over his shoulder to see the black sedan pull in two spaces from his rental. The car door slammed. A female figure approached his car. Jensen hit the unlock button and moved to face her.

The woman opened the door on the passenger side and slid in, pulling it shut behind her. The mask she wore muffled her voice. "How did it go? Did you get the material I asked for?"

He shook his head. "I rifled the desk. Couldn't find any of the fucking stuff you talked about. But you didn't tell me the fucking broad would be home when I got there."

The woman shrugged. "I didn't think she would be. Assumed she'd still be on the run or maybe at the hospital."

"Well, there she sat at her computer." He paused. "I had to do her."

"You had to what?"

"Goddamn, don't get all spastic on me. I looked around the house and couldn't find anything so I went into the den. Guess what, there she sat. She must have been asleep at her computer. Cause when I opened the door, she jerks awake and looks right at me. She could identify me. What the hell else could I do?"

The woman stared at Jensen, her eyes seeming to bite into him, making him uncomfortable.

Jensen tapped his fingers on the steering wheel. "Then the fucking female colonel shows up."

"The what?"

"His sister. I heard a motorcycle and looked out the front window. Hoped she'd keep on going down the street, but the dumb broad came into the house to look around. Found me in the den. She's tough for a broad, but I got away."

The woman sat there, silent. Jensen began to sweat, his stomach twisting. "What are you thinking?"

"The heat's going to be on. You can't go around killing people and not expect the police to react. Fairfax County probably knows who you are. They'll have the FBI scanning their files for you. You're hot."

"No problem. Give me my money and I'm outta' here. I'll head down to the Islands and disappear for six months. Some sun, a hair dye job, and I'll add a beard. Then I'll be good as new."

"I don't think so. Not this time. The FBI will be looking hard for you. They'll find you even in the Islands."

"You'd better help me. If I get caught, you know what it means for you."

"Yes, I'm afraid I do."

Jensen looked down to see the gun in her right hand. "Wait a minute." Nausea built in his stomach. "I was kidding about ratting you out. No way would I say anything."

"I know you won't."

A pop from the silenced gun was the last sound he ever heard.

A round dark mark appeared in the center of Homer Jensen's forehead. Jensen jerked a couple of times, then fell back against the car door and slid down in the seat.

The woman checked for a pulse in his neck. She knew there'd be none. There wasn't. *Stupid shit killed the Asian bitch, then got into a fight with Garcia. How dumb. Couldn't afford that now they were so close. Ready to operate and now Jensen fucks it up.* Pissed off, she shot him again. *Fucking men. Not worth a damn.*

She reached up and shut off the interior light so it wouldn't shine when she opened the door. She got out of the car and walked around to the driver's side.

The quarter-moon had disappeared behind a cloud. The darkness of the woods overlooking the Potomac River enveloped her. An owl hooted in the distance. The traffic on the far side of the tree line moved back and forth on GW Parkway even at this time of night.

Opening the door, she pushed the body over to the passenger side and slid into the front seat behind the driver's wheel. She started the car, backed up and drove it around the corner to a break in the wall.

She got out of the car, reached back inside to slip it into neutral. The car started rolling, gained momentum as it moved down a slight incline. It went over the embankment and bounced on the boulders until it burst into flames about two thirds of the way down the hill and ended up on the river bank.

The woman climbed back into the stolen car. She pulled off the two-sizes larger overshoes and threw them in the back seat. Satisfied with her work, she tightened her gloves, then started the engine. She drove off into the darkness, reaching for the special cell phone to make her report.

Zack hurried a half-block down the street, checking left and right, then cut toward the water along the fence. He stayed on the outside of the lot, taking his time, being quiet.

Climbing a small mound and standing on his toes, he found one spot where he could see over the fence. A number of windows in the house faced the bay. Quite a place. Whoever owned it must have a huge stash of cash.

Interior lights shone from a porch on the main floor and three floor-to-ceiling windows on the second level. Floodlights bathed the yard between the house and the shore line, although the fence cast a shadow, forming a blind spot. A large wooden building stood centered in the yard, probably used for storage.

He waited at the water's edge, watching the waves lap against the yard. The sun had long since dropped below the horizon with a final splash of orange. *Did the estate have sensors? How many guards, if any, walked the perimeter? And, what about dogs? Better not be any dogs.*

Taking off his shoes, Zack waded into the water to a point about four feet from the shore where the fence ended. He eased around the fence to the house side.

What could he say if he were caught? Maybe he had waded into the water and gotten confused. Story might not float, but it was now or never. He picked his way back toward the house using the fence as a guide. He pulled out his flashlight and held it by his side in case he needed it. Didn't dare turn it on yet.

In about ten steps he waded out of the water and reached down to pull on his shoes, cursing when he almost lost his balance.

Creeping toward the house, he stayed next to the fence. He needed to reach the windows and look inside. Two voices and a motor echoed from the bay. *Fishermen?*

It took him about fifteen minutes to reach the corner of the house. When he stood up to look in the closest window, he heard a sound that chilled him.

Barking dogs. Oh crap. Where are they?

He got his answer when a woman came around the corner, carrying a rifle in her right hand and holding the leashes of two pit bulls in her left. "All right, who are you and what the hell do you think you're doing? This is private property and you're trespassing."

Zack took a deep breath. "Look, I waded out into the water to enjoy the evening and somehow stumbled back in on the wrong side of your fence. I was trying to find my way back out to the street when these dogs came up. Sure caught my attention."

The guard kept the rifle pointed at him. "That's bullshit. What are you doing here? Hurry up and spit it out before I tell these dogs to go to work on you. And don't think they won't."

Another woman approached. Tall and thin, in a pair of shorts and a sleeveless blouse, she wore a fishing hat pushed back on her head. An M-16 rifle hung loosely in her right hand. "It's him. He's the guy from back at the inn."

Oh, shit, the woman at the table. Zack tried to fake it. "Do I know you?"

She smiled, showing a missing tooth. "Don't get cute with me. You're way out of your league. Come on, asshole, you're coming with us."

Zack pulled back. "Wait. I stumbled in here by accident. Call the cops. I'll take the charge."

"I'll give you one more chance to move your ass before I shoot, starting with your foot."

"All right." Zack faked a limp to slow down. He walked in the direction the woman pointed, keeping an eye out for any advantage. He could hit the woman on his right in the face with his elbow, but the dogs. If they got loose . . ..

The woman with the hat led him around the corner of the house toward a door. Pushing it open, she motioned with her rifle. "Inside."

Zack glanced at his watch. Twenty-two minutes until Wilson called Garcia and a team.

When Zack got inside, the woman in the fishing cap grabbed his shoulder to turn him around. She motioned toward her companion. "Keep an eye on this guy so I can pat him down."

"Wait a minute. You've got no right to search me."

"You know, one more dumb-ass comment and I'll knock your head off with this rifle." She found the pistol and Zack's cell phone. Slipped the M-9 in her own belt and threw the cell phone on the floor, crushing it with her boot. "I enjoy the M-9 myself. Think I'll keep it."

"Hey, what the fuck are you doing? That's my cell phone."

She pushed on his shoulder again. "Downstairs, asshole."

He decided to go along until Wilson could get there with help. When he reached the base of the stairs, she opened a door. "In there."

"This is all a misunderstanding. Look, let me talk to the guy in charge."

"Fuck you, ain't no guys here." She raised the rifle and brought the butt down on Zack's head.

Lights flashed, pain streaked through Zack's body, then everything went black.

27

Fairfax County, Saturday, 1:00 a.m.

When they reached the kitchen, Scott motioned for Garcia to sit in one of the chairs around a rectangular kitchen table. "I asked one of my guys to get us coffee. He should be back in a couple of minutes. Hope you wanted a cup."

Garcia tossed her uniform hat on a chair and sat. "Sounds great. Maybe two or three."

Scott sat across the table. "So far nothing on Jensen. We're checking the backyard for any clues and interviewing a witness who may have seen him drive off about an hour ago."

Garcia closed her eyes, exhausted. She snapped to at the sound of another voice, "Here's your coffee, Lieutenant, and there's an Agent Harper and Agent Fairchild out here."

Scott stood and reached for the coffee. "Thanks, I gave them a call. Tell them to come in."

The two stepped into the kitchen. "We came as soon as we could." Fairchild stopped when she saw Garcia. "Looks like you got sliced."

"I'll live." Garcia took a few minutes to share all that had happened since she'd arrived at her brother's house. "I had to choose between nailing Jensen and helping Soon. I picked Soon, but it was too late." She lowered her head. How would she ever tell her brother.

Harper reached into a cupboard and pulled out a glass, filled it with water. "You could have been killed."

"Nah, but he shaved off one of my nine lives. If I'd only gotten here thirty minutes earlier, maybe I could have saved her."

"Don't play that game. You'll drive yourself crazy." Lieutenant Scott started pacing around the kitchen, hands behind her back. "Let's go over what we know so far. We've got an artist's drawing of the man. He's a small-time hood named Homer Jensen who must be trying to hit the big leagues. I hit up the judge for a warrant, but when we raided his apartment, Jensen had already left. I don't know if someone tipped him or not. We put out an APB on him."

"Who would tip him off, Lieutenant?" Fairchild asked. "If we have a leak in our system, we've got to find it."

Scott reached down and took another sip of coffee. "I don't know anything other than Jensen wasn't there. We've got to consider all alternatives."

"Don't forget what's going on with Zack Kelly." Garcia summarized the conversations she'd had with Zack and the FBI director. "This whole mess could have international ramifications."

Garcia's cell phone rang. "Colonel Garcia."

"Rene, this is your mother."

Garcia looked at her watch. One thirty. Uh, oh, this can't be good. Her mother had never called this late before. "I'm pretty busy right now. Can I call you tomorrow?"

"It's your father."

Garcia gulped, shook her head to try and clear it. "What about him?"

"We're at the hospital. He's been so upset for the past several days and hasn't eaten right for a long time. His overall health has continued to decline. And now this thing with David."

The anger flared inside Garcia, but she muted it.

Her mother's voice jarred her back into focus. "He had a heart attack this afternoon. The doctor says it's serious. Oh, Rene, I'm so scared."

Garcia sat up straighter in her chair, the phone hanging from her left hand. Outside, the moon lit the tall oak trees behind the house, casting shadows across the windows.

She heard the echo of her mother's voice. "I think you should come to the hospital tonight. Before it's too late."

———————

While the elevator crept up to the sixth floor, Garcia thought of all the things she should say to her father. None of them seemed to be right.

When the doors opened, an orderly rushed by, pushing a medicine cart. "Excuse me," he called. "Coming through."

A voice on the loudspeaker called for Doctor Hathaway. Garcia stepped back as a nurse hurried down the hall, an anxious look on her face. She disappeared into one of the rooms.

Her mother waited in front of the double doors to the ICU. Garcia took a deep breath and followed her inside. The drapes were drawn, giving the room a cold, dark look and feel.

Garcia walked over to the bed, surprised at how small and shriveled her father seemed. Tubes poked out of his left arm and a constant series of numbers ran on the monitor next to his bed. She stood quietly for several moments, not sure what to say. Finally she put her hand on his arm. "Father?"

His eyes opened and he looked at her without expression, then his eyes widened as recognition must have dawned. "Rene?"

"Yes, it's me. Mother called. I wish you'd told me you had such serious heart problems."

He tried to lean forward, but fell back against the pillow. Reaching out, he placed his hand on her arm. "I'm . . . . I'm glad you're here."

Garcia fought back a tear. "You lay back and get better, then we'll talk."

28

Great Lakes Naval Lodge, Saturday, 7:05 a.m.

Lieutenant Nancy Smith arrived on the early morning flight from Dulles, her heart hammering in her chest. Could she really go through with this? The Dark Angel told her everyone had doubts before they did things for the sisterhood.

She passed through security, immediately spotting the tall, auburn-haired woman smiling at her. She tried to return a smile, but couldn't. The woman offered a hand and Nancy took it, her own hand trembling. "Hello, Nancy. I'm Phyllis."

Phyllis pulled her into a hug. "I love you for what you're doing. Those officer clowns will never abuse women again at one of their big parties. They won't be able to forget about you any longer. Come with me. We need to hurry."

Yes, Nancy thought, *we must hurry.* They had less than an hour until eight o'clock.

Phyllis had parked her car outside in the arrivals lot. The sky brightened, looked like a lovely day. Nancy shuddered to realize she'd never be able to enjoy it. A balmy breeze caressed her face, probably for the last time. How she loved that breeze.

Nancy climbed into the car and glanced in the back seat. There it sat, the briefcase. *Oh, God, the briefcase.* Waiting for her like a bad omen.

Phyllis drove to the gate, paid the ticket, then pulled onto the Bobby Caldwell Expressway. They continued on the expressway, Nancy wasn't sure for how long. She shut her eyes and prayed that she would find the strength to do her duty. To take a step for all of her sisters who had been raped and abused like she had. To make the military pay attention. She'd picked the perfect place to get her revenge.

She glanced out the window as they turned right onto Route 137, the sign read Buckley Road. Funny how she was interested in such a minute detail, a detail which didn't matter anymore.

They turned left on to Green Bay Road, then right onto Meridian. Nancy knew what that meant. They were almost there. *Oh, no, almost there.*

The lodge would be full of navy aviators attending their annual party. She'd attended it herself in past years, but after they slipped her that drug and got her stripping she could never go back. Three of the bastards who had raped her would be here. She pushed her shoulders back. Yes, she could do this. She had too. This could never happen again to another woman aviator.

Phyllis stopped in front of the Great Lakes Navy Lodge. She reached over and took Nancy's hand. "Have strength, my sister, have strength."

Nancy looked out the side window at the building. People walked around inside, people who would soon be dead. *Easy for Phyllis to say,* Nancy thought. *She wasn't going to die.* But Nancy had agreed to do this and she would. Her life had been ruined by that animal and she wanted to make a statement so other lives wouldn't be destroyed.

Phillis looked at her watch. "It's time."

Nancy's hand shook so hard she couldn't open the door.

Jumping out, Phyllis walked around and opened Nancy's door, then she reached in back and retrieved the briefcase.

Nancy exhaled when she saw it. Stared at it. This was her mission, her destiny. She watched the sun rising in the East casting a red haze, heard the cars idling in the driveway, horns honking from the road, people talking, all the sounds magnified.

Eight o'clock. Nancy took a deep breath, said a prayer for strength, and stepped forward, briefcase in her right hand.

Two naval officers stood next to the door, talking and laughing. *Did they look at her strangely?* She took another deep breath. Kept walking.

She opened the door and walked up to the counter. A man behind the counter turned from his desk and came over to her. "Good morning. May I help you?"

"Yes," Nancy replied. "I'm looking for a room for one night."

"Are you an active duty naval officer on travel orders?"

"I'm a navy pilot."

"Active duty on orders?"

"No, not anymore. I resigned my commission."

"I'm sorry, but we only accept active duty officers in advance. You can wait and if we're not full, I can help you on a space-available basis after three o'clock."

That gave Nancy strength. "But the reason I left the service is that my supervisor, another navy aviator, slipped me one of those pills at this party, raped me, then other aviators who are here joined in. They blamed it on me. Said I asked for it. The government did nothing about it, nothing to help me." She started to cry. "Now my ex-boyfriend refuses to touch me. Says I'm damaged goods."

The man looked at her, mouth open, as if he didn't know what to say. "I'm sorry, Lieutenant, but the rules are that only active duty officers on official orders can reserve a room in advance. Again, I can help you this afternoon on a space available basis."

This guy doesn't care about me. Doesn't care about any of my sisters. Determined, she wiped away the tears, then reached down and flipped open the latches on the briefcase, like she'd been shown. Saying another short prayer, Nancy pushed the red button. A flash of light filled the room.

Consciousness pulled at Zack. He struggled, but the ropes around his hands and feet held him fast. His head ached. The tape over his mouth made it difficult to breathe.

He tried a gimmick from his football days to check for any broken bones. First, he wiggled his toes, then his fingers, then he worked his way up his body. As far as he could tell, his body worked, his head just hurt like hell.

A Tiffany lamp on an oak dresser to his right cast a dim light in the room. He glanced through the tinted window to the right of the dresser, but couldn't judge the time.

The muffled drone of voices came from behind him, but Zack couldn't make out words. He struggled and was finally able to roll onto his left side. A heating vent opened at the base of the wall. He had to stall until Wilson got here with help.

Zack tried holding his breath, but could barely make out the words. Cocking his head, he listened. A female voice sounded familiar. "I say we shoot the bastard right now. He knows too much." Shit, that sounds like the woman who had brought him inside.

"We need to question him. Find out what he knows. Can't afford to have the cops here until after tomorrow." Another female voice. "Sometimes you are too trigger-happy."

"Wait, let's not argue," A third female voice. "It won't be long before we will take over. Then it won't matter. . . ."

Zack strained to listen, but he couldn't hear the rest of the sentence.

That same, deep female voice. "Relax, we'll soon have everything we want. Then we'll show those bureaucrats how to run things."

"What about Kelly? Is he awake yet?"

Another voice, the deep smooth voice. "Go downstairs and check. If he's awake, call me."

Okay, Kelly, get ready.

Lieutenant Scott stood next to FBI Agent Frank Harper at the overlook parking area just off the George Washington Parkway, the morning sunrise creeping over the horizon. Divers used a hoist to pull a red Chevrolet Impala up the river bank. They pried open the driver's door and pulled out a body and placed it on a gurney, then moved it toward an ambulance.

Scott drew in the gravel with the toe of her boot. "Guess we can cancel the APB on Homer Jensen. We know where he is. Good thing the car didn't sink in the river or we might not have found it for months."

"Yep," Harper replied. "You're sure it's him? I couldn't believe it when I got your call this morning."

"I ran the license plate number. Jensen rented the car three days ago with a credit card in the name of Herbert Johnson. We showed a picture to the attendant. He identified Jensen."

Trees swayed in the morning breeze. Men in white coats scrambled around the parking area, taking pictures, checking for footprints, and gathering other evidence.

"The problem with Jensen's death," Harper said, "is we've lost our chance to find a link to his boss."

Scott blew a smoke ring and watched it float away in the wind. "I'm sure that's the idea. Whoever did this must have realized we were getting close."

Harper fanned the cloud away from his face.

"Sorry." Scott continued to observe the divers below. "How did someone know we were on to him, enough to kill him? Very few people knew we were even looking for Jensen."

"Not quite true," Harper replied. "Wasn't the APB put out on him last night? It looks like he died early this morning."

"I would have liked to take a chunk out of him myself," Scott replied. "And I know that Colonel Garcia would, too. What do you think?"

Harper thought for a moment. "Okay, Jensen's ransacking the house when Soon wakes up. I'm not sure what he wanted, but I'll bet a month's pay it's tied to the truck hitting David Garcia. Anyway,

Jensen knifes Soon, then Garcia shows up. Good thing she's tough and quick on her feet, otherwise we might be investigating . . ."

Scott took another puff on her cigar. "Garcia arrived at Soon's house about nine-thirty last night. So Jensen's alive and running out the back door thirty minutes later. Two or three hours after that, the guy's bouncing over the rocks and down to the river bank." She paused. "With a hole in the center of his forehead, execution style."

"Any witnesses?" Harper asked.

"None yet. It appears no one heard any shots."

"The murderer probably used a silencer," Harper replied. "Anyway, these sites near the parkway are pretty deserted early in the morning."

Lieutenant Scott took another puff on her cigar and turned away to blow out the smoke. "I'm sure that's why the killer met Jensen here."

Agent Tara Fairchild hurried across the parking lot. Her trench coat hung open, showing her navy-blue suit, white shirt, and red and white striped scarf.

When she reached Scott and Harper, she took a deep breath. "Sorry I'm late."

"I tried to get a hold of you earlier," Harper said, "but you didn't answer and my call went into voice mail."

Fairchild shrugged. "I had a couple of things to check out, then I heard on the radio about the car along the river. What do we know?"

Harper summarized the status for her.

"So we know for sure this is Homer Jensen?"

"Yes," Scott replied. "But don't you think it's funny that we just find out about Jensen, then a couple of hours later he's dead?"

Fairchild rubbed her face. "Do you think our investigation has been compromised?"

Scott puffed on her cigar. "I don't know. Do you?"

29

The White House, Washington D.C., 10:00 a.m.

Admiral Steele strode into the conference room. The group at the table made a half-hearted attempt to rise. "Sit down, dammit, I feel like the rest of you look. All right, give me an update."

Garcia stood. "At eight o'clock this morning Nancy Smith, a recently separated navy lieutenant, carried a black suitcase into the guest house at the Great Lakes Naval Base blowing herself up and killing at least ten officers and injuring about twenty more. The area is still being combed for survivors and other bodies. It's a mess."

"What do we know about her?" the admiral asked.

"Lieutenant Smith was assigned to the Seventh Fleet as an aviator and seemed to be well-liked by all who knew her," Garcia said. "She accused her boss, a Lieutenant Commander Sacks, of raping her at a party. One of those date-rape deals. Sacks, another aviator, has an outstanding record. He denied it and said the sex was consensual. Unfortunately, it was his word against hers."

"One interesting bit of information," Blake said. "Many of Smith's fellow aviators were attending a reunion and staying at the guest house. I guess they all gather there annually. Kinda like a frat party."

Garcia looked down at her notes. "Maybe she was getting even."

"I checked the backgrounds of some of the aviators who were killed," Blake said. "They had the reputation of being ladies' men.

During the investigation, Smith claimed that after Sacks slipped her the drug, they all had had sex with her. They denied it. Said she was promiscuous with all of them."

"Could she have been getting even?" Steele asked.

Blake nodded. "This would sure provide a motive for her going after those particular guys. Hard to believe she'd just kill innocent officers."

Garcia looked up. "I don't have much more than what I've told you. Whatever the facts, Lieutenant Smith felt she was wronged and never received any justice."

Blake nodded. "It looks as if she has her justice now."

"Yeah," Steele replied, "but it's awful."

"Anyway," Blake continued, "it's going to keep on happening until the government realizes this is serious stuff and does something about it. What's been happening to these women is inexcusable."

"All right," Steele said, "this is the third bombing in three days. We've got to stop it. Garcia, what do you hear from Zack?"

"Nothing in the last twelve hours from Zack or T.J.," Garcia replied. "I've tried both of their cells several times. At least one of them should have their cell on." She stepped up to the board and began to write. "Now, as we look at the bombings, the first one was at the Army War College, the second at the Naval War College, and the third at the Great Lakes Naval Yard." She circled the first letter in each title.

Steele stared at the board. His eyes lit up in recognition. "Holy shit . . ."

Garcia pointed at him. "Right. If you pull out the first letter of each one, the first three sites were hit in the order of the word ANG. It could be a coincidence, but I don't think so. The first three letters in the word angel."

Admiral Steele tightened his lips. "So simple."

Garcia rubbed her eyes. "Now we've got to anticipate that the next bombing, if there is to be one, will be at a place beginning with the letter E. What sites within a reasonable distance of Washington begins with the letter, E.?"

Silence while the group thought about various sites.

Barclay Morrison snapped his fingers. Everyone looked at him." What about Fort Eustis. It's less than 100 miles from Washington and Eustis begins with an 'E'."

Garcia gave him a thumbs up. "You may have hit on something. I'll put out an alert to all facilities, but especially ones with an E in their title. So goddamn arrogant. Spelling out your name by killing people."

"Wait a minute," Blake said, "how many women have been ruined by these assholes and never had any justice, never had any way to come back at their male bosses?"

"That's true," Steele replied, "but at what a price. In any event, we need to get ready for a possible incident at Eustis. Blake, will you gather all the information you can about any sexual abuse incidents at Fort Eustis? Also, what forces are there? What facilities?"

"Will do, sir. I don't like this any more than anyone else, but the latest stats show that over 5,000 women complained this year about sexual assault. Very few have resulted in convictions."

"Let me know what you find out," Garcia said. "I'd like to fly down to Eustis and check out their preparations. Make sure they're taking the threat seriously. If the Dark Angel selects that site, we need to intercept the bomber before he or she gets near a target. I'd like to take the woman alive if possible."

Blake raised her hand. "Sir, one other thing we need to discuss this evening. The president is due to deliver his speech tomorrow night at the Liberty Bell in Philly. Zack was concerned about a possible plot to kill the president. I've found no evidence to support that as yet."

"Wait a minute," Garcia said. "Liberty begins with an L Could the Dark Angel be looking to end her reign of terror by assassinating the president?"

"I'll discuss it with the chief," Steele said. "Let him know our concerns."

"Maybe the vice president should go in his stead," Barclay said.

"That's one alternative," Steel replied. "But I don't want her to get hurt either."

"In the meantime, I'll go back and talk to Director Burnside," Garcia inserted. "Let him know what we've found out. He may not be ready to step in, so we could be on our own."

Steele tapped his fingers on a notebook. He looked up. "Okay, what about the plot against the DOD computer system."

"Agent Fairchild and I are working with Lieutenant Scott from Fairfax county on that one, sir," Agent Harper said. "We'll be checking the drone training site at Fort Shelby and the main site outside of Vegas. General Harding is doing everything she can to increase security in case there may be trouble. Scott is leading the investigation of who has tried to kill David Garcia."

"Okay, stay with it." Steele said. "The next twenty-four hours will be critical."

Footsteps approached the door. A click sounded as a key slid into the lock. The door opened. Zack stayed on his side, motionless.

The woman in the fishing hat looked down at him. She turned and walked out the door, slamming it shut.

What now? Zack waited.

The door opened again. He glanced over to see a female figure in a long green robe looking down at him. A scarf covered her lower face so all Zack could see were eyes. The woman wore sandals. A large diamond ring flashed from the little finger of her right hand.

"Ah, I see that you are awake," she said. "I'm sorry I have been forced to treat you with such minimal hospitality, but you should have left well enough alone when you had the chance."

The voice didn't sound familiar. Zack tried to sit up, hoping the woman would untie him.

"I know you are uncomfortable, but your discomfort will soon be over. I'll remove the tape from your mouth, but if you yell I'll put it back in place." She sat on the edge of the bed and chuckled. "It doesn't matter anyway. No one will hear you."

She pulled on the tape. It burned his face as she ripped it off.

Zack worked to keep a blank look on his face. "One hell of a way to treat a visitor. I stumble into your yard by mistake, then your security people knock me out. Now I demand you untie me and let me out of here before I sue your ass."

"You have guts," she replied. "Not much judgment, but certainly guts. I'll grant you that."

"Who are you?" Zack asked. "I don't know you."

"People call me the Dark Angel." She looked out the window for a moment and fiddled with the diamond on her finger.

So this is her. "Why are you doing this?" Zack asked.

"Time and time again, women in the military are abused and no one cares. No one does anything about it. Well, I'm doing something about it."

"But it's not right," Zack replied. "I saw in the paper where you're killing innocent officers and their families by bombing those facilities."

"Such a righteous man. Where was all that righteousness when women committed suicide, left the military in hopeless depression. A number of those killed were guilty as hell, but got away with it. They'd done hideous things to female subordinates. Where were you then? You should have been as disgusted as I was. I regret the collateral damage of officers who were not involved, but the government has brought this on itself and needs to pay."

Zack shook his head. He didn't have an answer for her.

"Did you hear about the army general accused of sexually assaulting a junior officer? He threatened to kill her family if she told anyone about their three-year affair. Then he did the same thing to two other female officers. The clown had a ream of pornography in Afghanistan. An army general. What happened to him? A slap on the wrist. A fine. Retirement. No jail time. What about those he raped? And no one cares. The army hierarchy swept it under the rug. Well, no more."

She rose and looked down at Zack. "I will send someone for you."

Rene Garcia walked down the hallway and spotted Officer Coats in front of the door to her brother's room. "Hey, Coats, how are you doing? Everything okay?"

Coats stood. "Yes ma'am, I'll keep a watch on things. No one 's going to get by me and hurt your brother any more. You can be sure of that."

Garcia patted him on the shoulder. "Thanks." She entered the darkened room, pulled up a chair beside her brother's bed and sat. Leaning forward, she took David's hand in hers.

Nothing had changed since her last visit except the room location. Monitors beeped, lights flashed and the smells of medicines and disinfectants enveloped her.

"Hi David, it's me again, your sister, Rene. How are you feeling?"

The constant beeping of the monitor and the squiggly lines across the screen almost mesmerized her. She stared out the window at the gray day. The dark sky matched her mood. How would she break the news about Soon to her brother? Would her father recover from the heart attack? Too much to think about right now. Too much.

She wasn't sure how long she sat there holding her brother's hand before she felt a movement in her finger, a tingle—no, movement, definitely movement. Turning away from the window, she stared down at her hand. It moved. She wasn't moving it.

Holding her breath, she looked up to see her brother's brown eyes, eyes she thought she might never see again.

He squinted at her.

She smiled and stroked his hand. "Hi, David, it's me, Rene."

He watched her, his head not moving.

"You've been asleep, but now you're awake. I'm glad." She wiped tears from her eyes with her shirt sleeve. She hated to blubber, but she couldn't help it. Not this time.

"You were in an accident." She formed the words slowly. "You are at Fairfax Hospital. I'm going to push the call button, then walk out into the hall to make sure the nurse comes."

Carefully setting David's hand on the bed, she edged her way to the door. When she looked back, David seemed to be following her with his gaze.

Garcia pushed open the door and stepped out into the hallway, letting the door close behind her. Her mother stood in the hallway talking to Officer Coats. Face drawn, her navy blue skirt hung on her slender frame.

Garcia wiped her eyes, then smiled.

Her mother stared at Garcia, bloodshot eyes wide, forehead arched in a frown. "How can you smile at a time like this? Your father and brother might die."

Garcia stood there, overcome with emotion, unable to talk.

"Rene," her mother said, "what is it?"

"David's awake. Mother, he just woke up."

Her mother jumped as if an electrical current had coursed through her body. She put her hands to her face. "David…" She pushed the door open, Garcia standing behind her.

David stared straight ahead. His head moved slightly at the sound of the door opening.

Garcia stepped back and turned toward the nurse's station. She met the nurse coming down the hallway. "David's awake."

The nurse hurried to the room. She checked David's pulse and looked at the monitors, then she reached for a phone and pushed some buttons. "Page the chief right away."

In a moment the phone rang. The nurse picked it up and listened. "All right, I'll call the neurologist on duty. We'll see you in about an hour."

She hung up the phone and whispered, "Remember David has been in a deep sleep for three days. Speak slowly, one person at a time. Say simple things to him. It's important you think of his recovery as a long-term event. His return to consciousness isn't like an on-off switch, but rather like a dimmer switch where each step is slow and halting."

His mother stood next to the bed and stroked his arm. "Oh, David."

The nurse started for the door, then turned back. "We'll be looking for appropriate responses to stimuli such as David moving his finger when asked. Don't expect much for a while."

Garcia sat down and smiled at her brother. "Your name is David Garcia. You were in an accident. You are going to be fine. My name is Rene Garcia. I'm your older sister."

David watched her speak, his eyes barely slits.

David's mother continued to stroke his hand gently, speaking slowly. "Hello, David, I'm your mother. You've been in a coma since the accident, but you're awake now and it's wonderful."

Garcia stepped out into the hallway and dialed Lieutenant Scott's cell.

Scott answered on the third ring. "Scott."

"It's Garcia," she whispered. "My brother just woke up. I thought you'd want to know right away."

"Wonderful news," Scott replied.

"The nurse has called the doctor. He should be here soon."

"Can David answer any questions yet?"

"I don't think so. He's pretty out of it."

"I'm happy he's awake. What a relief."

"I'll let you know as soon as he's able to talk to you."

As she disconnected, her mother stepped out into the hall, a huge smile on her face. She brushed a tear from her eye. "The nurse asked me to give them some space for a few minutes, then we can go back in. Maybe you can stay here with David. I'm going up to tell your father. This news should help his recovery."

"I called Lieutenant Scott to let her know." Garcia was glad she'd confided to her mother about the death of Yun Hee Soon. "We'll have to ask the doctor when David can stand to hear about Soon."

"I wonder if he'll be looking for her right away."

The nurse came out. "You can go back in."

"What do you think?" Garcia asked.

"He looks good. Vital signs are stable. The chief will be here shortly. He can tell you more."

Garcia sat quietly with David for about forty-five minutes. The door opened and the chief of service strode into the room. He walked over to the bed and checked David's pulse. "Would you mind waiting outside for a few minutes? I need some time with Mr. Garcia to check him out. We'll talk in a few minutes."

"Of course."

Garcia stepped into the hallway to see her mother coming from the other direction. "I told your father about David. He smiled when he heard."

In a few moments, the door opened and the doctor came out. "His vital signs look good. But remember, he's had a serious head injury. We have no way of knowing how long it will take for him to recover or,…," he paused, "if he will ever completely recover."

Garcia thought for a moment how to frame the next question. While her mother knew about Yun Hee Soon, she didn't know yet about the baby Scott had placed with Social Services last night. Tricky. Scott was still checking to see if they were married.

"Ah, what about his partner, Yun Hee Soon?" Garcia asked. "She was murdered last night. What do we say if he asks about her?"

The doctor's mouth formed an "oh," and he held his finger up to his chin. "I'd skirt talking about her for a while. I don't want to shock him until I see how well he reacts to routine things and I definitely don't want him to fall back into a coma again."

Garcia's cell rang. She stepped a few feet down the hall. "Colonel Garcia."

"It's Blake. Still no word from Zack or Wilson."

"What about a possible attack tomorrow?" Garcia asked.

"We'll be on a secure conference call in a half hour to determine strategy. How's your brother?"

"He just woke up. The doc's not sure how long it will take him to recover or if he will."

"Oh, man, you've had more than your share of crap."

"Can't worry about that now. I'm on my way. See you at the strategy session."

She hung up and glanced at her mother. "I need to go."

"You can't go. Your brother and your father."

"Mother, it's my job." Garcia started down the hallway, then turned. "You've got to give me space to do what I have to do."

30

Strathmere, NJ, Saturday Morning

Zack lay on the floor, his body aching and his throat parched. He strained at the ropes binding his hands, but they wouldn't budge. *T.J. should have notified Garcia by now. Help should be here. Where the hell were they?*

The door opened. The woman he'd seen at the inn entered. "If it were up to me, I'd kill you right now, but the Dark Angel believes you might have useful information and she's the boss. We'll see if she's right."

She bent over and slapped Zack's face with the back of her hand, snapping his head to one side. "All right, dumb shit, how did you find us?"

Zack knew from his survival courses that he needed to answer questions without conveying vital information and to keep her talking long enough to devise a method of escape. "I told you I stumbled in here by accident. Why are you doing this to me?"

"My job is to move your ass and that's what I plan to do right now."

With that, she grabbed Zack's left shoulder. Another woman came in, a tall woman with spiked blond hair. Together they pulled him through the door to the hallway, then dumped Zack near the outside door.

The bumping on the floor hurt, but he wouldn't give them the satisfaction of complaining. The sound of their receding footsteps echoed down the hall.

He heard approaching footsteps again. The taste of blood filled his mouth and his back burned. Zack clenched his teeth, focused on what he'd do to them once he got free.

The two women grabbed his feet and pulled him outside, dumping him on the concrete patio like a sack of potatoes.

The late morning sun beat down on him. The woman from the inn reached down and spread duct tape over his mouth. Zack turned and stared into the face of a pit bull growling at him. His heart hammered in his chest and a shiver ran down his spine. *Would the damn thing bite him? It could tear him apart and he wouldn't be able to defend himself.*

Looking around, Zack tried to gauge distances. A one-story, circular cement building stood in the center of the otherwise open yard. *Place for any hostages? Were there more here? He hadn't heard anyone in the basement of the house.*

Along each side of the yard, an eight-foot high fence stretched from the main house behind him to the waterfront. A boat dock stood at the end. Looked like three boats moored at the deck. *An escape? Maybe?*

A second dog had joined the first, both of them snarling at him. *Damn, if they got loose . . .*

The woman must have sensed his thoughts and sounded a throaty chuckle. "If you move, these dogs will tear you apart."

He moved slightly to his left. The nearest dog growled and crept toward Zack. He reflexively pulled back. Didn't want any part of that fucker.

Zack's hope lay in getting her to listen to a deal. Had to think through something she'd want.

Zack risked another growl from the pit bull and shifted to the left so he could see more of the yard. The only possible escape route lay toward the water.

The woman who called herself the Dark Angel stepped out of the open doorway, followed by two other women in robes, all with scarves over their faces. She leaned over Zack. "You've left me little choice. I can't leave you here and I can't take you with me. Unfortunately, I must get rid of you unless you can help me."

———————

Garcia stalked around her office like the proverbial caged panther. She reached into her desk drawer and pulled out two more aspirins. Her head hurt and she still had flashes of dizziness, but now she had to think. *Come on, brain, work.*

The latest bombing had been more disastrous than originally thought. Seventeen people had died and many more injured. The FBI continued to question witnesses. Surveillance videos showed a car, maybe a Buick, leaving the site right before the bombing, but the video wasn't clear enough to show a license number.

The press screamed for more information, causing panic among the public. At the last press conference, Admiral Steel shared what he could, but that didn't quiet the roar.

What the hell had happened to Zack? He'd been out of contact for over twenty-four hours. Missed two scheduled check times. So far his friend on the Sea Isle City Police Department as well as the New Jersey state police had come up empty in searching for him.

She called Blake, who picked up on the first ring. "When are you planning to fly to Fort Eustis?"

"I'd like to leave about three in the morning," Blake replied. "We've got to be ready at six in case there are more bombers. I've got a chopper on call. Want to ride along?"

Garcia debated for a moment. She sure as hell wasn't doing any good here. "You bet. I'll be ready."

Garcia had to update the director. She picked up the phone and dialed. It rang.

"Director Burnside's office."

"It's Colonel Garcia at the Pentagon. I'm calling on behalf of Admiral Steele and need to talk to the Director again. Is he available? I only need a few minutes."

Remembering what she'd said about his needing to help her, Zack shook his head to signal the Dark Angel to remove the tape. No Garcia. He was on his own. He needed a different strategy.

She ripped it off. "Yell and my dogs will tear you apart."

"Look, I work for the president's national security advisor. If you release me, I'll provide information on what the Federal government has on your group and the ongoing status of our investigation."

"Don't believe this bastard," the woman from the inn said with a sneer. "He's full of it."

The Dark Angel glared at her. "I'll judge for myself." She motioned for Zack to continue.

Zack had to talk fast. "The Operations Center in the Pentagon is the coordinating point for the investigation. It consists of representatives from the major elements within the government plus many of the other federal agencies, including the DEA and Homeland Security."

One of the dogs sniffed at Zack's foot, but he ignored it. "We've developed files on your group and other groups like it in the country."

Zack watched her eyes but couldn't gauge a reaction. "You must realize that I wouldn't have come up here without backup. You can kill me, but your life won't be worth a nickel if you do."

The Dark Angel paused for a moment. "Don't think you'll have help. I have your backup man. He is a guest in my house."

Zack coughed to cover his surprise. *How did she find Wilson?* "Who?"

"We captured your friend waiting for you in the truck. He's inside that building. We also took pains to park your truck in our garage. So you see, no one knows where you are." She chuckled.

"He was most insistent that he knew nothing about you, but I didn't believe him."

What to say. Plan your next step carefully. "My friend?"

"Yes, it's true, I have your Mr. Wilson. He's waiting to die just like our next candidate, Major Caldwell. All three of you will die before the day is out unless you can change my mind."

He needed to develop another plan of action. Maybe figure out how to work with her until he could escape. "But I can help you," Zack insisted. "Let you know what the Feds have on your group and what their next move will be."

Hands on her hips, the other woman cut in. "Don't believe this bastard, he's lying."

The Dark Angel glanced at her. "You don't listen to me. Now you must pay." She nodded to one of the dogs and pointed at the woman. With a growl, the animal lunged straight at her. The woman turned to run, but the dog wrestled her to the ground, digging dagger-like teeth into the soft skin of her throat.

The other dog joined the first and the two tore at her as if they were ripping meat off a bone. Made Zack sick to his stomach.

Arms folded, the Dark Angel watched, ignoring the soft whimpers, until the woman quit kicking. She called off the dogs.

Zack's heart beat fast. He couldn't believe what he was seeing. What a cold-hearted son-of-a-bitch. He was powerless to stop it. *Could he be next?*

The Dark Angel pondered the bloody chaos, then glanced at the other two women. "I'm tired of people not listening to me. Move what is left of the body to the building and throw her in the trash like the rest of the garbage."

The two women stood transfixed, seemingly rooted to the ground.

"Do I need to provide another demonstration of what my dogs can do?"

The two grabbed the remains by the legs and dragged her toward the building—leaving a trail of blood and tripping over their own feet. They unlocked the door and disappeared inside.

A loud clank sounded, then silence. The two women came back outside and locked the door. Hung the key next to the door. Blood stained the front of their robes.

The Dark Angel waited until they returned and stood behind her. "She will not interrupt our conversations any longer. Colonel Kelly, I have to tell you I'm suspicious of your proposal. I already have all the information I need. However, I'd like to think about what you're saying and make a phone call. If you're lying to me, the dogs will get their chance. If you are telling me the truth, at least you can die without pain."

She glanced at the two women who appeared frozen in place. "Take Colonel Kelly back inside. Let him wait for me to decide his fate."

The two hurried over to Zack, reached down and pulled him back inside the house. His head banged against the door frame, sending another jolt of pain through his body. The rough, concrete floor scraped the skin on his face. They lifted him onto the bed and placed the tape over his mouth.

After they left, he lay on the bed wondering why the hell he hadn't waited for backup. *Dumb.*

31

Strathmere, NJ, Saturday, Daytime

The door opened and a slender blonde Zack hadn't seen before entered the room. Dressed in street clothes, she wore a scarf around her neck, pulled up covering the bottom half of her face. He wasn't sure how much time had passed since they'd left him on the bed. He watched her.

She pointed a pistol at him and motioned for Zack to roll over. She cut the ropes binding his legs, but left his hands tied. Zack pivoted to sit up and swung his legs around to the floor. He started to wiggle his toes. *Could T.J. still be alive? Caldwell? Who's this woman?*

She backed toward the door, keeping the pistol leveled at him. "Upstairs."

Zack struggled to his feet, flexing his legs and bending over to stretch. He needed to get feeling back into his legs and arms. *What about the dogs? The damn dogs.*

"Go ahead, Kelly, after you."

As he walked out the door and down the hallway, Zack wiggled his fingers to get the blood flowing again. He passed a window. The sun shone brightly. People walked along the street within a few yards of the front door, headed toward the beach with no idea of the nightmare playing out behind these walls.

"Who are you?" he asked. "Where are you taking me?" No response. He didn't really expect any. Hell, he didn't know what to expect.

At the top of the stairs, she pointed toward a hall and they entered a grand foyer. Paintings of women in military uniforms lined the walls and a thick Persian rug covered the floor. Zack didn't recognize any of the women in the paintings.

An ornate chandelier, with crystal pendants dangling from the edges, graced the center of the hall. *How did the Dark Angel obtain a place like this? Rent it. Bought it?*

Each step carried him closer to what? Zack steeled himself for whatever lay ahead.

The woman pointed him toward a den, paneled in a heavy, dark oak. She moved to her left and sat at a small circular conference table, placing the pistol on the table in front of her.

The Dark Angel stood in the center of the room, dressed in street clothes, slacks and a blouse. She like the other woman, wore a scarf covering the lower portion of her face.

Motioning for Zack to take a seat at the conference table, the Dark Angel said, "You are very lucky, Colonel Kelly. My partner convinced me to give you a chance. So, it's time for you to make a decision. Please follow me to the window."

Zack kept flexing his legs and wiggling his toes, while trying to loosen the ropes around his wrists as he walked. He had to get feeling back in his wrists and hands.

When he reached the window, the Dark Angel pointed to the round, cement building in the center of the yard. Two dogs sniffed near the door of the building.

"Your friend is in that building, as is Major Caldwell. They are both perfectly safe for now. But that is about to change and you are going to take care of it for me."

Zack glanced at her, eye brow raised, trying to figure out what she meant.

"Yes, that's right. I plan to let you go in a few minutes, but before you go, you will open the door and let the dogs in on the two men. After you watch them die, you will leave and get the information I need. Is that clear?"

Zack's temper exploded. He strained at the ropes. "You're crazy. I won't do that."

"Oh, but you will. The question is do you want to live? Whose life is most important to you? And remember, I can get to your daughter, Laura, whenever I want."

Oh, God, he thought, *not Laura*. "You can kill me but leave her alone."

She watched Zack, eyes flashing. "If you agree to do something for me and don't, then Laura will be the one to pay and her death will be most unpleasant."

Zack had to forcibly stop himself from launching at her. *Wait a minute. Remember what your shrink said. Keep your cool. Use your head. Think, Zack, think fast.*

"You don't have much choice, Colonel Kelly, now do you?" The Dark Angel moved back toward the table and sat. "Now, let's get down to business. After you complete your mission here, you will leave the compound in a few minutes. Contact your friends in the Pentagon. Tell them you were unable to find any trace of illegal activities. You will need to be innovative and develop a story to cover your absence. Is that clear?"

Zack nodded, almost absent mindedly, as he glanced around for a weapon. Didn't see a thing to help him. "Can you untie my hands?" Zack asked. "They've gone numb."

The Dark Angel paused, then nodded. The other woman moved from the table to cut the ropes around his wrists. She kept the pistol trained on Zack.

"Don't even think about trying to pull something, Kelly. I'll kill you and I'll kill your daughter if you don't do exactly what I tell you."

The bitch meant it. How could he gamble on Laura's life? Blood flowed back into his hands making them tingle. Zack rubbed his arms and continued to flex his leg muscles as inconspicuously as possible. He saw a pitcher of water on the desk with a number of glasses. An idea formed in his mind. Maybe, just maybe. "Do you mind if I help myself to water? Been a long day. I'm thirsty."

"Not at all," the Dark Angel replied. "We are partners now and partners take care of one another. Would you like something to eat for the road?"

Should he stall? Get something to eat? His mind didn't seem to respond. *Stall.* Decided against it. He needed to act and he needed to act now before she got suspicious.

"No, not now, but thank you anyway." Zack had no idea what had changed, but he could play the nice game too. "I'll pick up something after I leave." He walked to the desk and poured a glass of water for himself. As he set the pitcher back down on the desk, he made a decision. Not much of a chance this would work, but it was better than nothing. And he had to do something.

Zack poured a second glass. He picked up both glasses and turned to face the women.

"Come over here, Colonel Kelly and quit stalling. You have things to do and I expect you to get to it."

Zack walked over and stood next to the Dark Angel. He knew that while she might release him to do her bidding, he couldn't stand by and watch Wilson and Caldwell die. Their lives were in his hands. He had to make it happen. Now. "Would you like some water?"

She looked up at him. "No. Now, sit down, Colonel Kelly. You're making me nervous."

As Zack bent over to sit, he threw the water from one glass in the Dark Angel's face and water from the glass in his left hand at the woman with the gun, simultaneously dropping to the floor and rolling under the table.

Broke both glasses on the floor and stabbed upward at the Dark Angel, hitting her in the stomach, hearing a satisfying scream of pain. Two gunshots sounded as he stabbed at the leg of the other woman. Another scream of pain.

Zack pushed up and tipped the table toward the woman with the gun, turning it on top of her. Spotted her hand and stepped on it. Another scream of pain. Whirled and sent a karate chop to the throat of the Dark Angel, causing her to bend over and start gagging.

The gun flew across the floor. He reached down and scooped it up. The woman under the table moved to get up and Zack shot her in the chest twice. The shots were sure to bring reinforcements.

Zack turned back toward the Dark Angel. She lay on the floor, appearing to choke from his karate chop to her throat. Blood poured from the glass cut. She tried to speak, but could only whisper. Motioned to him and pulled off the scarf.

It surprised Zack that he didn't recognize her. He pulled her up to hear her. Damned if she didn't smile. "The Dark Angel will kill you." With that she choked once more, then fell silent.

Zack felt for a pulse. None. *What did she mean the Dark Angel would kill him? Wasn't she the Dark Angel?*

Garcia thought she noticed movement as she walked down the back hallway of the hospital toward the parking garage after a quick visit to her father. It started as a feeling of someone watching her, then she sensed actual movement. She turned back toward where the movement had been, but saw nothing.

Standing at the door leading from the hospital to the parking garage. She debated contacting security. *No, I'll hustle to my motorcycle and get out of here.*

Garcia remembered all of the tricks she'd learned at a self-defense class in the Pentagon. Attacks on women happened all too often in D.C. *Be alert, focus and concentrate. Don't think about anything else.*

She pulled out the keys to her Harley and removed the canister of mace from her bag just in case. *Assume the worst.*

Her hearing upped a notch as she took the elevator to the third level. Walls blocked much of the outside light. Getting off, she sensed the garage darker than before. *Bulb must have burned out.*

She walked along the line of parked cars, keeping her weight balanced equally on her feet. Another glimpse of movement. Her breathing grew more rapid. She strengthened her stance, what she'd been taught to do in karate.

Garcia stopped. Listened. Silence. Directly across the concrete floor stood a narrow staircase with a tiny exit sign over it. The staircase turned back on itself until it disappeared into the floor above. She didn't see anyone hiding up there.

She heard measured footsteps. Looked back again but saw no one. Still she felt a presence so picked up the pace again.

Her Harley stood parked about ten cars away when a hand grabbed her shoulder. Pulled. Tried to spin her around. Ragged breathing in her ear. A woman's muffled voice, "If you value your brother's life, leave this alone."

She spun around toward the woman, spotted the upraised hand with what looked like a sap. Garcia raised her arm to block it but the sap connected with her temple.

She fell, clutching her head. Pain. Darkness crept around her. *Fight it.* She tried to pull herself up, but the woman kicked her in the side, throwing her against one of the cars.

Garcia's legs failed her. Falling.

The woman stood over her, face covered with a scarf. "Leave this alone before your family gets hurt. It's none of your business."

The sound of running footsteps.

Damn, she's not going to get away.

Garcia pulled herself to her feet, using the car for support and shook her head. A car door slammed. The roar of an engine. Lights came toward her. She jumped out of the way as a large dark car swung by. Blew down the exit ramp, scraping the right fender.

Her mind told her what she wanted to do, but the message broke down on the way to her legs.

She fumbled in her purse for her cell. Managed to push in Scott's number.

32

Strathmere, New Jersey, Saturday Afternoon

Zack locked the hallway door to the den and blocked it with a chair, then hurled another chair at the window, shattering the glass. He had to get away before the others in the house could get organized.

Grabbing a piece of cloth, he brushed away the shards from the sash, then pushed a chair to the window. Standing on the chair, he leaned out and looked down, estimating his fall to be about ten to twelve feet. He heard pounding on the door behind him. *Get the hell out.*

He jumped, landing on the ground with a thud, doing his best airborne roll. His leg and arm ached from the jarring fall. Shit, landed on bed of stones. He pushed up from the ground. Looked around. *Where were the damn dogs?*

Pulling one gun out of his waistband, he half ran, half limped across the yard toward the building. Heard the dog. It lunged at him from the right. Zack wheeled and fired, hitting the animal in the forehead. The dog fell to the ground as its teeth grazed his arm.

Zack limped on toward the building, his leg giving way. He almost fell.

At a movement behind him, Zack turned. Shot the second dog as it leaped at him. *Keep moving.*

At the door of the brick building, he heard the panting of a third dog. *Where the hell had it come from?* Zack turned. Fired as the dog charged. The animal dug its teeth into Zack's left leg. Blood spurted from the wound. *Pain.* His leg felt as if it were on fire.

Zack fired again. The crazed animal loosened its hold on the bloodied leg. Fell to the ground.

He grabbed the key and unlocked the door. The door creaked as he pushed. It stuck. Putting his right shoulder against the door, he shoved it open. Charged inside, checking both left and right with his weapon, pausing to let his eyes adjust to the darkness.

A man, maybe Caldwell, lay tied to a post in the center of the room, his clothes in rags. Wilson had been tied to a chair. Looking up when the door opened, Wilson motioned with his head.

Zack limped over and pulled the tape from Wilson's mouth. Bruises covered his swollen face.

"You okay?" Zack asked. "Mobile?"

"Just fucking beautiful. Get me out of these ropes. I'm going to beat the shit out of those little fuckers. Can't believe they surprised me. I owe them."

"Makes two of us." Zack worked on the ropes around Wilson's hands. They gave. Wilson went to work on his legs.

Limping to where Caldwell lay, Zack reached down to shake his shoulder. Damn face bruised and swollen, impossible to determine if he knew the guy. Zack pulled the tape from Caldwell's mouth and began to untie his hands.

Caldwell groaned. His eyes fluttered open "Who are you?"

"Don't worry about that now. We need to get you the hell out of here before these women get organized again."

Zack ripped the sleeve of his shirt into long strips and tied a tourniquet above the wound in his leg, using the other sleeve for a pressure dressing. He had to stop the bleeding otherwise he'd black out. Reaching down, he tightened the tourniquet.

Finishing with the tourniquet, he turned to Caldwell. "Can you walk?"

Caldwell rose to one knee. "I can make one hell of a try. My ass is too big for you to carry me." Using a chair, he struggled to his feet. Looked at Zack. "Shit, man, you're bleeding."

"Goddamn dog took a chunk out of my leg."

"We're one hell of a pair." He glanced toward Wilson. "Who are you?"

"Wilson. You?"

"Harrison Caldwell."

"Come on," Zack called, "let's get outside and see if we can slip along the corner of the building. If we make it to those boats, maybe we can get the hell out of here."

Zack peeked around the corner of the door. The dog that had taken a chunk out of his hide stared at him, glassy-eyed. Zack kept his pistol trained on the dog in case it wasn't dead. He motioned, "Let's go."

Zack limped around the building, keeping it between him and the house. Caldwell stayed close behind him, supported by Wilson.

Zack crouched, then ran across an open area, continuing to use the shelter of the building. Had to get to one of the boats. *Where were the guards?*

He waved for the other two to follow, then gave one of the two guns to Wilson. "I'll make a break for the water. Cover me. Give me about thirty seconds then get your ass in gear."

"Sounds like a plan," Wilson whispered. "We'll be right behind you."

Zack ran, hunched over, toward the water. No gunfire. Caldwell broke into a half-hop, half trot toward the water, Wilson balancing him as they ran.

A burst of gunfire. Wilson jerked up, then fell only a few feet from the boat, Caldwell collapsed on top of him.

Zack aimed and shot two rounds back toward the guard. It stopped the bullets for a moment. Reached Wilson. "You all right?"

"Fuckers got me in the left arm, but no sweat, I've got another one."

The three ran, staying low, reached a twenty-foot inboard. Zack and Wilson pushed Caldwell over the side, then followed, one at a time. The other providing covering fire.

"Hurt bad?" Zack asked

Wilson shook his head. "Son of a bitch burns, but I'll live." He tore his shirt into strips and wrapped them around his arm. "Fuck. Good as new."

Two women ran across the grass toward the boat. One dropped to her knee and took aim. Before she could fire, Zack took careful aim and squeezed the trigger. The woman flew back and crumpled to the ground. Maybe a break for a minute.

Wilson crawled toward the front of the boat. "Can you get it going?"

"I'll try. You cover me." Zack spotted a key hanging from the gear shift. Picked it up. Heard two shots. Wilson had picked off another woman. How many were there?

Shots ricocheted off the side of the boat. Zack could feel his strength ebbing as the blood oozed from his leg. Not taking time to aim carefully, Zack fired and hit one of the guards in the shoulder. She fell to the ground, lay still.

The motor kicked in. Zack yelled, "Untie the fucking line, or we'll take the dock with us."

Wilson crawled back, fired one shot, then lifted the rope from the dock. The motor roared. Zack called back, "Hang on, we're getting the hell out of here." He pushed the throttle forward. The boat leaped ahead.

Zack looked down at his leg, the shirt a dark red. He'd been so full of adrenaline he hadn't thought about it. Felt light headed. He saw a rag and tied that above the wound, hoping to slow the bleeding.

He looked back and his heart sunk. Three women were getting into the other boat.

"Better give it the gas," Wilson called. "The little fuckers are on the way."

Lieutenant Scott leaned against the door of the hospital security office and glanced at Garcia. "It looks like whoever attacked you shot out two lights in the garage. That's why it stayed so dark. Probably used a silencer so no one heard the shots. How's the head?"

Garcia rubbed her forehead. "Got myself one pisser of a headache." She looked down at her hands. "The bitch got away from me. I know I hurt her, but she still got away."

"Definitely a woman?" Scott asked.

Garcia nodded.

"Did you see the car?" Scott asked. "License number? Maybe a make?"

"Large and dark four-door passenger car, maybe a newer Buick. It's got a pretty big dent on the right front fender where she hit the wall on the way down the ramp.

"You're lucky," Scott said. "The woman probably had a gun and she's desperate. Showed a willingness to kill if she's the one who shot Jensen."

"Wish I could have stopped her."

Damn good that you're a tough lady, Scott thought. "Did you get a look at her face?"

Garcia shook her head. "A scarf covered part of her face although she seemed familiar to me. She did have on a dark trench coat and a hat. Seemed tall. Course everyone looks tall to me."

"I can understand that."

Garcia glanced at the security guard working at a computer. "Let's step out in the hall."

When the two reached the hallway corner, Garcia turned to her. "Just to let you know, Lieutenant, there's a meeting at the Pentagon tomorrow morning. They'll be talking about a possible hacking attempt on the drone program with General Harding. I'm not sure, but I can't help but think this is all related."

Scott pulled out her notebook. "Are you going to the meeting?"

"No, but we've got someone going."

"Do you have any idea of the number of staff who are aware of the arrangement with Sterling Software?" Scott asked.

"No, why?"

"I'm thinking it might be interesting to test out some of our theories. Maybe ask some questions at this meeting?"

"Not a bad idea. Let me talk to Admiral Steele. See what I can arrange."

"Might be wise to have the attendee wear a wire at the meeting. That way they could listen to it later and analyze what everyone said."

"I don't know. If our person was found out, it could be one hell of a problem."

"True enough," Scott replied. "But this could be critical in determining what's going on. And more importantly, how to get a warrant if we need it."

Garcia's cell rang. What now?

33

Strathmere, New Jersey, Saturday, 4:30 p.m.

Zack steered the boat past the Strathmere Inn, under the bridge and around the northern tip of the island, probably frustrating fishermen who shook their fists at him because he didn't slow down in the no wake zone. People partied on boats, drinking and looked to be enjoying the holiday.

He had to find a Coast Guard Station. When he looked back his heart sank. The boat behind them had closed the gap. One of the women raised a rifle and fired. Zack ducked. A bullet pierced the windshield. If they hit the fuel tank, it could explode.

"Kick it in the ass," Wilson called. "They're fucking gaining on us."

Zack pushed the throttle all the way forward. The boat leaped ahead in the waves. He risked another look back. Still gaining. Damn, go baby.

"Caldwell, can you hear me?" Zack yelled. "Answer me, damn it."

Caldwell moaned, managed to croak out, "Yeah, I can hear you. Don't feel for shit but I hear you. Can you make it to shore?"

"Don't think so," Zack yelled. "They'll follow . . . shoot the shit out of us and our boat."

Zack made up his mind. "Heads up. Time to give them the old fake out."

Turning the boat 180 degrees, Zack headed straight back toward their pursuers.

The eyes of the woman driving the boat widened. A second woman pointed her rifle at him and fired.

Zack kept the boat on a dead-on collusion course, his windshield shattered from the bullets. He stayed low enough to avoid being hit, only peeking up to insure he was still headed directly for them.

The other boat swerved, but Zack matched their moves.

"Get ready to jump," Zack called.

"I've got Caldwell," Wilson yelled.

Zack kept a straight shot toward them. "All right, now. Jump." He threw himself over the side as the two boats collided. An explosion shook the water, spinning him around. He sank low into the water, held his breath for a moment, then bobbed back up again. Pieces of the boats surrounded him. Flames spread around the remains. He searched for Caldwell.

Wilson bobbed up, hanging onto Caldwell's shoulder and head to keep him afloat.

Zack swam toward them, reached for Wilson's arm. "T.J., you all right?"

Wilson shook the water out of his eyes. "Been better."

"Can you make it to shore?"

"No sweat. I'm okay. But what about Caldwell?"

Zack felt for a pulse in Caldwell's neck. "He's alive. Don't know much more than that. Gotta get the hell out of here."

Wilson spit water out of his mouth and yelled, "Let's blow this place."

Zack launched into a strong side stroke, floating about every third stoke to conserve energy.

Wilson pulled Caldwell along, Zack helping as much as he could.

Caldwell floated behind the two of them. Fortunately the water felt warm, probably in the high 60s.

Zack glanced up every moment or so to get his bearings. The beach seemed about a hundred yards away. His leg burned. Pain radiated up his arm. Got to keep moving. Hold onto Caldwell. Keep moving.

"How are you doing?" Zack called back toward Wilson.

"Present for duty . . . not much more."

A row boat moved toward them. *Lifeguards?*

Lieutenant Scott stood in the doorway of Samuel Foster's office, trench coat over one arm. "Thanks for seeing me on such short notice, Mr. Foster. I know it's late on a Saturday afternoon and I'm glad you're here. I won't take much of your time."

"My wife and I have tickets to the Kennedy Center this evening. We're looking forward to a concert by the National Symphony Orchestra." He motioned toward the couch and sat behind his desk. "Have a seat. What may I do for you?"

Scott placed her coat on the couch, pulled out her notebook and leaned back, taking a moment to glance around his office. Nothing seemed to have changed. *What an egotistical bastard*, she thought. Someone tried to kill David Garcia and all Foster cared about was making it to a concert with the National Symphony Orchestra.

"You're aware someone murdered David Garcia's wife and may have made his little girl an orphan." She watched Foster's eyes as he answered. In the past she'd found eye movement to be key in determining if someone told the truth.

Foster lurched back in his chair, his eyes wide and his mouth open. "I had no idea." He looked down at his desk for a moment, rubbing his hand over his bald scalp. "That's awful. When did it happen?"

"Last night, about ten o'clock." Scott replied. "You should have read about it in the *Washington Post* this morning." *Why hadn't he seen the article? Was he lying?* "Did you met David Garcia's wife?"

He didn't meet her gaze. "No, I never did. I probably did see the article, but if I remember right, they have different last names so it didn't register. Do you know who did it?"

"Yes, I think so."

Foster's head jerked again, causing his double chin to jiggle. "Have you found him yet? David won't be safe until the murderer is in custody."

"Why do you think it's a him?" Scott asked.

"I, I ah, don't know," Foster stammered. "Why, I guess I assumed it was a man."

Scott decided to keep a few things secret. "We have some leads. It won't be long before we find whoever killed her. Should help us find whoever tried to kill David."

Foster pulled out a handkerchief and wiped his forehead. "We need to get murderers like him off our streets or none of us will be safe."

"We need to get the animals those murderers work for, too," Scott continued. "And I will."

"What does any of this have to do with me, Lieutenant?"

"I'm not sure."

Foster glared at Scott. "I don't like your tone, Lieutenant. Are you implying something?" He pulled off his glasses and wiped them with his handkerchief. "Do I need an attorney?"

Scott shrugged. "Not unless you've done something wrong."

"I can assure you I haven't. Be careful with accusations you can't support."

Scott scanned her notebook. Foster's hand shook as he put his glasses back on. She had him on a roll. "I'd like to look through your offices. I particularly would like to have our computer techs review the program David Garcia worked on before that truck hit him."

Foster's face twisted in a look of surprise, then he recovered. "I believe I already told you our program is proprietary. I'm not willing to share anything about it with you or anyone else for that matter."

"I had hoped we could work this out between us, Mr. Foster, you know like two people working together to solve two awful crimes.

I felt sure you'd want to help us find the person or persons responsible for killing Ms. Soon and attacking Mr. Garcia." She rose and reached for her trench coat. "But if you don't want to help us, I'll be back with a warrant."

"I don't understand why you insist on searching our system when you know we have a confidential agreement with our clients. What are you looking for, Lieutenant?"

"I understand that Mr. Garcia spent at least the last year and one-half working on this program. Then someone tried to kill him at the hospital. Yesterday someone, probably the same person, ransacked his house and killed his wife. You tell me what I should be looking for, Mr. Foster."

Foster picked at the skin around his lip. "I can assure you, Lieutenant, this awful business has nothing to do with me or any of us at Sterling Software."

"If you're right, why do you object to me looking at the program?"

"I've told you a number of times, it's a confidentiality issue. My client has given me explicit instructions that no one is to see it but the persons designated."

Scott paused. "I understand. We can protect your system."

"I'm sorry, Lieutenant."

"In that case, I'd like to meet with your client, Mr. Foster. Maybe I can convince him."

"My client doesn't want to meet anyone. There's nothing I can do."

"Too bad, Mr. Foster." Lieutenant Scott walked toward the door. She stopped and turned back. "There are two people in your office I haven't been able to talk with yet and I still need to."

"Who might that be, Lieutenant?" Foster asked.

"Megan Alcott and her deputy, Jason Helm. Are either of them in this afternoon? I need to close out this part of my investigation."

"You're too late, Lieutenant. It's a holiday weekend and both of them have left for the day. Megan may be here tomorrow."

"Give me their cell. I need to talk to them."

Foster got out his roster and read off numbers. "Now that I think about it, Ms. Alcott may be on the road this weekend. Jason should be here all next week."

"Thank you, Mr. Foster. I hope you'll reconsider letting a team look at the system including the supporting documents. Something doesn't add up and I intend to find out what it is."

34

Fairfax, VA, Saturday, 5:30 p.m.

Lieutenant Scott paced around David Garcia's house still fuming over another nonproductive meeting with Samuel Foster. She thought about what she had seen and learned in her search of the house. But there had to be more. *Where might David Garcia hide a package of software materials he needed to protect? Around here? In the cloud? Nearby?*

Then it hit her. She'd read in their papers that David and Soon spent much of their free time volunteering at a vet's office. What a great place to hide something. Scott reached into the top drawer of the desk and pulled out a roster with the phone number and address of a veterinary clinic. She ran her finger down the page. Doctor Henry Thurber at Bailey's Crossroads Animal Clinic, only a few blocks away.

Scott dialed the number. After two rings a woman's voice sounded. "Bailey's Crossroads Veterinary Clinic, may I help you?"

"This is Lieutenant Pamela Scott with the Fairfax police department. I'm investigating the incident with David Garcia."

"Oh, yes, Lieutenant, how's he doing? We've all been so worried about him."

"Finally some good news. David came out of his coma earlier today."

"I'm happy to hear that."

"He appears to be one tough guy. Say, is Doctor Thurber there?"

"Can you wait a minute? He's with a patient. I'll see if I can get him for you."

Elevator music played while Scott tapped her pen on the desk. She thought through the questions she wanted to ask. Wondered about how much she could trust Thurber. *He's probably okay, but be careful.* She'd learned over the years that one never knew who might be involved.

"Lieutenant Scott?"

Scott switched her focus back to the call. "Doctor Thurber?"

"Yes, Lieutenant, I'm Henry Thurber."

"I'm investigating what happened to David Garcia Wednesday morning."

"I heard about the accident. How's he doing?"

"He's out of the coma. Looks like he's on the comeback road."

"Be sure to greet him for me," Thurber replied. "Will he be able to have visitors? I'd like to drop by, but don't want to impose."

"Ah, I'm not sure, but I'll let you know as soon as I find out anything."

"How can I help you?"

"We're trying to find a package with some materials of David's. Did he by any chance leave something with you? Maybe for safe-keeping?"

Thurber stayed quiet for a moment. "He did leave a package here and asked me to secure it for him. I have no idea what's in it."

Scott did a quick thumbs-up to herself. "I wonder if I might stop by and pick it up. David may need it now that he's awake."

"I guess you could retrieve it for David, you being the police and all. I'll get it out of the safe and have it in my office with your name on it."

"Thanks, Doctor Thurber. I'll be over right away."

"Ah, we're closing for dinner in a few minutes and I have something else to do. I'll be back in the office at seven o'clock, but have appointments even though it's Saturday. You can come over at eight."

Scott looked at her appointment book. "I'll be there."

"That would be fine, Lieutenant. And please give my best to Soon."

"I'm afraid I have more bad news, Doctor."

Megan Alcott sat on the three-person couch, while Foster paced in circles around his office. He stopped and pointed at her. She wanted to tell him to quit pointing at her or she'd bite the damn thing off, but figured she'd better cool it, at least for now. *Everything in good time.* She ran on the fast track now and didn't want to mess it up.

He cursed under his breath. "We have to be able to sanitize Red Dog on a moment's notice if we need to. I have no doubt Scott will do everything she can to get a warrant for her computer experts to go over the system."

Alcott fluffed her hair, crossed her legs and laughed. "On what grounds? You're such a weenie, Sam." *Fun to taunt him. So damn up tight.* "That bitch can't do anything to me. How could she justify forcing us to break our confidentiality contract so she can sniff around our system?"

"I'm not sure she can, but I called Bernie. We need his legal expertise. Scott will claim that whoever killed David's wife was ransacking their house to find something he'd hidden, presumably something about Red Dog. Then what do we do?"

"It's a fucking trick, Sam. We don't have to worry."

"Don't patronize me, Megan." Foster burped as he walked to the window and pushed back the drape. "Have you asked yourself why the FBI is involved?"

Alcott bit her lip. "How do you know they're involved?"

"I just know."

"Sam, you can be such a prick." She squinted at him, annoyed she had to depend on him for information. "Do you think their involvement has something to do with Red Dog?"

"I don't know, but why else would she want to look at Red Dog?"

"I can't believe it. The system has worked perfectly. Our tests show I've been able to break into the Pentagon system whenever I want. We'll know in the next 24 hours if what we've been planning will really work. I think it will. Your client must be ecstatic."

"She's delighted with what we've done."

"What did she say?" she asked. "Tell me now."

"She complimented me and said it did exactly what she wanted."

"Why you? I'm the one doing all the fucking work and now you're getting the credit with our client." Right then and there Alcott plotted how she would get Foster out of the way. She should get the credit. "What's she going to do?"

"I think I'll keep it to myself for now, Megan. I don't want you getting any ideas about finding out who she is."

She stood and stretched, then walked over and stood next to him at the window, playing with his lapel, licking her lips and smiling. "You know, Sam, we're partners and partners have to work together."

"I know, Megan, but I don't completely trust my pretty partner." He patted her rear. "Why don't you get your cute little tail back to your office and continue monitoring Red Dog in case we need to bring it down? Leave the client to me."

"All right, Sam. But tell her I'm in charge of the system now and will take care of everything." She brushed against him when she stalked out the door. Pulling it shut, she laughed. In 24 hours, she'd be on top. Everything she'd always wanted stood within reach.

It was time she met and got some respect from the client. A shiver ran up her spine. It felt good. She laughed out loud and hurried down the hallway.

As she sat at her desk, the door opened. Her deputy, Jason Helm, stood in the doorway. She leaned forward to block his view of her computer screen. "What do you think you're doing?"

He shrunk back. "Whoa, I didn't mean to bother you. There are a few things we need to discuss now that David's not here and

I'm in charge of one of your teams. You've been busy so I figured I'd stop by late to catch you."

"You'll have to make an appointment." She pointed at him, her voice raising. "I've got things to do. Don't ever sneak into my office again. Do you hear me? Never again. Period."

Helm left the office shaking his head and pulled the door shut behind him.

35

Sea Isle City, New Jersey, Evening

Zack watched the row boat draw closer. A female lifeguard sat in the front facing the three of them, a male lifeguard in the middle rowing. The woman leaned over the side of the boat. "I'm going to toss you a life preserver. Grab it. I'll pull you in."

If he'd died and gone to heaven, Zack hoped this would be his reception. Finally some help. The white preserver landed about two feet from his good hand. He reached out and managed to grab it.

"Okay, hold on tight," she cried. "Are your friends hurt badly?"

"Yeah, both of them."

"We'll try and lift them into the boat but they both look pretty big. I've radioed for help."

When Zack glanced at Caldwell, his gaze met a fairly blank stare. He called to Wilson, "Help me get Caldwell into the boat."

"You bet, Wilson called. "Then we can get the fuck out of here and onto shore."

"Be careful now, you balance him," Zack called, "I'll push."

They helped lift Caldwell into the boat just as a second boat, this one with a motor on the back, pulled up next to Zack.

Two young men leaned out. "Come on, we'll get your friend in." He saw Wilson. "Goddamn, you're a big dude."

209

"Just get busy and quit talking." Wilson grabbed the edge of the boat and they helped pull him over the side.

Zack was surprised at how quickly they did it. One look at their muscles showed they must both be weightlifters.

When they had Wilson in the boat, the taller one reached down and called to Zack, "Come on, it's your turn."

After they helped Zack into the boat, the lifeguard turned the boat around to head for shore. The larger of the two men asked, "What about those other people? I don't see anyone. Another boat's coming out."

"Call the Coast Guard first. Don't attempt rescue without police support. Those women are criminals. I know it sounds crazy, but you've got to believe me. They were shooting at us. I rammed them so we had a chance of escaping. They would have killed us had they caught up."

Zack found himself talking fast. "Maybe the three of them were killed in the explosion. See if Lieutenant Powell is in her office. I've been working with the Sea Isle police on this case. You know, the bodies on the beach."

The young man stared at him and lifted an eyebrow. "Looks to me like this guy's been shot."

"Got hit once that I know of. Lost some blood. Have you got a cell phone?"

The lifeguard shook his head. "We'll get one up on shore. I'll call the Coast Guard."

"Do it," Zack said. "And find Lieutenant Powell. She's with the Sea Isle City police department."

"I'll call her," one guard called. "I know who she is."

They ran the boat up onto the beach, popping the motor up so it wouldn't drag in the sand. Two three-wheeled cycles idled nearby. One had a stretcher on the back. People crowded around the cycle, gawking, talking.

They were joined by two other lifeguards. The four lifted Caldwell onto the stretcher. The two who had brought Zack and Wilson in helped Wilson out of the boat and placed him onto a stretcher on the cycle. The motors roared as they raced up the beach.

"We'll get another one for you in a minute," one of the guards said. "How are you doing?"

"I'm not hurt like those two," Zack replied.

"I don't know what you've been up to," he said, "but it must have been something. I've called the Coast Guard and we're trying to find Lieutenant Powell. I guess she's on a trip somewhere."

"Okay," Zack replied. "I need to contact the Pentagon and the FBI as soon as possible."

The lifeguard's eyes widened. When the three-wheeler returned, the guards helped Zack climb onto the back. They reached a white building up the beach containing the lifeguard offices where an ambulance waited, red light whirling.

Pushing himself up to his feet, Zack said, "I've got to get to a phone."

A slender man in a golf shirt and a pair of shorts hurried over to Zack. He looked at Zack's leg. "I'm a doctor. Where are you hurt?"

"Nothing life threatening for me," Zack said. "I was bitten by a dog, hurts like hell but I managed to slow the bleeding. The big guy's been shot. The other was kidnapped . . . held hostage for at least a couple of days. Been through a lot."

"We'll get all three of you to the county hospital right away."

Zack whispered to the doctor, "Look, my name is Zack Kelly. I'm an army colonel who works for the president's national security advisor. The women chasing us could be involved in the explosions. You know, the explosions around the country at various military bases. Don't say anything to anyone else. I know it sounds crazy, but I think the president could be in danger. And I think they're involved in the murders here in Sea Isle City."

The doctor walked over to another man. In a moment he returned. "We're ready to transport you and your friends to the hospital. We can straighten everything out there."

Zack turned to watch the ambulance with Caldwell and Wilson pull out. "I've got to find a phone. It's a matter of life and death."

The doctor patted Zack's good arm. "Sure, sure, buddy, we'll see about that phone once we get you to a hospital."

"What day is it?"

"It's the third of July," the doctor replied. "Now hop in that ambulance over there and we'll be on our way."

———————

After stopping at the office to check e-mails, then running home for a hurried dinner, Lieutenant Scott pulled her truck up in front of Doctor Thurber's office. She got out and walked up to the door, surprised that the office looked dark. Thurber had said he'd be back before eight o'clock.

A bus lumbered by, belching a cloud of diesel smoke in her direction. *Goddamn pollution.*

Scott double-checked the office hours on the door. Saturday, closed from five to seven, then open from seven to ten. She stood, pondering her next move, when a red van pulled up.

The driver got out and coached a Saint Bernard out of the back seat. The dog let out a couple of deep-throated barks and jerked the man toward the door, surprising Scott. Dogs didn't normally like to go to the vet.

The man pushed his Washington Nationals baseball back on his head. "Do you have an appointment for eight o'clock, too?"

Scott shook her head. "No, I'm picking something up from Doctor Thurber. It doesn't look like anyone's in."

"Funny," the man replied, "the doc told me he'd be here for Herbert."

An uneasy feeling crept into the pit of her stomach. She tried the door. Unlocked. The uneasy feeling spread throughout her body and put her on red alert.

"I'm a police officer," Scott said. "Please step back. I'd better check inside." She pointed toward his van. "Why don't you wait in your vehicle."

She drew her .45, reached for the door handle and pushed it open. All of the lights were off. Scott flipped a switch and the lights illuminated the reception area. "Doctor Thurber? Doctor Thurber, are you here?"

No answer. Scott crept across the reception area, her heart beating faster and her palms sweaty. She opened the back door, the smell of gunpowder and something else assaulting her. She knew that smell.

Scott turned on the light. Blood spattered everywhere. A young woman in a white shirt and trousers who must have been his assistant lay sprawled over the exam table. A tall man, who Scott figured must be Thurber lay on the floor, sightless eyes staring up at her.

Scott's shoulders slumped.

———————

"Did you get it?" the voice on the phone asked.

"Yes. But there may be a problem," the woman said.

"What?"

"The package isn't sealed."

"We must assume they've seen the contents. That's bad."

"Yes."

"Kill the colonel before she can talk to her brother."

"I don't think it's wise. There's been too much killing. Killing a cop will bring the entire law enforcement world down on us."

"All right, Ms. Genius, what would you do?"

"I think I scared the hell out of her."

"All right. Will anyone be able to check out the trace on the phone?"

"Not a chance. I made sure of it."

"Destroy the material in the envelope."

"Don't worry. I'll take care of it."

A click. She sat alone in her car at the overlook. The lights of downtown Washington blinked back at her. A plane came in low, probably headed toward Dulles Airport.

Things had gotten out of hand. She hated working for the bitch, but had no choice. This was the way to settle all the scores against fucking men.

She picked the envelope off the seat and turned it in her hand. It would be easy to destroy the material, but she'd keep it for awhile. It paid to be cautious. The package might come in handy for insurance purposes in case the boss tried to double deal her.

She prepared a second envelope and placed the one she had taken inside it. She put a note on the outside, "To be opened in the event of my death." Tomorrow, she'd place it in her safe deposit box.

36

While she waited for the medical examiner and the lab staff, Scott wandered around the veterinary clinic. Drawers had been pulled out and their contents dumped. Various pieces of equipment had been thrown on the floor, along with a cabinet of medicines. A real mess.

Was this a random burglary or someone looking specifically for the Red Dog papers? Scott almost immediately ruled out a random burglary. Evidence might prove her wrong, but for now she bet this had something to do with that damn computer system. Could Foster be involved? Maybe.

Scott bent down and checked Thurber. She could tell from the knife cuts he'd been tortured. The poor man had really been put through it. Made her want to cry for these two people.

The anger built inside her. Who the hell did this? How did they know to come here? Then it dawned on her. The phone at David Garcia's house. Did she screw up by using that one? Should she have used her cell? Was her mistake responsible for the death of these two innocent people?

It took three minutes for a squad car to arrive, followed by an ambulance about four minutes later. Their sirens sounded, drawing Scott outside.

An orderly jumped out and slammed the vehicle door. "What ya got, Lieutenant?"

"Two adults, one male and one female, both in the back room of the clinic. Both dead."

The orderly hurried past her. "Sounds bad."

"Yep." Scott's morale had dropped to the floor. She'd get the squad to check the phone at Garcia's house, but she knew in her heart it had been tapped.

They started processing the site once the medical examiner arrived. While she went over everything at the clinic, one of the squads went over to the house.

Her cell rang. She didn't want to answer but she did. "Scott."

"Scott, it's Morrow. . ."

She shut her eyes. *Please don't let me be stupid and have caused these deaths.* "What did you find?"

"I took the receiver apart and sure enough, found the tap."

Scott lowered her head. What the hell had David Garcia gotten into?

Scott walked outside the clinic and pulled a business card out of her pocket. She pushed in Agent Harper's cell number.

"Harper."

"This is Lieutenant Scott. You asked me to tell you if I found anything at David Garcia's house that might figure into what Jensen had been looking for."

"Sure."

"I discovered that David Garcia and his wife spent time volunteering at the Bailey's Crossroads Veterinary Clinic. I called the vet around five o'clock to see if David might have left a package with him for safekeeping. He did."

There was silence for a moment. "Agent Harper?"

"I'm wondering what we should do."

"Wonder no more. I went over to pick it up."

"Great. What did you find?"

Scott walked around the end of the building to get away from the gathering crowd. "Two dead bodies."

"What?"

"Yeah, it looked to me like the vet had been tortured. The poor bastard had knife wounds over much of his body."

"My god."

"Yeah. Someone went over him long and hard, a real mess."

"How did they know . . .?

She couldn't stand still and started to pace. "Sounds as if you're getting it."

"Tapped Garcia's phone?"

"I've been kicking myself." She banged her hip with her fist. "I should have used my cell not their phone to call the vet."

"You couldn't have known."

"I'm not sure that's true, but it's a moot point anyway. The question is, what do we do now? We're obviously dealing with pros. And serious pros at that."

Silence.

"Agent Harper?"

"Now that's really interesting and . . . other things are starting to add up now."

"What are you talking about?" Scott asked.

"I don't think I can say anymore on an unsecured line."

"How about if we meet at my office?"

"I can be at your place in forty-five minutes."

"I'll be there. See you then."

Scott disconnected. She had to quit blaming herself for the murders. Focus on getting the bastard behind all of this. She headed for her truck. When she reached it, she called Colonel Garcia. Scott needed her involved, too.

———————

Samuel Foster took out his handkerchief and patted his forehead. Things were unraveling. If the FBI computer experts got their hands on the program, it would be all over for him. He couldn't let that happen. Not after all he'd done and he was so close. It wasn't fair.

He reached into his desk drawer and pulled out a black cell phone. Consulting the list next to the phone, he dialed a number. It rang twice.

A female voice answered in a hushed tone. "Yes."

Foster composed himself. "Lieutenant Scott with the Fairfax County Police Department is threatening to get a warrant to go over Red Dog."

"You can't let that happen. Get your goddamn lawyer. If he's any good, he'll be able to prevent anyone from looking at the program. Be prepared, Foster. You know, like the boy scouts." She laughed. "Now, pay attention, I have finalized an assignment for you."

Foster grabbed a pad of paper from his top desk drawer and retrieved a pen from his pocket. He took a deep breath to slow his pounding heart. *Couldn't make a mistake. Get the directions absolutely correct.* He'd made a mistake once in the past and he couldn't let it happen again.

"You must make sure the computer system is ready to take over management of the drone tomorrow afternoon at two o'clock. Do you understand me? Two o'clock."

Foster sat back. "But what about the FBI? And the warrant?"

"I'm not used to being questioned. Two o'clock."

"I understand."

A click and the phone went dead.

Foster murmured to himself, *why doesn't the boss realize how dangerous this is?* But that didn't matter. He had to do what the boss said or risk everything.

Placing the cell phone to be destroyed in a covered red box in the back of his desk drawer, he walked down the hall to Megan's office.

Alcott sat at her desk pushing in keys on her computer. She looked up when he entered. "Fucking Scott called me but I let it go to voice mail. Keep her away from me, I've got things to do. Now, what do you want? I'm trying to get some work done."

Foster cleared his throat and looked at his notes. "The boss wants you ready to strike tomorrow at two o'clock."

"Shit, I was going through the system to make sure I could wipe the code in a hurry if I had to."

Foster wiped sweat from his forehead again. "The boss says two o'clock."

Alcott smiled. "All right. Once I start the process, the military won't be able to control anything in their system unless I release it." She jumped up and gave Foster a kiss, then rubbed her body against him. "God, all this money makes me so damn excited."

Foster felt himself getting hard and backed away from her. He couldn't believe this woman. "I need to get back to my office to make a call."

Damn Alcott.

37

Cape May County Court House, New Jersey, Saturday, 7:45 p.m.

The ambulance stopped and the back door swung open. Two men in white uniforms helped Zack out of the vehicle, set up the wheels on the stretcher and whisked him through the emergency room entrance and down a long hallway. People sat in chairs in the waiting room, some looking at magazines, others with bored expressions on their faces watching him. The orderly pushed him into an examination room and two of them lifted him onto a table.

A nurse hurried in, leaned over him, and asked, "Where are you hurt?"

"A dog bit me in my right leg and I injured my wrist in a fall, but my injuries aren't as serious as the other two. Take care of them first." Zack leaned forward and whispered, "Look, I've got to get to a phone right away. It's critical."

The nurse squinted, stared at him for a moment. Then she began to cut the pants off his right leg. "We need to look at that leg. See how serious it is."

The doctor Zack had talked to earlier appeared next to her. He touched the nurse's arm. "He told me there's a plot against the president."

The nurse leaned back. "Didn't I see him on television a little while ago? I think he's going to Philadelphia tomorrow to make a speech at the Liberty Bell about all that's happened during the past few days."

The doctor whispered to the nurse, "Poor guy was on the boat that exploded. He's probably suffering from a concussion."

Zack overhead the doctor and tried to push himself up. "Look, I know it sounds crazy, but I think the president's life is in danger. I need a phone right now."

She smiled down at him. "It's going to be all right. I'll find a phone for you as soon as we get you and your friends fixed up."

This conversation was going nowhere. Zack rocked forward and tried to swing his legs off the bed, but he felt dizzy and fell back. Tried to get up again.

The nurse took his arm. "Look, stay down until we check you out. Then I'll find you a phone."

"You've got to help me. If you don't believe me, at least call Lieutenant Powell with the Sea Isle City Police Department. I've been working with her on the murders of the men found on the beach in Sea Isle. She'll know what to do. Please, it's critically important."

The doctor came in. "You've been through a lot and you need to rest now. Everything is going to be all right."

A pinprick in his arm and Zack's mind started to swirl. Darkness descended. He grabbed the nurse's arm. "Please, for god sakes, call Lieutenant Powell." He called out her cell phone number before all went black.

Samuel Foster made a U-turn and swung his van into the third overlook off the George Washington Parkway. Shutting off the engine, he looked at his watch. Seven forty-five, fifteen minutes early.

No other cars parked at the overlook, although a steady stream of traffic flowed by on the parkway from the normal Saturday evening crowds. Never seemed to stop. He had brought the company van so even if the cops watched his car, they wouldn't know his current location.

Foster leaned back in the seat and thought about his family. Maybe he should move west and make a fresh start. He had computer skills and experience. No money problems. Then a picture of Megan clouded his mind. Nude, smiling, walking toward him. He couldn't leave her. She did things for him no woman had ever done before. God, she was electric.

The sun began to set, its golden tentacles reflecting off the Potomac. The hum of traffic on the parkway diminished. Two cardinals flitted around in the cedar tree limbs above the stone wall lining the parking lot. They chirped and whistled.

His frustration grew. *What happened to the bitch? She said eight o'clock—now it was eight thirty. How long should he wait?* As he considered leaving, a car pulled in behind his van. The driver blinked her lights. Foster started to climb out of the van, but she motioned him back inside.

The woman opened the passenger side door of the van and slid inside.

"Where the hell have you been?" Foster yelled. "I've been sitting here since before eight o'clock waiting for you. I almost left. Maybe I should have."

She ignored his question. "Tell me exactly what needs to be done to bring down the system if we need to do it in an emergency. Give me details."

Foster shifted in his seat and focused on the figure in the trench coat sitting next to him. "These programs are complex and detailed. Once Megan sets the time bomb, she needs to let the threat play out. There's no way she can cancel the viruses until after the program runs its course. Then she can delete it and we'll be in the clear. I suspect it'll take about twelve hours to do everything. And the boss says we must begin the process at two o'clock tomorrow afternoon."

The woman, seeming to be thinking. "The system must be cleared before the cops get there or you're going down."

"If I go down, I won't be alone." Foster rubbed his forehead with the back of his wrist. "What does the boss say?"

"I shouldn't have to tell you. She wants the program set for six hours, then you've got to cover up what you've done. It's simple. You started on the right track and made her happy. Now there are a number of complications and rest assured, they don't set well at all."

"It's not my fault the cops may have figured out a link with Red Dog. What the hell am I supposed to do?"

"Is it fixable?"

"If someone who knows computer systems looks at Red Dog before we finish taking control of the drone control launch system, they'll spot the time bomb and the virus. No question they'll be able to backtrack and determine what we did."

"Are you sure?"

Foster almost shouted. "Yes, of course, I'm sure."

She looked out the window a moment then back at Foster. Shifting in her seat, she reached into her coat pocket. "I'm sorry to tell you, Foster, you're now collateral damage."

Samuel Foster found himself staring at the silencer on a pistol in the woman's right hand. "Wait a minute. What are you doing?"

"The boss told me I need to take care of any collateral damage and that's what I intend to do right now."

Foster heard a pop and felt a tearing blow into his cheek. Then darkness.

The woman pushed in a number on her speed dial.

A female voice answered on the second ring. "Yes."

"It's done."

"Good. We've eliminated the last link to us. Once we complete the program, we'll be in charge. Even if the cops uncover the system, which I don't see how they can, they won't be able to trace it back to us."

"What about David Garcia? He's out of the coma now and might be able to lead the police to us."

"You'll have to take care of him."

"I can't get to him. The room is under guard twenty-four hours a day."

"You have always figured these things out in the past. We've come this far. Don't fail me now." The woman laughed. "I'm going to call Alcott and make sure she's ready to move on with our plan. I've heard she's really sharp."

"Foster told me she's ready to implement at two o'clock to-morrow."

"Good." A click and a dial tone sounded in her ear.

She sat in her car. *How had she gotten in so deep?* But she knew the answer. Fucking men. Well, she'd finish this one last step, then she could move up in the government and fix all the things that are broken. Men, they'd better pay attention when she took over, or they would feel her wrath if they didn't. Yes, she'd soon be in charge.

38

Fort Eustis, VA, Sunday, 6:30 a.m.

Garcia stood along the wall about ten feet to the right of the main gate and glanced at her watch. Lieutenant Timothy Felter, the head of the Virginia State Police Bomb Squad, stood next to her, watching and talking into his microphone to one of his men. Anywhere from thirty to ninety minutes until show time if this bomber followed previous patterns.

When Felter got off his radio, Garcia turned to him. "The bomber has beaten security at three other bases and you know the death and destruction that caused. Guards didn't react quickly enough. We can't let that happen here."

Felter, a tall, well-built man, talked with an air of confidence. "We'll be ready."

Garcia hoped he was right. She'd been in a number of these situations and they never went according to plan. Murphy's Law always seemed to strike. She had placed Blake with three guards on the opposite side of the gate.

Garcia spoke into her microphone. "See anything yet?"

"All quiet on this side," Blake's voice came through the ear bud. "How about you?"

"Nothing so far."

Her head pounded and her leg throbbed from the fight at the garage. She had convinced her doctor to let her go back to work with the understanding that she would take care of herself and not do anything strenuous. He'd probably have a coronary if he saw her now. But she had to be here. Gotta stop the nightmare.

Blake seemed really tired, too. Almost missed the chopper. Well, hell, they were all beat.

Ignoring the dizziness and the aches, Garcia slipped down a little further behind the wall. She gambled the bomber would enter through the main gate of the post as the previous bombers had done at the other sites. Since the guards had orders to stop anyone suspicious, whether on foot or in a vehicle, no way this woman should get on post.

Twelve tactical operations team members had been airlifted in by helicopter three hours ago. She had deployed them to cover all of the entrances.

Soldiers encircled the post from the inside, partially hidden by trees. Military police cars idled at specific locations, waiting for her order to move. She'd told the officers to be alert, but to stay inside their cars until she notified them via radio.

She watched. Tapped her foot. Checked her watch. Watched some more. Didn't like to wait.

Time crept by, then it happened. Garcia's heart jumped and pounded in her chest when she spotted the woman in a trench coat. Focusing her binoculars, she studied the slender face and long black hair. Why was she walking and not planning to enter by car? Still a block away. How would she try and get on post?

Garcia whispered into the microphone. "Be alert. Suspect walking toward the gate on the north side of the street."

"Roger," Blake replied. "I see her."

She leaned over to Felter. "Look at her lips move, like she's saying a prayer. What do you think?"

"Do you see something that looks like a clicker in her right hand. I bet it's her."

Garcia spoke into the microphone again. "I'm going to give the woman another half block, then challenge her. Shoot to stop her, but not to kill. We need to be able to question her. All right, be ready."

"Roger," Blake replied.

Garcia held her breath, watching each step the woman took. Brushed sweat from her forehead. She couldn't be wrong stopping the woman. When the suspect came within twenty-five yards, Garcia stood and called to her, "I'm Colonel Garcia from the military police. I need to talk with you."

The woman turned toward Garcia as if in a trance. "Ah, are you talking to me?"

Garcia drew the pistol out of her holster. "Stop right there. Open your coat."

The woman stopped. She stared at Garcia, then started walking again.

Garcia's heart raced. What if she was wrong? Just a woman walking down the street. But in that trenchcoat buttoned all the way to her neck. Didn't think so. "Stop," Garcia called again.

The woman kept walking. Her lips moving, eyes locked dead ahead.

"I won't warn you again," Garcia called. "Stop and open your coat."

She called out. "This is for all those bastards who get away with raping women."

Garcia leaned forward, targeting the woman's legs with her Glock. Had to convince her to stop. Don't kill her. "I understand your concerns and only want to talk to you."

"Better stop her," Felter called. "She's getting close."

As Garcia took aim, three shots rang out from her left. The woman's body snapped up, then crumpled backward to the ground.

Felter and his team sprang into action. Two men moved out of the gate, lead shields blocking them from the woman. They reached the woman who lay prone on the ground, Felter behind them.

Garcia ran to the gate. Waited.

Felter motioned her forward as he opened the woman's coat. "She's dropped the detonator."

Garcia reached the woman and bent down. Saw a bullet hole on the left side of the woman's forehead. Felt for a pulse. None. Saw the bomb vest. Dammit. Why? Why would she do this?

Blake hurried up to Garcia and knelt down. She had her gun out, eyes wide. "Oh, god, I panicked when I saw her ready to push that trigger. Meant to hit her legs but she must have bent over. We'd have all gone up in that explosion."

Garcia couldn't believe it. They were only going to wound the bomber so they could interrogate her. But Blake may have been right. If they only wounded the woman, she may have been able to detonate the bomb.

It wouldn't help to jump all over Blake. Garcia had to take the hit for putting an inexperienced person in such a high-stress position. Shit. Shit. Shit.

———————

When Scott arrived at the hospital, David Garcia sat propped up in bed, holding his mother's hand. Scott walked over to the bed, nodded to Mrs. Garcia, then leaned down to David. "Hello, David, I'm Lieutenant Scott with the Fairfax Police Department."

David looked up at Scott, his eyes glassy. He opened them a little wider in reaction to her voice, but otherwise didn't acknowledge her presence.

"How's the patient doing?" Scott asked.

"Much better," Mrs. Garcia replied, a smile on her face. "So much better."

"Has he responded to any stimuli yet?"

"He moved his finger a couple of times when I asked him to, but not much else. I hope it wasn't only a reflex action." She stood and motioned for Scott to follow her to the window. "He still doesn't know about Soon, so please be careful what you say."

Scott didn't realize she knew about Soon. "Don't worry, I won't say anything." She walked back to the bed and smiled down at David, all the time wondering if his mother knew about the baby. "David, as I said before, my name is Lieutenant Scott. I'm with the Fairfax Police Department and investigating the incident when you were hit by the truck. I understand you're doing much better."

David watched Scott's face, but didn't respond.

Scott tried another tactic. "Do you remember working at Sterling Software?"

David frowned, then his eyes widened and his hand started to shake. He nodded, then nodded again.

Scott put her hand on David's arm. "It's all right. I don't want to scare you. I'm only wondering if you remember working at Sterling."

Mrs. Garcia clapped her hands. "He remembers. He remembers. Oh, that's wonderful."

Scott didn't want to push him, but based on what Harper had told her, lives could be on the line. Maybe even the president's life. "Do you remember a system named Red Dog?"

David continued to nod, his movements becoming more pronounced.

Scott leaned over the bed and looked closely at David. "This is important, David. What does the name Red Dog mean to you? Do you remember talking to your sister, Rene, about Red Dog?"

More nodding.

"Does the name Agent Frank Harper with the FBI mean anything to you?"

David leaned forward, the speed of the heart monitor beeps increasing. He opened his mouth and started to stutter. He grabbed Scott's hand and stammered out, "Stop them."

Mrs. Garcia reached over the bed to touch her son's shoulder. "It's all right, David. She glared at Scott. "Oh, you've upset him."

Scott kept watching David. "It's all right. I'll take care of it." She patted his hands. "It's going to be fine. You relax now. I'll take care of everything."

David settled back into his pillow, his mouth still trying to form words. One word sounded like "dron . . .."

Scott straightened. "Thank you, Mrs. Garcia, but I need to leave."

On her way down the hallway, she punched in the cell phone number for Garcia. In a moment she heard Garcia's voice. "It's Scott. I just left your brother's room. He seemed to remember Agent Harper. And get this, he said his first words when I asked him about Red Dog,"

"What did she say?" Garcia asked.

"Stop them."

"Oh, man, we gotta do something."

"On the way out, it sounded like he said something like the word, dron . . I couldn't understand anymore."

Garcia exhaled. "Could he have been trying to say drones. That's what General Harding's outfit works on. Do you think those bastards are going to try and hack in to the system controlling drones?"

"Agent Harper told me a little about General Harding's outfit." Scott thought about that for a moment. "That's enough for me. I'm going to a judge to get a warrant. Then it's off to Sterling to go through that place and see what I can find. It all fits."

"Let me know when you get the warrant," Garcia replied. "I'll join you if I can. For your information, we just killed a bomber at Fort Eustis."

"I thought you were only going to wound her so we could question her."

"I did too," Garcia replied, "but we fucked up. The president will be speaking later today at the Liberty Bell in Philadelphia. I'm worried he's the one they're after."

"Oh, shit. Wish me luck with the judge."

"Go get 'em. And Scott, keep me in the loop."

39

Cape May Court House Hospital, Sunday, 8:30 a.m.

Zack registered movement. Someone shaking his arm. He tried to focus, but his mind wouldn't respond. The shaking continued. Finally, he forced his eyes open.

Lieutenant Powell stood over him, concern written on her face. "Zack, can you hear me?"

Zack stared at her, forcing himself to concentrate. Powell. Damn, it's Max. Her voice echoed in his ears like she was speaking through a microphone. "Have I died? Are you an angel?"

She started to laugh. "Hey, great line, Kelly. You've been a busy boy. First I get a call about gunshots a block away from the Strathmere Inn, then I hear from the state police they have three dead bodies at the site. I'm on my way to check that out when a boat explodes and the Coast Guard gets the call."

Zack kept watching her, trying to sort out what she was saying. Gradual understanding came to him. So damn confusing, but it was good so see her.

"I arrived at the house and my team started to work with the state cops when I get a call from a nurse at the hospital. She told me this Zack Kelly guy is trying to get a hold of me. So in a moment, it all becomes clear." She smiled. "Someone has let Colonel Kelly loose in my community and he's made one hell of a mess. Am I accurate about that?"

"Ah, yeah," Zack stammered. "Guess that's pretty accurate. I'm trying to figure all this out."

"Zack, you were on a boat that collided with another boat and exploded."

His mind went back. "Sounds familiar."

"They brought you to the hospital here at Cape May Court House. You must have somehow impressed the nurse because she called and asked me if I knew who you were. That you needed to contact me."

"The damn doctor wouldn't believe me."

"I would have been here sooner, but I was on a conference call briefing for our governor. Unfortunately we don't know much. Happily, Sprite took most of the flack from the big guy."

Zack pulled himself up onto one elbow. His head felt as if it would blow out. "Thank heavens you're here. The doctor thought all my concerns about the president were from the concussion."

Max sat down in a chair next to the bed and crossed her leg. "He must have figured you were a nutzo." Another smile. "Which probably isn't too far from the truth. Maybe you'd like to share with me a little of what you've been doing to entertain yourself the last couple of days."

"Let me see if I can get my act together."

"Take your time, Zack. The doctor told me about your wrist and the dog bite. How are you feeling?"

"Like a train hit me and bounced me around. I'll try and be as coherent as possible. Here goes." He told her about eating at the Strathmere Inn with Wilson, noticing the women and driving to the house. "We were damn lucky to get out of that place alive."

"Sounds like it." She turned a page in her notebook. "What happened next?"

"I was able to convince the Dark Angel I wanted to work with her, so she agreed to release me if I would let her killer dogs in to attack T.J. and Caldwell. I had to watch her dogs kill one of her own people. Never seen anything like it and hope I never do again. God, it was awful."

"Caldwell?"

"Major Harrison Caldwell. We need to check his military file. I suspect he's had a problem with sexual abuse and that's why they were holding him prisoner. T.J. and I were able to get him out of there, but he's in pretty tough shape."

Max made a note. "Harrison Caldwell. Got it. Did you kill the Dark Angel?"

"I assumed the woman who seemed to be in charge was the Dark Angel. But as she lay there dying, she said the Dark Angel would get me." He shrugged. "Don't know for sure who she was, or if the Dark Angel is still alive."

"We'll get the ID on her and see if it's possible she could be the Dark Angel."

"I was able to escape and rescue T.J. and Caldwell from where the women held them captive. Three women chased us, but I turned our boat around to collide with them. Thankfully, theirs exploded and who knows what happened to the women on board."

"The Coast Guard is investigating the explosion. I haven't heard of any survivors. They'll want to talk with you. And the nurse told me you should take it easy for a day."

"Can't do that." Zack shook his head to clear it. "What's got me worried is that the president is speaking in Philadelphia on the Fourth of July. He's in danger there. What time is it?"

She glanced at her watch. "It's ten minutes after nine in the morning of the fourth."

Zack jerked up. "You've got to help me alert people."

She put her hand on his arm. "The nurse told me they're planning on evacuating Caldwell to a Philly hospital. The med evac helicopter will be leaving in about thirty minutes. I'll see if I can get you on it."

"That would be great."

"I suspect they'll make room for you, but not Wilson. That's okay cause I need to talk to him as soon as he's able. He can show me what happened at the house, then I'll turn him over to the Coast Guard." She smiled again. "He's going to be popular."

Zack sat up, swaying slightly and tried to move his legs.

She took his arm. "Be careful. Don't move too quickly."

"Where are my clothes?"

"The nurse told me they had to cut them off. I'll see if I can get you some blue scrubs."

Zack tried to stand and fell back on the bed, his head throbbing.

She hurried over to him. "Hey Zack, you've got to take it easy. The stuff the doctor gave you to knock you out will stay with you for a while."

"I just realized that."

Max opened a drawer and pulled out some scrubs. She tossed them to him. "Can you put these on?"

"I can sure as hell try."

"Okay. I'll check on Wilson and Caldwell, then I'll be back to see how you're doing." She turned back at the door. "Don't worry, I'll make sure they hold the chopper for you. You know, I'm a cop. Got some pull around here."

"I think Wilson's in the next room."

"I'll call on my super-sharp investigative skill." She hurried out of the room.

She did make him smile. Zack pushed himself up and began pulling on the scrubs. Max had set a pair of slippers on the floor next to the bed. He slipped his feet into them. The doctor had sutured and wrapped his leg, then put a splint on his wrist. Using the wall for balance, he took a few steps, finally making it to the hallway.

The sun shone through a window at the end of the hall, a perfect Fourth of July day. A number of staff hurried up and down the hallway, pushing carts, talking to one another. A man in blue scrubs stood three doors down, looking at a chart.

Lieutenant Powell stuck her head out of the room next to his. "In here."

He limped down the hallway, still balancing against the wall, his left leg refusing to move properly.

When Zack entered the room, Wilson sat on the bed, a glazed look in his eyes.

Zack took his arm. "Powell got me on a helicopter to Philadelphia. I think someone is going to try to kill the president when he makes his speech."

Wilson stood and began to weave, then fell back down onto the bed. He pushed up again.

"Take it easy, friend, you've been through a lot. We both need to move slowly."

"Here." Max handed Wilson a set of blue scrubs. "The nurse said she thought these would fit you. Big guy. One hell of a challenge."

She started out of the room.

"Wait," Zack whispered, "you've got the two stooges here. I don't think he can get into these scrubs without some help. More than I can do."

Max glanced at Wilson. "I'll help in any way I can."

Wilson managed a smile. "I apologize in advance for any disappointments."

"Don't worry," Max said. "I'm a cop. I've seen it all."

The two helped Wilson pull on scrubs.

"T.J.," Powell said, "you need to stay here and give me the details on what happened at the house. The Coast Guard will want to talk to you later today also."

"Let's get moving." Zack limped out into the hallway. The nurse pushed a wheelchair down the corridor.

"That's Caldwell," Powell said. "I need to talk to him, once he's better. His story will be helpful in determining what charges are filed and what we can prove. Hopefully he'll recognize some of those women."

When they got to the helipad outside the third floor, the blades of the chopper spun, kicking up dirt and gravel. The crew chief stood next to the chopper and shouted, "Can I help you climb on board? Once you two are belted in, we'll get going."

Max and the nurse helped Zack onto the chopper. Max patted him on the rear and whispered, "I thought you looked really cute in that open-back nighty back there in the hospital."

Zack laughed as he settled in a seat. "Yeah, right." He waved to Max and gave her a mock salute. "Let me know what you find at the house. I look forward to seeing you again when this is all over."

"Count on it." Max stepped back and blew him a kiss. "I'm going to check the records and see who owns that house."

The crew chief pulled the door shut and helped strap the two into their seats. The helicopter lifted up into the late morning sky. They flew parallel to the Garden State Parkway, circled past the beach, then headed northwest.

Zack leaned forward. "Do either of you have a cell phone?"

The crew chief pointed behind Zack. "Put on the headphones. We can patch you into the communications network."

Zack turned and grabbed the headphones.

"What number do you want?" the crew chief asked.

Zack gave him Garcia's cell number.

He listened as it rang. "Come on, Garcia," he whispered, "answer the damn phone. Answer it. Please."

It rang four times before he heard, "Garcia."

Her voice had to be the best sound he'd heard in a very long week. "It's Zack. Thank god you're there."

"I got a message from a Lieutenant Powell in Cape May, but she didn't answer when I called back. Where the hell have you been?"

"Probably because she was with me at the hospital. Just listen. T.J. and I have been held prisoner by the Dark Angel, but were able to get away yesterday afternoon. I thought I'd killed her, but now I'm not so sure."

A gasp from the other end of the phone. "The Dark Angel?"

"We've just lifted off from Cape May on a medevac chopper headed for Philadelphia. Wait a minute."

Zack motioned to the crew chief. "Where are we going?"

The crew chief switched his mike to the frequency with Zack. "What was your question, sir?"

"Where are we headed?"

"Philadelphia Memorial Hospital. We should be there in thirty-five minutes."

"Got it," Garcia said. "Let me update you on what's been going on. We stopped a bomber at Fort Eustis, an Army Specialist four by the name of Sandra Johnson. Unfortunately, Blake shot and killed her so we didn't get a chance to interrogate her."

"Oh, man," Zack said, "that's a shame."

"Yeah, Blake panicked when she saw the woman trying to activate the bomb and killed her. My error."

Zack blew out a breath. "Can't go back. Say, would you check and see if this Johnson worked for an Air Force Major Harrison Caldwell? T.J. and I rescued him at the hell hole in Strathmere, New Jersey, just north of Sea Isle."

"I haven't had a chance to check out Johnson yet, but since she's Army, they may not have come in contact."

"Well, check Caldwell and see if you can find out any reason why he crossed the Dark Angel. I suspect he must have done something to warrant her ire."

"Will do. I'm working with Lieutenant Scott on getting a warrant to examine the computer system at Sterling. Blake and Admiral Steele are up in Philly. I'll call them and tell them you're on the way and ask them to meet you at the hospital pad. They can provide you more details on everything that's happening here. Been busy."

"How's your brother?" Zack asked.

"That's the good news. He woke up yesterday and seems to be getting better as time goes on."

"That's great," Zack replied. "Keep me posted on what you find out about Caldwell. He's on the medevac with me. Pretty screwed up so they evacuated him to the hospital in Philly."

"Okay. Glad you're out of there."

"Damn straight. Me too."

Zack disconnected and leaned back, watching the sun shining over the water. It was one of the most beautiful sights he'd seen in a long time.

Then it dawned on him. Laura. He motioned to the crew chief. "I need to make another call."

"Go ahead, sir. You're still on the network."

Zack gave him the number. After four rings, a female voice said, "Hello."

Dammit. Ellen. "It's Zack. What are you doing there? I thought you were headed back to Minnesota."

"I had to stay. You disappeared on Laura."

"Let me talk to her."

"I don't know if she'll talk to you. She's pretty upset. Said you had plans for the Fourth."

He didn't have time for this. "Damn it, put her on."

"Oh, my, yes sir."

Zack needed to settle down. Laura had every right to be pissed. "Hello."

"Hi Laura, it's me."

"Yeah."

"I know you're upset, but I can explain."

"Yeah, whatever. Mom tells me you used to do this all the time."

Damn Ellen. "Look honey, I'm on a helicopter headed toward Philadelphia. I'll call you again as soon as I can."

"Whatever."

A dial tone. He motioned for the crew chief to disconnect and leaned back. *Damn Ellen. Filling Laura's head with crap.* But he did let her down. When he had a chance to explain, she'd understand. Wouldn't she?

40

Philadelphia, Sunday, 1:00 p.m.

As the helicopter dipped toward the pad, Zack glanced out the side window. Blue and red lights twirled on a multitude of vehicles below, most of them military.

When the chopper bumped down, the crew chief pulled the door open and jumped to the ground. Blake Lannigan ducked down and hurried over to the chopper. Admiral Steele stayed back a little, holding onto his hat.

Zack had never been happier to see two people in his life.

Behind Blake, drivers and orderlies stood in front of army ambulances, stretchers between them. Zack lifted his legs over the side of the chopper and gingerly stepped to the pavement. His wrist throbbed, his leg burned and the bruises hurt like hell, but he couldn't worry about any of that now. Help had arrived and he had things to do.

Blake ran over and gave him a hug. "Are you all right? Do you need a doctor? A stretcher?"

He winced.

"Oh no, did I hurt you?"

"Nah, the hug felt good. I'm not too bad, but Major Caldwell needs help. Lots of help."

Blake patted his good arm. "We've got a couple of medical teams here. One of them can take Caldwell to the hospital. Can you move around? Do you need a wheelchair?"

Zack shook his head. "Lieutenant Powell has a team up at the house in Strathmere where we were held captive and T.J. stayed with her. I'm not sure how long the Dark Angel held Caldwell. Once he's cleared medically, Powell wants to talk with him. I also talked to Garcia on the phone and asked her to see if Caldwell has any sexual assault charges against him."

"Got it." Blake motioned with her hand. One of the pairs of orderlies ran up to the side door of the chopper, pushing the stretcher between them. "She probably told you I panicked and shot the bomber at Fort Eustis. An army specialist named Johnson. Feel like shit about my mistake."

"Shake it off. Mistakes happen to everyone. There are a number of bullets I wish I could have back. Do you know if Johnson had sworn out any charges against Caldwell? Maybe that's the tie."

"Not yet, but we're checking that out now."

"I had a tough time convincing the medical staff in New Jersey of the possible danger to the president. They thought my head was all screwed up from the explosion on the boat."

She laughed. "Which may have been the truth."

Zack had to smile. "Yeah, but thankfully, the nurse did get things moving by calling Lieutenant Powell."

Blake wrapped her hand in Zack's good arm to help him walk. "Admiral Steele figured we'd better only use soldiers until we know who we could trust." She pulled out her cell phone. "Let me check with Lieutenant Powell and see how things are coming at the house."

Zack moved out of the way of the orderlies as they wheeled Caldwell away from the chopper. "Take good care of him, Doc."

One of the two orderlies waved over his head as they pushed the stretcher toward the waiting ambulance. Four military Humvees surrounded the ambulance. Soldiers stood in the hatches, weapons pointing away from the ambulance, covering all approaches in case someone tried again to kill Caldwell.

Admiral Steele walked over to Zack, the medals on his dress uniform sparkling in the late morning sun. "Welcome back."

Zack gave him a salute. "Thanks, sir. Believe me, it's good to be back."

The admiral put his hand on Zack's shoulder. "Can you walk?"

"Yes sir, but slowly."

"Okay. Come on, let's get away from this chopper so I can hear what happened. I called the presidents' chief of staff and told him you were here and I would update him later once I knew more."

Zack followed the admiral across the tarmac with the aid of the cane the crew chief gave him, his leg bending a little as he stepped.

Admiral Steele noticed the limp and the cane. "Are you sure you're okay?"

"I'm one hell of a lot better now than in that house in New Jersey."

Steele leaned over to whisper, "I'll need a complete update from you on what happened, but just a summary now."

"I don't know all that's going on," Zack said, "but I'm convinced we need to get to the president right away. I honestly believe someone is going to try to kill him. We need to advise the president without tipping anyone working for the Dark Angel." He thought for a moment. "Course, they already know we escaped from the house in New Jersey."

"I've arranged for us to meet with Director Burnside as soon as he arrives. He's on his way to Philadelphia by chopper as we speak." Steele looked at his watch. "We'll meet him at the courthouse in about thirty minutes."

The admiral glanced at Zack. "We need to get you into some other clothes. Hopefully we can find some inside the hospital. A quick change and we'll be on our way."

"How about a cell phone and a Glock. I feel naked without them."

Steele nodded. "Shouldn't be a problem."

Zack watched the medics loaded Caldwell on board the ambulance. "Blake is coordinating with Lieutenant Powell to get all the information she needs to bring in the FBI and Homeland Security. Don't want any of those killers to get away."

"She told me," Admiral Steele replied. "We need to convince Director Burnside of the possible threat to the president."

Zack followed Steele toward the hospital. "And I sure hope we're not too late to stop it."

Rene Garcia sat at her desk, staring at the electronic copies of the two service records the personnel staff had sent over. The first one belonged to Specialist Fourth Class Sandra Johnson, the bomber at Fort Eustis. Johnson had left the Army after unsuccessfully making a sexual harassment complaint against her supervisor, Master Sergeant Grady Sullivan. Sullivan claimed the complaint to be a misunderstanding and charges were never brought against him.

Garcia called and asked the battalion commander, Colonel Henning, about Johnson.

"Specialist Johnson appeared to be career army all the way, having come from a military family," Henning said. "She worked on my headquarters operations staff and I really liked her. Efficient as hell. But, after the army dropped her complaint against Sergeant Sullivan for lack of evidence, she seemed to lose interest in everything and began to get in trouble. Small things. Sloppy work, picking fights, stuff like that. She left the army at the end of her first tour."

"What about Sullivan?" Garcia asked.

"A good soldier and a strong supervisor. Other than Johnson's complaint, I never heard of any problems in his section. Although I remained a little uneasy about the relationship between Johnson and Sullivan. They worked well together and it surprised me when she lodged the complaint."

Garcia told him what happened. "The police shot and killed Specialist Johnson this morning to prevent her from setting off a bomb at Fort Eustis."

"Johnson associated with this Dark Angel business? I find that hard to believe."

"Well believe it," Garcia replied. "It just happened."

"Oh, man, I feel awful. If I missed something that brought this on, I'll never forgive myself."

Garcia wondered if he had. "It's possible if you'd checked a little more carefully, you might have found the truth about her complaint. I have to hang up now, Colonel."

She slammed down the phone. Another good soldier dead and maybe because the system had failed her.

Garcia picked up Caldwell's file. His latest assignment had been to Creech Air Force Base. Why did that ring a bell? Hell, that's the base where the drone program is located. She wondered if General Harding knew him. Paging through the file, his efficiency reports showed an average officer who managed an operational portion of the drone program. On his latest report, he received an unsatisfactory rating in getting along with others. What was that all about?

Garcia grabbed the phone and dialed the number for General Harding.

When the sergeant major answered, Garcia asked to talk to Harding.

"She's in a meeting," the sergeant major replied.

"Please get her out," Garcia said. "This could be critical."

In a moment, she heard, "This is General Harding. What may I do for you Colonel Garcia?"

Garcia told her about the rescue of Harrison Caldwell and the entry in his file. "What can you tell me about him?"

"Let me think a minute," Harding replied. "Let's see. Overall, Harrison seemed to be a good officer, but he did get in trouble over a sexual abuse problem. I remember the case well. An air force sergeant named Emily Kine alleged he had been sexually abusive to her. The two worked together in the drone program. She claimed he'd made a number of unwanted advances, then one day tried to rape her."

"Were charges ever filed?" Garcia asked, glancing at her watch. Time was getting away from her.

"Yes, and the file came to me as court martial convening authority. This is another case of one person's word against another. There were no witnesses and no DNA evidence. Eventually I had to drop the charges."

"Damn. Can you check and let me know where Kline is now?"

"You think she could be involved in the Dark Angel thing?"

"It's certainly possible. Zack Kelly just freed Caldwell from the Dark Angel."

"I'll call the unit right now and get back to you."

"Please hurry," Garcia replied. "Time is critical." She texted the information to Blake.

Megan Alcott checked her watch again. Two o'clock. She reached for the cell phone she'd retrieved from Foster's office and pushed in the first number on the list. Alcott's heart beat rapidly as she waited. *This had to be the boss. Her big chance. Don't screw it up.*

It rang twice, then a female voice came on the line. "Yes."

Alcott cleared her throat and wiped a bead of perspiration from her face. "This is Megan Alcott at Sterling Software. Samuel Foster isn't here. I'm calling you myself."

"What do you need?"

"I'm ready to block the communications control system at the launch site, but I haven't been told how long to keep it on."

"I need it blocked for six hours."

Megan tried to contain her excitement. "Maybe we could meet after this mission. I've never met you and would like to talk to you face to face."

A pause. Breathing. "Wait until this is over. Then we'll talk. I've heard you are an intelligent woman. I may have an opening in my new organization for someone with your skills. Don't forget to call me at the end of six hours before you leave your office."

"You can depend on me."

Disconnecting the call, she placed the cell phone in the red discard box. Her fingers tingling from the excitement, she followed the written instructions to block any outside communications to the launch system. It took about thirty minutes to complete the checklist.

Heaving a sigh of relief, she walked over to her closet and pulled out two small boxes hidden under a blanket in the back. One box held a set of false IDs – passports, credit cards and an extra driver's license. The other box contained two wigs, one black and one red, plus another untraceable cell phone.

Smiling at her foresight, she hurried back to her desk. She'd show those bastards. No one would ever take her for granted again.

41

Philadelphia, Pa, Sunday, 2:25 p.m.

When they arrived at the Federal courthouse, Zack, Blake, and Admiral Steele hurried up the steps and entered the front door. An agent escorted them along the tiled hallway to a conference room. Two agents stood guard at the door.

Steele flashed his ID. One of the agents, a burly man with black hair, checked his identification, then pushed the door open.

FBI Director Burnside sat at the head of the conference table, Agents Harper and Fairchild to his left.

Burnside rose when they entered. "Hello, Admiral Steele. I understand you have something critical to talk to me about." He nodded at Zack and Blake.

Admiral Steele sat and motioned for Blake and Zack to join him at the table. "You know Colonel Kelly and Blake Lannigan. Zack, please summarize for the Director what you know."

"Director Burnside," Zack began, "I arrived in the small town of Strathmere, New Jersey, two days ago with another officer from our task group to see if we could find the Dark Angel. I was able to locate the house where I thought the Dark Angel might be holding one of the hostages."

"Did you call for back up?" Burnside asked.

Uh, oh, Zack thought, *may have screwed up.* "There wasn't time. If we didn't move, they could kill the hostages, then escape."

"I see. What happened next?"

He explained being held as a captive. The director grimaced when Zack described the two dogs killing the woman. "Major Wilson and I rescued a severely beaten air force major by the name of Harrison Caldwell. He's been transferred to a hospital here in Philadelphia."

"Do we have him under guard?" Burnside asked.

"Yes," Admiral Steele replied. "I have a team of MPs watching him."

Zack figured he might as well go for it. "Sir, we managed to escape, but I believe someone is planning to kill the president when he arrives here in Philadelphia."

Burnside's eyes widened. "Philadelphia? Why Philadelphia?"

"You know the Dark Angel has been killing officers and tattooing her name on their chests."

"Kelly, please keep this moving," Burnside said. "I don't need to hear things I already know."

"Yes, sir. We tracked the four explosion sites – Army War College, Naval War College, Great Lakes Naval Base, and Fort Eustis. We anticipated Fort Eustis because the first three are the first letters in angel—a— n – g – and Eustis adds the 'e'. Plus Eustis is close to D.C. Our concern is that the last letter is 'L' and that could be the Liberty Bell where the president is speaking later today."

"You can't be serious," Agent Fairchild broke in. "You really think the Dark Angel will try and get to the president here because of an 'l' in her name? I'm sorry, but that's ridiculous."

"It's something we have to consider," Zack replied. "It may well be the president's life is at risk and I recommend we ask him to not speak here this evening."

"That's an easy one," Burnside said. "He won't change his plans. I talked to him about the potential risks of speaking in Philadelphia to a large group with all the explosions and he's determined. He believes not showing up will make him look weak at a time when the country needs strength and leadership."

Admiral Steele leaned forward. "I understand the president's concerns about looking weak, but we must at least talk to him about it. The Dark Angel has shown herself to be resourceful and willing to take chances."

Burnside took a sip of his coffee. "The president will say that's what he has a Secret Service for. To protect him from nut cases like the Dark Angel."

"While I don't think the spelling of her name is a reason for the president to change his plans," Fairchild said, "it's very dangerous to believe the Dark Angel is a nut case. We all know the problems our country is having with sexual abuse of females, particularly in the military."

Burnside held up his hands. "I'm perfectly aware of the reasons this Dark Angel is killing these officers and setting off explosions, but you can't defend killing people for what seems to be her cause."

"Well," Fairchild replied, "she certainly has our attention. Some were actually involved in the abuse."

"That's true," Blake said. "The Dark Angel has achieved her purpose of bringing focus to the issue. Just think if she is able to stop the president from speaking or worse yet, kills him."

"I understand what you're saying," Burnside said, "but he's not going to change his mind."

"My other concern," Zack said, "is this plot could involve the highest levels of government. This Dark Angel seems to be aware of what we're doing. We may have a mole." He talked about Sterling and their possible efforts to hack into the DOD computer systems.

"I agree with Zack," Admiral Steele said. "As a minimum we should advise the president of our concerns. The secret service is good, but not infallible."

Burnside stared at Admiral Steele, then at Zack, tapping his fingers on the table. "All right, what do you suggest?"

"Contact him on Air Force One," Zack said, "and share our concerns with him. We owe him that. If he decides to go ahead, then that's his decision."

"It's better if I talk with him face-to-face. I'll meet him at the Liberty Bell and see what he has to say."

Oh, shit, Zack thought, *that's going to be too damn late.*

———————

Air Force One angled slowly out of the sky on a trajectory toward Philadelphia International Airport. All of the air traffic in the skies around Philadelphia had been placed on hold to allow the Boeing 747 to land without interference.

President Sheldon Bradford leaned back in one of the two spacious leather chairs in his personal office and talked to his chief of staff, Richard Pearson. "I'm trying to make sure I've got the right tone for this speech."

"You do, sir. We've acknowledged all those who have died in the last three days and emphasized the sacrifice of our soldiers and their families. Don't forget the families. Many of them will be in the audience as well as watching you on television. People need to hear from you at this time of crisis. It's the perfect Fourth of July speech."

"Do you think eight o'clock is too late?" Bradford asked. "We're past prime time."

"I would have preferred we schedule it a little earlier, but with all of the conflicts, this is the best we could do."

The press secretary opened the door and looked into the lounge. "Sir, we're close to final approach. Do you want to come back and greet the press? Hand out a copy of your speech and give them a scoop on what you're going to say? It'll help put their stories together."

Bradford stood and reached for his coat. "Good idea. I was just telling the chief that I wished the speech could have been a little earlier to catch more of the prime time audience."

"It's a holiday night, Mr. President, so people will be celebrating. They should be inside from their picnics by the time you give your speech and they can watch the fireworks later. You'll actually have a bigger audience than if we had scheduled it earlier."

Bradford pulled his coat tighter to hide his slight paunch, which had been growing over the past six months. "Too many damn state dinners. I need to cut back on what I eat."

The press secretary opened the door for the president and the two made their way past the staff compartment. They both greeted his senior military advisors who were dressed in their dress uniforms and walked back to the compartment where approximately two dozen members of the White House press corps awaited him.

The press secretary opened the door. "Ladies and Gentlemen, the President of the United States."

As the president walked into the room, the reporters rose from their seats.

Bradford liked the members of the White House press corps and knew how important they were to a successful presidency. "Good evening, everyone. Please be seated. I hope you enjoyed our short ride. We'll be on the ground in a few minutes. I thought I'd share with you a little of what I plan to say to our audience tonight during this time of crisis in our country."

Garcia tapped her fingers on her desk and kept looking at her watch. Goddamn, where was the general? Doesn't she realize we're on a deadline?

Her phone rang and she pushed the button.

"We have a problem," Harding said. "Actually two problems. Specialist Kline has gone AWOL and no one has any idea where she is. More importantly, we've lost control of our computer system. It's blocked."

"How the hell long has that been going on?" Garcia asked.

"I'm told it went down at 2:28 p.m. That's a little under three hours ago."

"And you're just finding out about it now?"

"Oh, no, we've been working on it. I've called all of our techs in to solve the problem."

"Is it possible Sterling has done something to take control?" Garcia asked.

"I wouldn't think so, but I don't know. With the computer system down, we have no idea what the status is of our inventory. My staff is working with Megan Alcott to get it back on line, but so far without success."

David's warning rang in her ears. "This is exactly what my brother told us might happen. We assumed Sterling would go after money. Now I'm worried the Dark Angel is going to use that system for her purpose." Another flash hit her. "Shit, would she be going after the president tonight? What is the status of all those drones?"

General Harding sucked in her breath. "Oh, my god. What have we done?"

"Okay," Garcia said, "let's think this through. I need to alert Admiral Steele so he can get to the president. But what about all those people at the site? Could the Dark Angel really do this?"

"We need to stay calm and think," the general replied. "You contact Admiral Steele and alert him to the problem, I'll get back into what's going on with the computers in our research center. It may be a coincidence."

"General, I don't believe in coincidences. After I talk to the admiral, I'm going to drive out to Sterling. Lieutenant Scott is trying to get a warrant to go through that place. If I remember right, the president is due to speak at eight o'clock."

"Good luck. I'll keep my phone line open so we can stay in touch."

"I forgot to ask, what is Kline's job?"

Harding gulped. "She is one of our top drone flight controllers."

"What kind of threat does this pose if she has control of a drone?" Garcia asked.

"The Predator is an unmanned area vehicle used primarily by the Air Force and the CIA for reconnaissance and forward observation roles. The system carries cameras and other sensors."

"I know that, General. What about the weapons system?"

Garcia waited for a moment. "Hey, are you there?"

"Ah, the Predator has been upgraded to carry and fire two AGM 114 Hellfire missiles."

"Oh, shit, could she have that capability?"

"I won't know until we can get our system on line," the general replied, "but it's possible."

"Oh, man, I gotta call Admiral Steele."

"I'm going to get into the middle of this one and will update you as I find out more."

Garcia hung up. Why the hell wasn't Harding in the middle of it before? She dialed Zack's phone and got voice mail. Damn, probably had it taken away in New Jersey. Called Blake. More voice mail. Why the hell didn't Blake have her phone on?

She ran out the door, pushing in the number for Lieutenant Scott.

42

Fairfax, VA, Sunday, 6:50 p.m.

Garcia barreled down Arlington Boulevard, the siren on her military police staff car leading the way, a light mist spattering her windshield. Why couldn't she contact Blake? Blake always has her cell on. She needed to alert her to this threat that now seemed so clear. Dammit Blake. Answer.

If Kline had control of that system, she might be able to fire a drone into Philadelphia during the president's speech at the Liberty Bell. God, what a nightmare. She had to get to Sterling and see for herself what was happening.

Garcia came within a couple of inches of sideswiping a Hummer that didn't get out of her way when she turned right onto Route Seven from Arlington Boulevard at Seven Corners. She pressed down on the accelerator. Double checked the GPS. Seven minutes away.

The mist reflected light off the pavement, making it more difficult to see. She squinted through the windshield and spotted the sign for Sterling Software to her right.

Her car squealed into the parking lot, nearly brushing one of the three parked cars. She screeched to a stop in front of the building and kept the flashing blue light swirling on the top. Jumping out, she raced to the front door. Stop this madness.

When Garcia hurried into the lobby, the guard glanced up at her, startled. "I'd like to see Foster right away." She flashed her badge. "This is a police emergency."

The guard, a tired-looking black man in a navy-blue uniform with a name tag that read Simpson, stood. "Excuse me. Your name is?"

"Lieutenant Colonel Garcia, military police. Please hurry. It's imperative I see Mr. Foster right away. Is he here?"

The guard checked the sign out roster. "Mr. Foster isn't here and I don't expect him back today. You know it's a holiday."

"How about a Ms. Alcott? Is she here?"

"I'm afraid I can't give you any information without clearance from my supervisor even if you are the police. Mr. Foster is very concerned about security."

Garcia leaned across the desk again and grabbed the company roster. "I understand your concerns, but I can't wait for Mr. Foster. How about if I check myself."

Simpson put his hand on Garcia's arm. "See here, you can't do this. I'm going to call 911." He reached for the phone. "You can't bully your way past me. I've got my orders."

Garcia skimmed through the roster. "Simpson, I am the police. All I want to do is talk to someone."

"Young lady, you're in enough trouble already. Please step back while I call."

Garcia bit her tongue to keep from lashing out anymore. "Simpson, this is an emergency. You've got to tell me where I can find the person in charge of Red Dog. Please help me. It's critically important."

The guard shrugged. "All right. Ms Alcott is in the third office on the left. But I have to call and let her know you're here."

"She's here? Working? Now?"

He nodded.

Garcia started around the desk. "Don't bother to call her. She probably knows someone will be coming."

"I'm still making that other call."

"Do it. Ask for Lieutenant Scott. Tell her I need back up."

Air Force One taxied up to the red carpet that led to the welcome area. Flags adorned the platform and a host of local VIPs waited for the president. Snipers on the roof of the terminal kept an eye on the crowd.

The presidential motorcade consisted of two black limousines, a communications van, counter assault troops, a bus for the press corps, a vehicle for White House staffers, a medical unit, as well as vehicles for photographers, military aides and the Secret Service.

Three Secret Service agents stood at attention next to his bullet-proof limousine.

Once the 747 stopped and the door opened, the governor of Pennsylvania and the mayor of Philadelphia stepped forward. They waited at the foot of the ramp.

President Bradford stepped out and waved to the cheering crowd. As he walked down the stairs, the cheering increased in intensity.

The governor extended his hand. "Welcome to Pennsylvania, Mr. President. We want you to know that we're behind you in this time of crisis."

"Thank you. I'm glad to be here on this Fourth of July evening. Thank you for your support."

The governor turned. "I believe you know the mayor of Philadelphia."

The president extended his hand. "I certainly do. You were very helpful during my campaign. Your efforts helped me to be standing here."

The mayor shook the president's hand. "Mr. President, your car is waiting. We'll go directly to the site of your speech."

"That's my understanding," Bradford replied. "Let's go."

The president took a minute to walk over to the line of people standing behind the ropes where, accompanied by anxious-looking agents, he shook hands and waved to the rest of the crowd.

The Secret Service formed a cordon around the president as he stepped into the waiting limousine. With the sound of sirens and screeching tires, the motorcade swept off into the early evening dusk.

43

Sterling Software, Fairfax, VA, Sunday, 7:05 p.m.

Garcia hurried down the hall, glancing at her watch. Time had to be running out. No waiting for backup. She shuddered to think of the consequences.

Her footsteps echoed in the night-time stillness. All the office doors closed and locked. Only the security lights glowed in the long corridor.

She stopped. Listened. No voices or movement anywhere. Well, what the hell did she expect? A holiday evening.

Reaching the third door on the left, she turned the knob and pushed on it. Locked. She banged on the door. "Ms. Alcott, this is Colonel Garcia with the Military Police. I need to talk with you. Open this door. Right now."

No response. She pounded again. It sounded like a radio playing from inside the office. "Alcott, open this door." She pushed on the door. Must be hardwood. Could she bust it down? No way in hell. Time for a little breaking and entering.

She pulled a credit card out of her wallet and slid it between the door and the frame. Thankfully, no deadbolt. Jiggling the card, she felt the catch move. At the same time she pushed against the door as hard as she could. Keeping the card in place and jiggling it, she put all of her weight against the door and pushed it open.

A small office, typical spread. Desk with computer, a conference table with four chairs, three drawer file cabinet, and a two-person couch.

A woman with long blond hair sat at the desk. She glanced up at Garcia. "Get out of my office." She turned back to her computer, but didn't stop typing.

Garcia flashed her badge. "Megan Alcott, I'm Colonel Garcia with the Military Police. Please stop what you're doing. I need to talk with you."

The woman didn't turn again, kept typing.

Garcia stepped up behind Alcott, grabbed her shoulder. "Move away from the computer, Alcott. Stop right now."

Alcott turned, screamed, "I don't know you. You can't barge in here. I've got work to do. If you don't leave, I'll call security and they'll throw your ass out."

Garcia grabbed Alcott's shoulders to pull her away from the desk.

Alcott whirled, knocking Garcia's arm away. "Get your fucking hands off me, you clown."

Surprised, Garcia fell backward and tripped over the waste basket next to Alcott's desk, barely catching herself.

She swung her arm and slapped Alcott on the side of her face, pushing her aside. Alcott fell to the floor, hair astray.

She looked up at Garcia, laughing. "You can't stop me now. No one can stop me. Do you hear me? Never again."

Garcia's hands clenched. "Tell me how to stop this program, you bitch, or I'll really hurt you."

Alcott laughed. "Fuck off. When the program is completed, it'll self-destruct." She leaned back on her elbows and laughed again. "You'll never prove a damn thing. You're finished. Give it up."

Garcia pushed in the speed dial on her cell phone for Scott. "Scott."

"Garcia. I'm in the computer room at Sterling. Where are you?"

"I had to go to the station to pick up the warrant and our computer guys. We're about twelve minutes out."

Garcia looked back to see Alcott sitting on the floor. "Alcott's off her computer, but she won't stop the program. Says it will self destruct when she's finished. I need those computer guys if we've got a chance to stop this thing. Need them now."

"We're hurrying."

"Dammit, we don't have time." Garcia glanced over at Alcott. Still on the floor.

"Work on her. I'll be there as fast as I can."

Sirens sounded through the phone. Garcia disconnected.

———————

The siren screamed as Scott and the two computer experts raced toward Sterling Software.

Her driver turned left onto Columbia Pike. Two minutes to Arlington Boulevard, then four minutes before they reached Bridge Lane.

"Goddamn," Scott called, "Seven minutes to Sterling. Push this thing, we gotta get there."

"I'm going as fast as I dare on this wet pavement."

She turned back to the computer guys. "Once you get there, you've got to figure a way to stop that program." She explained what she knew, which wasn't much. "Come on, give this damn thing the gas."

———————

Garcia turned to Alcott. "Listen, please listen to me. If by some chance, Specialist Kline can get possession of a drone, your actions could result in the death of innocent people. If she launches that drone, not only will the president die, but also hundreds who happen to be near the Liberty Bell listening to him. You've got to stop this madness."

Alcott's eyes glistened. A smile lit her face. "Fuck you."

Garcia sat down at Alcott's computer. She didn't know where to start. Would Scott get here in time with the computer geeks?

"Get away from my computer," Alcott screamed. "It's mine. Mine."

Garcia turned. Alcott stood behind her, smiling and pointing a .38 at her. She measured the distance to Alcott, probably fifteen feet. No way could she knock the gun out of her hand before the bitch had a chance to fire.

"Alcott, think of all those people. For God's sake, don't do this. You've proved your point. You're a brilliant software engineer. Give those people a break."

Alcott laughed. "No one ever gave me a break. They don't care about me. Why should I give a shit about them?"

Garcia knew it was hopeless but she had to try again. Find the right message. "They're people, Alcott, real live breathing people. Not only adults, but children, babies."

The pistol shook. "Screw them. I earned everything I've got. Put up with dumb shits like Foster manhandling me time and time again. Outsmarted all of them. Don't talk to me about giving anyone a break. The hell with them. I'm going to get out of here and cash in. Now, move away from my computer. Don't make me shoot. Make no mistake, I will."

Frustration welled up inside of Garcia. *So close.*

44

Philadelphia, Sunday, 7:30 p.m.

The staff car sped east on Interstate 676, the siren allowing them to maneuver through the traffic jams. Blake sat in the front seat next to the sergeant who was driving. Zack and Director Burnside rode in the back.

Blake took out her cell and checked for messages. Saw the four voice mails from Garcia and called her.

"Where have you been?" Garcia yelled. "I've been trying to get a hold of you for thirty minutes. I'm in Alcott's office and she's got a gun pointed at me. I'm lucky she hasn't shot me."

"Oh, no."

"Yes, listen to me. Get the president out of there and clear that area. Harrison Caldwell worked at the drone site in Mississippi. A Specialist Emily Kline is AWOL. They can't account for all the drones. One of them may be armed with Hellfire missiles. Blake, I'm here at Sterling and Alcott's computer may have allowed Kline to take over the launch computer. Alcott won't stop the system. Gotta go. She's threatening to shoot."

"Garcia," Blake called into the phone but only heard static. She told Zack and Burnside what Garcia had said.

"We've got to get the president out of here right now," Burnside called, "I'll get agents on their way to Sterling."

"Get them there, fast," Zack called. "And we need to clear the audience at the Liberty Bell."

"I have to notify my people and the Secret Service." Burnside punched in keys on his cell phone, advising his staff of the emergency.

The driver switched lanes, greeted by the blaring horn of a garbage truck. "Goddamn Philly drivers," the driver muttered.

"We need to find the president as soon as we get there," Burnside said. "He won't stop for a phone call and I doubt he'll let the Secret Service interfere."

"I've got a complete schedule," Blake replied. "The president should be arriving in a few minutes. He's due to address the crowd at eight o'clock."

Zack looked at his watch. "Seven thirty-five. We haven't much time."

"His speech is to last twenty minutes," Blake continued, "then they'll start the fireworks on the mall. The president is scheduled to depart after greeting VIPs. He'll head to the airport at nine o'clock where Air Force One will take him back to D.C."

Burnside sat quiet for a moment. "We must meet the president as he arrives. I've got to convince him the threat is real. How are we to prevent a panic?"

"The answer is," Zack said, "we can't. But the president, the Secret Service can get him out of here."

"Unfortunately he thinks I'm an alarmist after all of my concerns about his safety. I have alerted Agents Harper and Fairchild to check for anything suspicious and coordinate with the Secret Service. Fairchild is former Secret Service so she will be in charge of that part of it."

Something about Fairchild bothered Zack. Maybe her attitude. "In addition to the drone strike, the Dark Angel may have assassins or bombers on the ground here. It'll be like checking for the proverbial needle in a haystack." Zack searched his mind. *What was working on him?* A thought he needed to come up with. He closed his eyes. Tried to visualize. Nothing.

The driver curved off Highway 676 and onto Sixth Street, slowing to a crawl even with the siren blaring. Police worked to clear a path for the staff car through the mobs of people. Yellow tape blocked off much of the mall. A group of young girls ran across the street in front of them. People continued to stream across the street, many pushing strollers or pulling wagons filled with children.

Zack jumped when a firecracker went off.

Market Street had been closed between Third Street and Eighth Street. Their car arrived at the barriers across Market Street. A police officer walked over as the driver rolled down the window.

Blake flashed her credentials. "The FBI Director, Mr. Henry Burnside, is in the backseat. We need to get through right away."

The police officer checked. "I'm sorry, but you're not on the access roster."

"Get me a supervisor," Burnside shouted, "and do it now."

"Yes, sir." The officer spoke into the microphone on his collar.

In a moment a man in a dark suit with light brown hair hurried over. "Yes, sir, can I help you?"

"I'm FBI Director Henry Burnside. I need to get through and talk to the president. It could be a matter of life and death."

"I recognize you, Mr. Burnside, but I still need to see your identification. I also need to see the identification of those with you."

They showed their cards, Burnside having to vouch for Zack.

"Has the president arrived yet?" Burnside asked.

The agent looked at his sheet. "Maverick arrived at the airport thirty-five minutes ago and his ETA here is in two more minutes." The agent listened and held up his hand. "Sir, we have the arrival of Maverick."

Sirens sounded behind them.

The agent opened the barrier and their staff car drove into the controlled area and pulled over as the beginning of the president's motorcade flowed in behind them.

Garcia watched Alcott, hoping for an opening. Counted the steps to the woman again. She'd never get to her before Alcott could fire.

Alcott waved the pistol and pointed for Garcia to move to the other side of the room. "I'll count to five. If you don't move away from that computer, I'll shoot. Is all this really worth dying for?" She smiled. "I'll get paid whether you live or die. If the mission goes through like it's supposed to, I'll be in one of the top positions in the country. Gain the respect I should have had all these years."

Somehow Garcia had to stall her. "Look, Alcott, I'm going to sit down at the computer and try to stop this nightmare before all those people die."

"Move, dammit," Alcott yelled.

Garcia shook her head, turned back toward the computer when a motion to the right caught her eye.

"What's going on?" A slender, sandy-haired man called from the doorway.

Alcott whirled toward the voice, startled.

Garcia launched at Alcott, ducking low and executing one of her best cross body blocks. Her right shoulder hit Alcott's legs. Alcott crashed to the floor, the gun discharging harmlessly into the ceiling and flying across the floor.

Garcia jumped up and grabbed the gun, clicked on the safety. Pushing Alcott back to the floor, she slipped the gun into the waist band of her slacks and called, "Who the hell are you?"

"Jason Helm. I work here. Who are you?"

"Colonel Garcia, Military Police. I'm investigating the attempted murder of my brother, David Garcia. The program on this computer is blocking DOD from preventing the launch of a drone which may be targeting the president. Time is urgent. Can you help me stop it?"

"This cop is mad," Alcott screamed. "She doesn't know what she's talking about."

Jason's gaze moved from Alcott to Garcia, then back to Alcott. "Simpson called. Told me you were here." He pursed his lips. "All along, I've suspected something terrible was going on, but I couldn't prove anything."

Garcia motioned toward the computer. "Any idea how to stop this program?"

"It's probably set on a time bomb," Helm replied.

"Get away from my terminal, Helm," Alcott yelled. "You're fired. Now get the hell out of here."

"No, I believe the colonel."

———————

The sun had begun to disappear below the horizon with a splash of orange as the black Cadillac pulled up to the raised stage decorated with American flags and blue and white bunting.

Market Street bisected the site, with the Independence Visitors Center on one side and the Liberty Bell Center and the President's House on the other. The stage had been set up across from the Liberty Bell. Zack couldn't believe all the people.

Their staff car crawled along at the end of the motorcade. When they stopped, Burnside and Zack jumped out and ran forward to catch the president. They had to push through a line of guards and army personnel protecting the route.

A secret service agent jumped out of the front seat of the Cadillac, his gaze searching the crowd. The Marine Band stood off to the right side of the stage. As the band director brought down his baton, the first notes of "Hail to the Chief" floated across the crowd.

Reaching back, the agent opened the door for the president who stepped out. The president turned, surprised to see Burnside.

Burnside hurried up to him. "Mr. President, you're in terrible danger. We have credible evidence a drone may be targeting this site to kill you."

The president's eyes widened. "Have you gone mad? I told you I didn't want to cancel this speech. What in the world has gotten into you?"

"We believe that an air force enlisted woman has launched a drone and is guiding it toward this site. Mr. President, we must get you out of here and clear these people."

"Do you have any proof of what you're telling me? I mean real proof, not just a feeling."

"No, sir, not right at this moment."

"Henry, I'm going on. The people need to see their president at a time of crisis. Not running off somewhere because some specialist didn't get her complaint approved."

Burnside took his arm. "Mr. President . . .."

"Take your hand off my arm or I'll have you arrested."

45

As Garcia punched in General Harding's number on her cell and put it on speaker, Jason Helm took off his sport coat, tossed it on the floor and sat at Alcott's computer.

Alcott glared at Garcia as the phone rang. When Harding answered, Garcia asked, "What's going on at your end?"

"It appears Specialist Kline is controlling a drone," Harding replied. "Can you find staff at Sterling to deactivate the program? So far, the president doesn't understand the threat and seems determined to go ahead with his speech."

"I've found a guy who works here. He's gonna try."

"Can we trust him?"

Garcia glanced at Helm who nodded. "Our best chance. Here he is."

"This is Jason Helm. What's the current status?"

"The Red Dog system is blocking us from communicating with the drone we believe is headed toward Philadelphia and the president."

Alcott charged at Helm with her fingernails in an effort to scratch him. "You're fired, now get out."

266

Garcia stepped between them, took Alcott's arm, pivoted and pushed her back down to the floor. "Stay down there and be quiet."

Alcott fell back and looked at her arm. "You hurt me. I'll have a bruise."

Jason wiped perspiration from his forehead and began typing, pushing in codes, then deleting and punching in more codes.

Garcia's stomach knotted and sweat dotted her forehead. "He's working on it, General. Doing the best he can."

"We're only seven minutes away from the start of his speech," Harding called.

Jason's hands trembled as he typed and he nodded toward Garcia.

Garcia's heart hammered as she called into the phone, "Anything?"

"Nothing. Nothing. Hurry."

Jason's fingers slipped as he pushed more keys. He deleted a line of code and typed more.

"Anything?" Garcia called. "Anything?"

"I'm trying to bypass the time bomb," Jason called. "Gotta do that to get to the main program."

Garcia looked down at Alcott who smiled. How could anyone do this? "Anything, General?"

"Nothing," Harding replied. "Only minutes away. He's got to break into that code. Got to."

"Hang on," Garcia called. "He's working on it. Doing his best."

"I've dismantled the time bomb," Jason called. "Now, I've got to stop Red Dog." More typing on the keyboard.

"Not gonna make it," Garcia called. "Can the Air Force stop the drone?"

"I called to alert them," Harding called. "Even if SAC verifies the risk, they can't get there in time to shoot it down."

Oh, no, Garcia thought. *Too late. Too goddamn late.*

Static over the phone.

Harding's voice busted in. "President's on the stage. Refuses to stop. And all those people, damn, all those people . . ."

Garcia couldn't believe it. She was powerless to stop a catastrophe. "Hurry, Jason," she whispered. "Hurry."

"Wait a minute," General Harding called, "A signal. I'm told the security operator has a signal. Maybe, just maybe . . .."

"Goddamn, is it possible?" Garcia heard a cheer in the background.

General Harding's voice broke in. "We may have control back."

Garcia took a deep breath. Said a silent prayer.

"Yes, we do, but now we need to divert the drone. Our comptroller is working to modify the arc. With any luck we should be able at least to aim it toward the water."

Garcia held her breath. Please . . ..

Two minutes, which felt like two hours, passed before Garcia heard, "We've adjusted the flight path of the drone to fly over Philadelphia—then head toward the Atlantic Ocean. Now our comptroller must angle it away from any boats that may be in the harbor. This is pretty chancy." Silence for another two minutes. "Yes, it's dropping down. Yes, it's in the water." More cheers.

Garcia turned to Alcott. "You lose." She talked to air. Alcott had disappeared. Oh, shit, can't believe I let her get away. Dammit. Too focused on the computer. She pivoted around and ran toward the door.

The Dark Angel found out the drone had been diverted and would not strike its target. She needed to implement her alternate plan. The president must die. A new leadership team would then be organized to give women any chance at equality.

Checking around the site of the Liberty Bell, she didn't spot Kelly or Agent Harper, but saw the staff car. That was all she needed. She elbowed her way through the crowd gathered around listening to the president. People ignored her as they were focused on the speech.

When she reached the car, she took out the extra key she had made and unlocked the trunk. Reaching into her backpack, she pulled out her .45 caliber pistol. The answer. She would not live to reap the benefits of her plan, but that didn't matter. Thousands of innocent, hard-working, military women would gain from her sacrifice.

She shoved the .45 under her belt in the back, pulled down her jacket over the lump, then shut the trunk lid. Checking around again to make sure, no one appeared to have noticed.

Edging toward the stage, she slipped past group after group intent on the president. Her heart beat fast. She wiped sweat from her forehead. She continued to push through the crowd, careful not to alert anyone. *Take it slowly,* she thought, *slowly*. Secret service agents surrounded the stage, circulating through the audience, hell, everywhere, watching, checking, looking. Fortunately she had a badge showing her authorization to move around the site without drawing attention.

She continued forward toward the stage. Toward her destiny.

Footsteps sounded in the hall. Garcia looked up, the sweat lining her face.

Lieutenant Scott hurried through the open doorway, three uniformed officers behind her. She pulled Megan Alcott along by the arm. "Look who I found running down the hallway. I thought you might want to talk with her."

"Jason's the good guy. He prevented the assassination attempt." Garcia stopped to take a breath. "The DOD comptroller was able to divert the drone into the ocean, hopefully without hurting anyone." Garcia had to stop again to take another breath. "Alcott's the one you want. Arrest her and don't let her touch anything."

The door banged against the wall. A heavy-set man in a brown trench coat and felt hat walked in. "I'm Bernard Hirsch, Mr. Foster's lawyer. The guard called me. I demand you stop this illegal action immediately. I'll sue all of you."

Lieutenant Scott waved a piece of paper at him. "It's with pleasure I show you this warrant authorizing us to search Sterling Software. Now if you would step back, we can get to work."

"Let me see that." Hirsch grabbed the document and began to read.

Scott smiled. "You bet, big guy."

She handed Alcott off to one of the officers. "Cuff her and take her out to the squad car. Keep her away from any computer." Scott pointed at the other officers. "Get keys and check to see that we've secured all the computers in the building. I believe there are seven offices here. Make sure each computer is sealed and we control the main server."

Scott's cell phone rang and she pulled it out of her pocket. "Scott."

"This is Agent Harper."

"I guess you heard that Garcia found a guy who unblocked the communications system. The DOD staff regained control of the drone, then diverted it into the ocean. Looks like no significant damage. How about at your end?"

"The president is finishing his speech and we're watching for any bomb attempts. Can you talk for a minute?"

She motioned to one of the officers. "Be sure to keep an eye on Alcott. I'll be right back."

Scott brushed past the attorney still reading the warrant and shaking his head, then stepped out into the hallway. "Ah, I'm right in the middle of things now. It's pretty wild, but I think we've got the system secured so no one can make any more changes. Let me put you on speaker so I can take notes." She fumbled with her phone. "I hate these fucking things." She pushed a button. "There."

Harper's voice sounded from the speaker. "The Park Police called me a few minutes ago. They found Samuel Foster dead in his van at one of the overlooks."

Scott sighed. "Good God, another one."

"Initially the D.C. police suspected suicide, but that went out the window when they found two additional bullet holes in him."

Scott chuckled. "Guess it's pretty hard to shoot yourself three times."

"Also, there are footprints from another person around the car."

"Any witnesses?"

"Not yet."

Lieutenant Scott thought for a moment. "Someone realizes we're getting close. They're eliminating all the trails."

"I agree. How much longer will you be there?"

"It'll probably be another half hour before I can turn it over to the computer nerds. Why?"

"Just checking. I'd better get going. I need to find Agent Fairchild and see what she knows."

46

Philadelphia, Sunday, 8:15 p.m.

Zack whirled around. Checked in all directions. He'd heard Harding had stopped the drone attack, but he'd bet money the Dark Angel had a backup plan. Not only could the president die, but thousands of others depending on what that monster had planned. Where the hell is Fairchild?

He searched his mind. Before she died back at that house in Strathmere, the woman pretending to be the Dark Angel had said something like, "You can't stop it. No one can. Our person is in place and the Dark Angel will do it." *Is the Dark Angel here? Now?*

All this time, something had been working on him. *Think, Kelly.* Then it hit him. *Damn, how could he have been so stupid? Gotta get to Powell.* He grabbed his cell to send a text to Powell and find out who owned the house in Strathmere.

Harper hurried up next to him. "Stopped the drone."

"Yeah, I know. Gonna be something else. Have you seen Fairchild?"

"No, and that surprises me."

As he pushed in Powell's number, Zack called, "See if you can find her."

Harper nodded and hurried off.

Zack finished the text, then elbowed his way toward the front, scanning the area. People yelled and waved American flags at the president. He stood on the stage, waving back at the crowd, putting his hands together in the air. Music by the Marine band drowned out everything else.

Zack elbowed through the crowd, looking, checking. Not exactly sure what he was looking for. His heart sank when he saw a woman pushing toward the stage. Couldn't make out a face, but she was hurrying, pushing past people. He ran toward her, but she had disappeared in the crowd.

Someone bumped into him and he lost his balance, catching himself before he fell. Had to find her. Couldn't let her set off the bomb. *But could he stop it?* Hell, he had to.

Two hands grabbed him. He pulled away but the hands held fast, then another set of hands, then another. "Stop," a male voice called out. "Let me see your identification."

Zack turned. Two Secret Service agents, one on either side of him, held his arms.

"Let me go," he called. "The Dark Angel could be headed toward the president."

One of the agents pulled out his pistol. "Don't move, not a muscle. You're one of those wackos who tried to stop the president from making the speech. We were told to watch out for you."

"You've got to let me go."

"Just stay where you are. You're not going anywhere."

The Dark Angel maneuvered through the crowd. Her life in ruins. All because of that bastard.

Only a few feet to the stage. Then she'd slip out the pistol. Killing the president would be the blow to help her sisters. And with his death the death of the policies that had imprisoned her sisters.

A couple more steps. He'd never suspect her. She could get the shot off and slip away.

When she reached the bottom step of the stage, one of the Secret Service Agents blocked her path. "Step aside," the agent said, "the president will be coming through."

She took a step back and watched as a scuffle broke out between someone and a group of agents. They blocked her. *Can't see. The president must be headed toward the plane. Meet him there. She could do that. The president couldn't get back to Washington. He couldn't. All their planning depended on that.*

She turned and hurried back to the staff car to put her gun back in the trunk. She could slip it out at the plane.

"Wait, let that man go," Henry Burnside called to the agents surrounding Zack. "Let him go. He's the one who helped stop the drone attack. He's with me."

The agents looked at each other, then at Burnside. One of the agents replied, "Director Burnside. Are you sure?"

"Yes, dammit, now release him."

When the agents let Zack go, he followed Burnside toward the stage. Heard Burnside yell, "Mr. President, we've got to get you out of here. We've diverted a drone, but there is still a credible threat. A serious threat to you."

The president stepped down from the stage. Agents hustled him toward the car, through the open back door. The president stumbled into the car. An agent slammed the door shut.

Zack yelled to Burnside, "Go with the president. I'll catch up with Blake and we'll meet you at Air Force One. I think Admiral Steele is with her."

Burnside nodded. "Find Agent Harper and Agent Fairchild and have them follow."

"Yes, sir," Zack replied. "We'll be right behind you."

Burnside ran around to the other side of the president's car, opened the door and got in. The car squealed off, behind the screaming sirens of the motorcycle escort.

Zack pulled his cell from the coat pocket and dialed Blake's number.

"Lannigan."

"It's Zack. The president is on his way to the airport with Burnside and Admiral Steele. You, the FBI agents, and I should meet him there. Where are you?"

"Toward the back of the stage. I can meet you at the car in a few minutes."

"Have you seen Harper and Fairchild?"

"Saw Harper a little while ago but not Fairchild. Wait a minute. There she is over by the staff car. We'll wait for you."

Zack disconnected his cell. Looked around for Harper. Spotted him and waved him over. "We're supposed to meet at the staff car and head to the president's plane."

Zack raced toward the car, Harper right behind him. *Get to Air Force One.*

47

Philadelphia Airport, Sunday, 9:22 p.m.

Their driver wheeled the staff car up to the steps of Air Force One. Security officers stood at attention around the plane. Snipers on the terminal roof watched from their various stations.

Two agents waited at the base of the stairs. The shorter one asked, "Colonel Kelly?"

"Yes."

Agent Harper stood next to Zack. "It's okay. These people are with me."

The agent checked the access list. "Agent Harper and Agent Fairchild, Colonel Kelly, and Ms. Lannigan. All right, go right on board, sir. They're waiting for you."

Zack limped as he hurried up the stairs, his leg still burning from the dog bite. He followed Blake and the two FBI agents. Admiral Steele sat on one of the couches in the front lounge of the plane next to Director Burnside, whispering to him.

The president came into the lounge from the back compartment. They all jumped to attention.

"Colonel Kelly, Director Burnside tells me I owe you my thanks. You were right all along. I should have listened to you."

"Mr. President, it was so unbelievable that I had trouble getting my head around it."

Everyone sat and adjusted their seat belts as the engines roared and the plane taxied to the end of the field.

The president turned toward the secret service agent by the closed door. "Would you please wait in the other room. I want to talk to these people alone."

"Are you sure, Mr. President? I have orders to stay with you."

"I'm sure. It'll be fine."

"Yes, sir." The agent turned and went into the next room, closing the door behind him.

"All right, now that we're alone, let's get started," Director Burnside said. "We've got to figure out what we're going to do and in what order. Let's start up in New Jersey. Zack, what can you tell us?"

"We've got a team there as we speak," Zack replied. "Lieutenant Powell from the Sea Isle City Police Department is coordinating the effort along with FBI agents and members of the New Jersey State Police. Lieutenant Powell picked up Major Wilson from the hospital about two hours ago and drove him to the house in Strathmere."

"How is he?" the president asked.

"Shot in the shoulder." Blake chuckled. "Says the dirty bastards got one of his wings, but he's still flapping with the other. I expect an update in fifteen minutes."

Zack continued. "They've cordoned off the town. Initial reports indicate significant damage to the house. Major Caldwell is here in Philadelphia under guard at a hospital. He should make a compelling witness for the prosecution."

"What about this Dark Angel?" Burnside asked. "I wonder if she's still alive?"

Zack wondered if the Dark Angel might be closer than any of them thought. He explained about the fight and his escape. "I don't know if that woman was really the Dark Angel."

"Why?" Burnside asked.

"She said something like the Dark Angel will get you. This happened right before she died. I can't see why she would lie."

The engines roared again and the plane took off. He glanced over at Fairchild. She sat quietly, looking down at her hands.

Fairchild looked up at him, then quickly away.

Zack couldn't wait any longer. "Agent Fairchild, in the last hour I didn't see you. Where were you?"

"Why are you asking?"

"Just curious. I saw everyone else but missed you. I asked Agent Harper, but he couldn't tell me."

"Colonel Kelly, I was doing my damn job. It's really none of your business what I was doing."

Zack shrugged. "Well, that's true. But I could have used your help during all the problems with the drone attack."

"That's true," Harper replied.

"What's this? Gang up on the girl? I was working with my former friends in the Secret Service trying to convince them of the danger and helping with crowd control."

Sounds reasonable, Zack thought. *But still . . ..* "I wish you had let us know."

"Get off it, Kelly, before I really get pissed off."

Zack leaned back feeling the reassuring touch of his Glock. *Why the hell hadn't Powell returned his text message about ownership of the house.*

As if on cue, his cell phone vibrated. *Probably Powell.*

He pulled it out of his pocket and read the text. His heart jumped in his throat. He looked at Blake. She watched him. He looked down again, but he knew that she knew. He leaned back, feeling the lump from the Glock behind him.

"Don't do it, Zack."

Blake had her pistol pointed directly at him. "Was that your little friend in Sea Isle City? Did she finally get around to telling you who owned my house?"

Zack's face remained impassive.

"No one else would have known except for you. Darcy took over the ownership after my shit-head father started preparing for the Supreme Court. Powell wouldn't have figured it out."

"That's true." Zack looked at a bewildered Burnside. "Darcy Quinn's name was on the ownership papers. She's Blake's aunt. Blake's father shot and killed her."

Blake watched Burnside. "Don't call for the secret service agents in the next cabin. If you do, I'll kill the president right now."

"All right," Zack said. "Take it easy."

"Fuck, take it easy. You all knew my father. He was the talk of Washington. Gonna be a Supreme Court judge until everyone found out about that damn whore house his sister ran. Who the fuck screened him?"

The president cleared his throat. "You're painting a very bleak picture of our procedures, Ms. Lannigan. I knew your father. I'm the one who planned to nominate him to the Supreme Court before the scandal broke."

"Yeah, great selection. Then he escaped from jail. I could feel everyone looking at me. Poor Blake. Seemed so nice and efficient, but all that went for nothing when I became Sean Lannigan's daughter. Odd man out. Bunch of fuckers."

The engines roared louder as the huge plane continued to lift into the darkened sky.

Zack leaned forward. "Why Blake?" Why kill people?"

"You men don't know what it's like. Having fuckers staring at you all the time, undressing you, acting like teenagers. Thousands of women go through the same thing, those in the military put up with harassment just to do their job. To try and get promoted. And none of the bigwigs in Washington give a damn."

Admiral Steele looked around at the group sitting like statutes. Harper, Fairchild, Garcia, the president. "But we were a team."

Blake's eyes teared. "Nothing else worked. Everyone knows the problem. It starts in college if not before. Universities are supposed to have procedures to help young women, to encourage them to report sexual assaults, but few have done anything. No one cares except the poor women. I got sick of it and so did my sisters. We decided to do something about it. Something you men couldn't ignore."

Blake looked at the president. Zack knew her thoughts. She planned to kill him. Then it dawned on him. The vice president would take over. Zack needed to keep her talking. Maybe Fairchild, who sat on the other side of the aisle, could get at her. "Why is this so personal?"

She wiped the tears away. "My sweet daddy used to come in and talk to me as I was taking a bath. He did it when I was little, then he kept on as I got older. When I was a teenager, he'd walk in on me. Can you imagine that? All the time to see his daughter's boobs. Then he'd want to wash my back. Then my front. What a bastard. I know how those women feel. You have no idea what they've been through. Well now, our new president will put a stop to it. She coordinated the hacking effort so the drone would do the job, but that failed. So now it's up to me."

"Wait," Zack called.

"No, you wait. I've waited long enough." She pointed the gun at the president.

As she pulled the trigger, Zack lurched toward the president. Had to stop it. But no noise sounded.

At the click, Fairchild jumped at Blake, jamming her against the wall, knocking the gun out of her hand. Blake slipped to the floor of Air Force One, holding her head. Fairchild whipped Blake's hands behind her back and slipped on the cuffs.

Zack turned toward the president. "Are you all right, sir?"

A shaken President Bradford looked at Zack, then at Agent Fairchild. "Thank you for saving my life."

Fairchild pulled Blake back into a chair and pushed a button for the secret service agents. "You're welcome, sir."

Three agents rushed in from the next room, guns drawn, their gaze searching the room.

Bradford pointed at Blake. "Secure her."

Zack couldn't believe it. "An empty gun."

Fairchild had to smile. "That's what I was doing, wise guy, when you couldn't find me. Following Blake. I had a feeling and watched her. I saw her take a gun out of the trunk of our staff car. Then she walked toward the stage. I stayed right behind her to stop her if she pulled the gun, but she couldn't get a shot off because of the secret service agents. She had to go back to the car. After she stashed the gun, I waited until she hurried away, then I took the bullets out of the magazine."

Zack felt like shit. "I really misjudged you."

"Damn right. I knew what you were thinking, Kelly, but you need to bone up on your game."

"You're absolutely right," Zack replied. "Now what do we need to do with the vice president after what we heard?"

"You can't prove a thing," Blake said. "I'll deny everything. Say you misheard me."

Fairchild reached in her pocket and pulled out a miniature tape recorder. "Let me see, Blake, I have your quote about the vice president here somewhere. I suspect your voice will come through loud and clear. Loud enough for a courtroom."

"You bitch," Blake screamed. "How could you turn on your sisters?"

"I don't like what's happening any more than you do, but I'm not going to kill innocent people." She turned to the president. "Besides, I think he's got the message."

The president nodded. "Definitely."

The pilot's voice came over the intercom. "Please take your seats. We'll be landing in twenty minutes."

Zack and Fairchild sat and pulled tight their seat belts.

The president checked his belt. "Once we arrive, I'm going to the White House and kick that bitch in the butt. When I think how close she came to pulling it off, I'm floored."

"Be careful, Mr. President," Burnside said, "there may still be agents looking to harm you."

"Thank you, Henry," the president replied. "I'll be careful."

Zack leaned over to Admiral Steele and whispered, "You know sir, with Blake gone, your task force is short one member. I know just the FBI agent to add to the group."

"Funny, Zack, that's exactly what I was thinking."

"Now," the president said, "here's what I think we should do."

48

The White House, Washington D.C., 11:00 p.m.

Zack and Admiral Steele followed Director Burnside and the president into the Oval Office. The president motioned them toward one of the two white couches that angled in front of the desk. "Take a seat, please, I'll call for the vice president."

In a moment there was a knock on the door.

"Come in," the president called.

The door opened and Vice President Townsend walked in, a smile on her face. Zack was amazed at how cool she looked in her long skirt and tweed jacket. She must know that things went very wrong.

"Good evening, Mr. President, Director Burnside. Oh, and Admiral Steele and Colonel Kelly. You've all had an awful day. I understand there was a problem in Philadelphia. Some terrorist with a drone capability?"

The president motioned her toward a chair. "That's right. I imagine you're surprised to see me."

She remained standing. "My goodness, no. I'm just glad that you weren't hurt."

"I'm sure you are," the president replied. "If anything happens to me, then you'd have to take over as president."

"Sir, I'd never want anything to happen to you."

The president stared at her for a moment. "A funny thing happened in Philadelphia."

"What was that, sir?"

"Well there was a woman who gave me some startling news."

"Oh." Townsend glanced at Burnside, then Admiral Steele. "What was that?"

"I brought her back with me. Zack will you let her in?"

Zack limped over and pulled the door open. Blake Lannigan walked in, escorted by Agents Harper and Fairchild.

Townsend's eyes got wide. She took a step back, shook her head, then gave another small smile. "I don't understand. What's going on?"

"Oh, but I think you do." The president pointed at Townsend. "Henry, arrest this woman."

"Wait a minute, Mr. President, you're making a terrible mistake."

She glared at him for a few seconds, then reached in her pocket.

"Wait, no, it's over," Blake called.

As the vice president pulled the pistol out, Zack dove for her. The gun discharged. Zack heard a groan as he wrestled her to the ground and twisted her arm to make her drop the gun. He turned to see blood gushing from Blake Lannigan's chest.

Fairchild helped Zack subdue Townsend. She slapped handcuffs on the vice president, then faced the president as the door opened and three secret service agents rushed into the room.

A shaken Bradford called, "She saved my life. Jumped in front of that bullet."

Zack knelt beside Blake. She lay on the floor, eyes closed. "Blake, Blake can you hear me? You saved the president."

She opened her eyes. "I'm sorry, Zack. I was wrong. So wrong. Forgive me. I'm glad I could do something right." Her eyes shut and she didn't move.

Admiral Steele grabbed a phone and called for a doctor. He hung up. "Blake blocked the bullet meant for the president.

The president walked over to Townsend and stared into her eyes. "I depended on you. But why? Why would you do this? Kill all these people."

Townsend glared at him. "You don't have a clue about what's happening to young women on your watch. They're getting raped, abused, and you're not doing a thing about it."

"That changes right now. This will be a priority. I'm going to fix what's happening to our young women. It must stop."

The vice president sneered. "You say. Well, I don't believe it. I've tried to get your support for legislation in the Congress and you sat by and did nothing."

"No more." The president motioned to Fairchild. "Get her out of my sight."

As the door closed, another opened and a slender man in a suit rushed into the room, carrying a black bag. He knelt beside Blake. Checked for a pulse. Looked at the president. "Mr. President, she's dead."

The president watched the door close behind the vice president. "How close she came."

Zack took Blake's hand. Couldn't believe all that had happened. "Oh, Blake, Blake . . ."

Admiral Steele put his arm on Zack's shoulder. "She's gone, Zack."

Zack nodded and stood. *Come on*, he thought, *get it together*, He looked at Steele. "Sir, I don't believe it's over yet. We need to figure out who else is involved in the plot."

"I'm already working on that," Burnside said, "beginning with the vice president's chief of staff."

"Makes sense," Zack said.

President Bradford walked over to his desk and sat. "We need to do a thorough review of people and procedures. I'm going to form a commission to address this issue and I'm not going to stop until I get it corrected." He turned to Zack. "Thank you for all you've done. If there is ever anything I can do for you, please let me know."

Zack thought for a moment. "Well, now that I think about it, Sir, there is one thing."

Laura Kelly sat in front of her television set, watching a late movie, sick and tired of all the news about the bombings. She still cried when she thought about her dad. They had such fun plans set for the Fourth of July and he never showed up. *How could he do that? Maybe her mother was right. Maybe she should go back to Minneapolis and enroll in Carlton College.* But that thought almost broke her heart. She loved her dad so much, but he'd just dropped her and ran off somewhere without a word except that phone call from Philadelphia. It made her so mad she threw a pillow against the wall. Then she started to cry again.

The phone rang.

Crying hard enough she would have trouble talking, she let it ring. But it kept ringing and she finally picked it up. "Hello."

A woman's voice asked, "Is this Laura Kelly?"

Laura almost hung up, but she asked, "Who is this?"

"This is the White House calling. Will you please hold for President Bradford?"

Laura took a quick intake of breath, put her hand over the receiver and yelled, "Mom, it's the president on the phone."

Ellen came running into the room. "What? Is this some sort of joke? Wait a minute, put the phone on speaker."

A male voice came on the line. "Good evening, Laura. This is President Sheldon Bradford."

Laura didn't know what to say. She recognized his voice.

"I wanted to take a minute to tell you how your father saved not only my life tonight, but the lives of hundreds of other people in Philadelphia. I know you were disappointed that you couldn't be with him over the Fourth of July weekend and he was too. But, I needed him and he agreed to help me even though it meant not getting to spend the time with you he wanted. Because of the extremely sensitive security considerations surrounding this operation, he couldn't tell you about it."

Laura finally managed to gulp out, "Really?"

"Yes, really," the president replied. "Now, I'd like to make it up to you. If you can be ready at eleven o'clock tomorrow morning, I'll send a staff car to pick you and your dad up and bring you both to the White House. The First Lady and I would like to give you a tour, then have you stay for lunch with us. It's the least I can do after what your father did for me, Then I'm going to insist he take two weeks off so you can spend time together. I'll be glad to fly you both to a place you've always wanted to go. And Laura . . ."

She had trouble getting the word out. "Yes."

"Thank you for understanding."

Laura couldn't talk. She looked at her mother and smiled, tears flowing down her cheeks.

49

Arlington, Virginia. Two Weeks Later. 8:10 a.m.

Zack and Laura walked up the hill just after sunrise and stood by the freshly dug grave, Zack not sure what to say.

He bent over and placed a bouquet of red roses in a planter in front of the gravestone. The incription read, *Blake Ann Lannigan, Born September 26th 1982, died, July 4th, 2015. Loving niece, good friend. She died saving her president.*

"Oh, Dad," Laura said, "it's so sad. How could something like this happen?"

"I never realized what a difficult childhood Blake had." Zack put his arm around Laura and hugged her closer. "Let this be a lesson to both of us. We've got to be able to talk to each other and tell each other how we really feel. I'll try harder, sweetie, I promise."

"I love you, Dad."

Footsteps sounded behind them and Zack turned to see Garcia walking up the hill, a bouquet of yellow roses in her hand. She smiled when he turned.

Zack gave her a hug. "You're back from your vacation. I see you like roses, too."

"I thought Blake would like yellow roses from Texas." Tears dotted Garcia's cheeks. "She was my friend. I knew her. How could I have missed her pain. That much pain."

"We all missed it," Zack replied.

Garcia reached over and gave Laura a hug. "Hi, Laura. What a sad time."

Laura nodded, unable to speak.

Garcia bent down and placed the roses in front of the grave stone. She bowed her head for a moment, then stood.

"I still can't believe it." Zack turned to Garcia. "So damn sad.

"I know," Garcia said, "I know."

"How is your brother doing?" Zack asked.

"Much better, thanks. The staff at Fairfax Hospital was terrific at preparing him for transfer to the rehab facility in Austin. It's only about ten miles from my parent's home."

Zack wasn't sure how to ask the next question. "Uhm ... did you ... I mean have you ..."

Garcia smiled and said, "Let me put you out of your misery. Little Lee Ann flew to Austin with us. She's a delight and we had a nice time. My mother is going full bore on her new role as a grandmother. She hardly ever lets that little baby out of her sight. Takes her over to the rehab facility every day to visit my brother. We had such fun together when I was there. Even my father had a good time."

"Oh, man," Zack said. "That's great news."

"My mother's been waiting for years to become a grandmother and now she and my dad are really looking forward to taking care of the baby and helping David recover."

Garcia looked down at the gravesite. "Oh, Blake, how did it come to all this?"

Zack kept one arm around Laura and put the other around Garcia. For a long time they stood by the graveside without speaking. Finally Zack said, "Let that be a lesson to all of us. Friends need to share their feelings with each other. I promise to do a better job."

Both Garcia and Laura murmured a quiet, "Me, too."

The three turned almost as one and started back down the hill.